RED MOON DISTRICT

Underground Voices

http://www.undergroundvoices.com

Edited by Cetywa Powell

ISBN: 978-0-9830456-6-3

Printed in the United States of America.

CONTENTS

FICTION

Rodger Jacobs	5
Jim Meirose	9
Jamez Chang	15
Carter Schwonke	18
Steven Loton	30
George Sparling	40
Mark Daponte	49
James Brown	57
Thomas Kearnes	70
Mary Krienke	79
Luke Tennis	88
Olyn Ozbick	95
Khanh Ha	97
Zachary Amendt	108
David Luntz	124
Dennis Kennedy	131
JeanPaul Ferro	146
Patti Abbott	156
Zdravka Evtimova	166
D.H. Schleicher	172
David Synder	186
Simon Friel	204
Kristen Falso-Capaldi	219
Michael C. Keith	228
Jenean McBrearty	234
Conor Powers-Smith	238
Timothy Bearly	242
Evan W. Stoner	249

POETRY

Ronan Barbour	26
Ken Poyner	28
R.C. Edrington	65
Cody Badaracca	66
Jose Hernandez Diaz	118
Mitchell Grabois	122
Ted Jean	127
Frederick Pollack	129
James Babbs	152
Stephanie Smith	170
B.Z. Niditch	185
Meg Johnson	215
Marc Pietrzykowski	217
Noel Sloboda	248

CONTRIBUTORS BIOS   **253**

RODGER JACOBS

No Style, No Grace, No Mercy

There was heavy conjecture after the fact. The pundits of pugilism all concurred that it had been too soon for Thomas Hudson to jump back into the ring after capturing the championship belt. The gossip mongers offered an unsubstantiated noir-ish spin, suggesting that the champ owed "a huge amount of money to some connected guys in Glendale," reneged on the payment arrangement, and that was what accounted for the last-minute substitution on the fight card that fateful night.

Then came the high priests of celebrity rehab who moonlight as cable news talking heads, insisting that Hudson's opponent, Geech McAndrews, was most certainly amped up on meth; the real medical experts, the men and women without a pricy Palm Springs clinic or a book to hawk, testified that McAndrews's actions were certainly consistent with the manner in which methamphetamine works on the human brain and central nervous system.

Setting aside the useless conjecture, rumors, and scientific musings, this much is very certain and was recorded by the TV cameras, sports photographers, columnists, and thousands of fight fans in attendance at the Grand Olympic Auditorium in downtown L.A. and via pay-per-view broadcast.

At 9:11 p.m. Pacific Standard Time on the night in question, the opening bell rang and the two fighters sprang from their assigned corners.

It was apparent immediately that Hudson and McAndrews practiced vastly different styles of boxing. Hudson was a classic out-fighter, a combination of reach, hand speed, reflexes, and delicate footwork. He kept a distance between himself and his opponents, fighting with fast, long-range punches and he jabbed frequently, wearing his foe down; in this way he controlled the pace of the fight, leading his rival.

Geech McAndrews, however, was a brawler, a slugger, lacking Hudson's finesse in the ring, with less mobility and a predictable punching pattern, but he compensated for his deficits with sheer brutal power and the ability to knock out opponents with a single stinging blow.

The first round was uneventful; some said "dull and boring." (One sports hack at a Long Beach newspaper observed that "Aside from my first marriage, it was the longest three minutes of my life.") But thirty-two-and-a-half seconds into round two, a moment viewed and downloaded by millions of worldwide users on YouTube and ESPN.com, all manner of hell paid a visit.

Geech McAndrews was not interested in a single knockout blow. He aimed to punish (hence the loan shark rumors), blasting out of his corner like a human tornado. Many seated at ringside swore they felt a strong wind in his wake, like a battleship passing a dinghy at cruising speed.

A flashy wide-sweeping undercut was thrown for distracting effect from the thunderous left uppercut that smashed Hudson's jaw and spilled blood on the faces of the judges.

Not content with spoiling his rival's ability to enjoy solid food, Geech rushed and struck with a series of merciless blows, his right repeatedly mangling Hudson's broken face. "No more beautiful trophy wives for Hudson," one radio wag quipped, eliciting a flurry of hate mail, death threats, and envelopes packed with white powder in the days and weeks following the event.

With forty seconds remaining in the second, the ref cowering in a corner, too terrified to intrude on the mad fury encouraged by the cheering mob that filled the auditorium, Geech pummeled Hudson's torso, backed him up against the ropes, and delivered a shower of heavy blows. Flailing in the ropes, Hudson resembled a panic-stricken fly ensnared in a spider's web. As the round came to a close it was not lost on anyone that Geech McAndrews had simply turned into a killing machine, offering a final series of blows that showed no style, no grace, and certainly no mercy.

And what of the spectators, some of whom paid five hundred dollars for a ringside seat, only to feel robbed and cheated when the contender for Hudson's crown was replaced at the last minute? Well, many feel that's where the true horror lies. For the spectators were not slack and taut during this display of brutality.

Immune to violence after a steady diet of endless wars, bloody terrorist attacks, mass shootings at schools, shopping malls, the workplace, and in quiet homes on quiet cul-de-sacs from Manhattan, Kansas, to Manhattan, New York, they offered no style, no grace, and no mercy of their own.

This was payback for the brutal blows they cowered from every time they dared to turn on their televisions or boot up their computer to surf the internet. Every man and woman in that overflowing crowd put themselves in the brawler's place, fighting back against every vapid cable news field reporter, every "emotionally troubled" punk who vented his frustrations with a high-powered rifle on innocents, every chainsaw-wielding mass murderer from Hollywood, all of the sick child abductors and rapists who made them pray daily for the safety of their children, and the reckless Wall Street gamblers who looted their pensions, all of the Columbines and Newtowns and Virginia Techs, all that fascinates and repulses and makes them feel shame and guilt for having survived such a ceaseless holocaust called modern life.

Throughout the carnage the house was on its feet in celebration, whooping and hollering, shouting out words of encouragement for the brawler, urging Geech McAndrews to slay his opponent, to pound Hudson into dust. Their fists pumped in the air, arms waved wildly in the manner of penitents speaking in tongues at a revival meeting, and they pelted the ring with paper cups full of beer and soda. Metal folding chairs were thrown. The beaten, bloodied, and defeated champ was enmeshed in the ropes, helpless to defend himself against the shoes being hurled at him, against the dozens of hands reaching and groping in an effort to remove his head from his shoulders and parade it in the streets.

Over the auditorium public address system a baritone voice pleaded for calm and sanity but it was far too late for such urgings. They were fighting amongst themselves now. Knives were drawn. Ears were bitten off and spit out. A churning mass of spiteful and hate-consumed faces, teeth bared like feral animals, flailed about on the floor, a writhing mass of pure malice.

A column of twelve young black men broke from the back of the auditorium, elbowing, punching, and kicking their way toward the ring. They extricated the fallen warrior from the ropes and hoisted his battered and broken body onto their shoulders.

"There they go," an ugly white man with a cigar parked in the corner of his snarling mouth barked at me. "Protecting one of their own. It wouldn't be that way if the circumstances were reversed, would it?"

I gave the sonofabitch a shove and turned toward the ring to see Geech McAndrews grinning from ear to ear, arms held high in victory, presiding over the chaos like the Lord of Darkness himself. He didn't care that Hudson's lifeless body was being hauled away. Garbage in, garbage out.

Ducking and dodging blows and flying chairs, I pushed and prodded my way to the exit, following the trajectory of the brave young men escorting Hudson's body out of the fetid cesspool of the auditorium.

By the time I finally emerged into the night air it was too late to be of any assistance. Eyewitnesses reported that a gang of white youths with shaved heads had overwhelmed Hudson's protectors, beating them down with fists, sticks, chunks of brick, and metal garbage cans.

Hudson's corpse was deposited at the base of a towering palm tree on South Grand Avenue. Someone provided the accelerant, possibly gasoline, and others gleefully provided the matches and lighters.

As sirens wailed in the near distance the slain fighter's body ignited in a whoosh of blue and orange light. Bright flames licked at the base of the palm tree and raced upwards, setting the fronds ablaze. The palm tree etched against the night sky as it was engulfed in fire was one of the most strangely beautiful things I had ever seen in Los Angeles. As I stood there, mouth agape, enraptured by the sight, someone punched me from behind and I dropped to my knees, wailing louder than the approaching sirens.

The riots began the next day.

JIM MEIROSE

Mania

Perry Manitoba and Parkie Stanley gun down the owner of the Krauszer's they're robbing on this Saturday afternoon and they run and run and run and Perry swerves into Our Lady of Lourdes Catholic Church and heads straight to the confessional – what luck what God-damned luck – and he cuts in line and goes in.

The priest opens the shrouded panel. A shadow is on the other side.

Yes my son.

Bless me Father I have sinned, says the shadow. It is a long time since my last confession. I don't go to church much. I should go more often, but – it doesn't occur to me to go to church I just never think of it – you know what I mean Father sometimes things just don't occur to you – but let me catch my breath a minute I been running Father just let me catch my breath –

The door next to Perry clatters open. Light bathes the shadow.

Come on let's go! What are you doing? cries Parkie.

No, no, I got to say my confession. We just did a sin. A big sin. I got to say my confession Parkie. What we did was really really wrong.

Well all right but be quick about it – we got to get home –

I will, said Perry. I'm always quick about everything, Parkie – you know that. I never do nothing to hold you up Parkie. I would never do nothing to upset you. I just need a second to catch my breath is all –

The door slams shut. The walls rattle. The darkness returns.

The priest speaks.

I am listening – why were you running son?

Father, I'll get to the point right off the bat. It's good to get right to the point; it's no good to make people wait while you talk and talk and talk. People that talk too much are a dime a dozen, my Mother used to say – a Goddamned dime a dozen – she had a friend lived across the street she stopped going over to see because she'd just go on and on like that. She called her a blabbermouth. A big fat blabbermouth – that's no good – it's rude, for one thing –

9

anyway, I just was standing there when Parkie shot Mr. Christian with a gun. There it is Father, there's the whole thing. Just like that. Simple as that. I could just get up and walk out of here now, Father, and you'd know the whole story. That's as simple as it was. I mean, I didn't even know Parkie had a gun. He had it hidden in his belt. It never occurred to me to own a gun. My Father and Brother had guns – but I never did. It just was never anything that interested me. I guess I should have figured Parkie'd have a gun though. He's the type that would have a gun. But we both just had baseball bats – that's true – but I thought that was what all we were going to use when we robbed that Krauszer's – baseball bats. I didn't know any guns were going to be involved. I'm afraid of guns to tell you the truth – scared to death of them. I mean, it's enough to threaten someone that you're going to brain them with a baseball bat if they don't hand over the money. Imagine being smacked across the face with a baseball bat – God how that would hurt, not to mention the damage it would do—knock teeth out, break cheekbones, jaws, break noses, blow eyes out – or all of these at once. It'd be a bloody mess. I mean, you could kill someone with a baseball bat. Imagine swinging it with all your might! Right into someone's face! You don't need a God-damned gun. It'd be worse than being shot. But Parkie just had to have one. Oh, Parkie's always the guy who has to have everything. God-damned Parkie. Goddamned big shot. Well, big shit I say – big shit who got me into this mess – oh I mean he's like a brother to me mostly but it always seems like he gets me into God-damned jams, the big shit –

Don't curse in the confessional, son –

Sorry Father – anyway, here I am confessing Father. Even though he's the one who did the shooting. But I went in there with him all set to rob the place. I suppose that's really what I'm confessing Father. We came up with the idea together. He asked me was I up to it? I said yes. I even got us the bats. My little brother's on the high school baseball team. Our house is full of bats. I got us two fat ones. And I guess that's a sin. Do you think it was a sin? I guess it's a sin huh? I mean I wasn't even going to use my bat – I was just going to wave it around to scare old Mr. Christian. Wave it around like I was going to use it you know? Wouldn't you be scared if somebody waved a baseball bat at you and said give me all your money? I bet you'd give all your money over just like that. But yeah.

10

I know it's a sin. Is it a sin, Father – oh, I'm talking crazy. I don't really need you to tell me it's a sin Father I know it's a sin that was a stupid question. I talk crazy a lot please forgive me but I talk crazy a lot – but maybe you could tell me if it's a sin or not maybe you could just tell me I'm not sure –

Hold it, son. Slow down – yes, it is a sin –

– I know, I know – I always got to slow down for Parkie too – he says stop jabbering – like that, just stop jabbering. Oh I jabber father. I been spending my whole life asking stupid questions and jabbering and saying stupid things, and doing stupid things too like hooking up with God-damned Parkie. I thought wow, this is cool, to be hooked up with such a cool guy – he has that look, you know – that look of being a really cool guy – when he looks you in the eye it's like he's looking through you – creepy somehow – but there's something about that that really looks cool – and he's got a really cool scar by the side of his face, and this really cool grin where he screws up his eyes when something's funny – but he really isn't so cool is he Father I mean look at the mess he's got me into like I told you, I was with him when he shot Mr. Christian – just not even a half hour ago – but it seems like ten years Father, isn't that funny? A half hour ago seems like ten years. Yeah, years, I will get plenty of years in jail for this Father. I never been in jail Father I never even been near a jail but Parkie has – he was in for a while for beating up a guy – he's tough, really really tough – he almost killed the Goddamned guy—he pulled off his belt and used it for a strap and really whipped the shit out of the guy. Then when the guy was down he used his boot – but listen, listen – I didn't mean for anybody to die – I never wanted to be the one to make someone die – even though Parkie pulled the trigger – I was with him. I thought it would be fun – really big fun – I went along with robbing the place – I thought it would be cool to do – you know. With Parkie – everything's really cool and fun with Parkie – but I am sorry now Father I'm really really sorry –

All right son. Just calm down. You say you're sorry. That's what matters to God. I will now absolve you of this sin. God the Father of mercies, through the death and resurrection of his Son –

– but anyway – like I said before, Father, we were just going in to wave around the bats and be real bad assed, you know, and we knew old man Christian would give us all his money he'd be scared

11

to death being like he's about a hundred years old or should I say he used to be a hundred years old because he's dead now – oh, but maybe just maybe he isn't dead – do you think he might not be dead Father? Maybe he's not. Not everybody who gets shot ends up dead. They might look dead and all when they're laying there, but they're not dead, they pull through. I didn't go check him out to see if his heart was beating he just laid there with a big hole ripped in his chest and there was a lot of blood coming out – he had a white shirt it was all turning black its funny blood is red but it was turning the shirt all black – but I never checked to see if he's alive, maybe you could say a prayer Father maybe Mr. Christian will pull through – would you say a prayer like that Father, after you're done with the one you're praying now –

– has reconciled the world to himself and sent the Holy Spirit among us –

– I mean I almost shit my pants when Parkie pulled the big gun out of his pants and pointed it at Mr. Christian and Parkie dropped his bat and it made that clattery noise, you know, like a bat makes when you drop it on the hard floor – but I held on to mine because this was just like a dream that was happening in front of me I was so surprised it was like the inside of the store got all hazy and there was like a white halo around Parkie and Parkie was waving the gun and yelling at Mr. Christian give us all your money give it now – and Mr. Christian stood there bugeyed I mean really bugeyed they say that word but its really true people can get bugeyed – he was bugeyed –

– for the forgiveness of sins; through the ministry of the Church may God give you pardon –

– and Mr. Christian tossed his head back and opened his mouth and just said go to hell son, you and your friend there – you can go to hell, all these years here and I never been robbed just who do you think you are I know your mother and your Father they come in here to buy the papers and the odd thing now and then so who the hell do you think you are – you're just a young assed punk – I seen you around – I seen the kind of shitty places you hang around – you and your buddy there – hey Perry yeah Perry Manitoba I know your name it's Manitoba you been in here with your mom to buy bread I know you what are you doing mixed up with a young assed punk like this – put that gun down now, you got no guts to use a fucking gun –

– *and peace, and I absolve you from your sins in the name of the Father, and of the Son* –

– yeah Mr. Christian was talking to us like that – it made me feel pretty small, the way he was talking – and I was ready to back down, I was ready to leave the place – Mr. Christian was yelling we had no guts, I was even starting to tell Parkie let's back down – but then Parkie pulled the trigger and there was a big boom, like my ears hurt the boom was so big – my ears are still ringing now it's like the biggest sound I ever heard in my life and Mr. Christian stopped talking and went down behind the counter and blood splattered across the wall behind where he had stood I guess the bullet blew right through him and Parkie turned to me and said there that's what he deserves he had no right to talk to me like that, talk to me and you like that, come on let's get the money, let's get the money and split –

– *and of the Holy Spirit.*

– so we got the money and we dropped the bats and we ran out with stupid Parkie still waving that big gun – we ran up and down some alleys and ran in here – I'm just drenched in sweat –

– *you're absolved my son are you truly sorry?*

– sorry well yes I'm sorry as hell, I'm sorrier than I ever been for anything before in my life – we shouldn't have done it I shouldn't have done it – but what's done is done Father right you can't turn back the clock my Father used to say that whenever anything went wrong you can't turn the clock back son what's done is done – when Parkie pulled that gun I should have brained him with my bat, looking back that's what I ought to have done – but I didn't. I'll get jail time Father I don't want to go to jail I seen what it's like on TV you know, I'd rather die than be in jail – they mess with you in Jail they mess with you even worse than Parkie messes with people – I should have brained him I really should have made him drop the damned gun –

Suddenly the door is once more flung open by Parkie and –

What are you telling this guy? What are you telling him, taking all this time? C'mon! Perry! Let's go right now!

Sorry Father – I'm sorry I'm so sorry – but I got to go now–

Say an act of contrition first, son – hurry –

Yes I remember it from when I was a boy it's one I've never forgotten yet it goes O my God, I am heartily sorry for having offended You and I –

I said come on!

– detest all my sins –

Perry struggles with Parkie, trying to get through the act of contrition –

But I remember it from when I was a boy! Let me say it, let me – because I dread the loss of heaven and the pains of hell – that's how it goes Father right? That's how it goes –

They scuffle. The priest sits agape –

– but most of all because they offend you, my God, who are all good and deserving of all my love – Parkie let go my arm!

They struggle. Something's slammed against the wall.

– I firmly resolve, with the help of your grace – to confess my sins, to do – penance and to amend my life – no Parkie no –

– and the gun goes off and a body drops and the door slams shut and the stunned priest is alone but for the faraway sound of sirens coming from beyond the thin walls of the cheap built church in the fading echo of the shot.

JAMEZ CHANG

Learning to Drive

My dad had gotten rich selling liquor on Olympic Boulevard, opening shop when I was five. After that, a small bodega in Van Nuys. And it wasn't long before a chain of Red Moon Liquor stores thumb-tacked all of East L.A. If Randall Pak wasn't selling booze to *penny-thug* addicts, he was teaching his son how to "drive" – behind a counter. It was a Sunday afternoon and I was riding shotgun, studying for the SATs from behind one of dad's counters, his store in Cypress. Straight-A student plucking index cards from a black plastic box, cash register to my right.

"If someone really wanted to steal from you, Joel, you'd know it the moment they walked in." Dad was hanging phone cards on the wall behind me. "You learn to see that."

For dad, the cameras took the edge off. No good. They blunted that healthy pang of paranoia every merchant needed when he faced his daily man. Customers, in for the ride.

He was hovering over my work now – taller – no matter the concrete platform beneath my feet.

"Study this instead." He closed the box lid and put his arm around my shoulder. "A test of the eye charts."

He pointed to some men inside.

Gripping a Sharpie like he was hammering nails in mid-air, dad pointed to a customer in the third aisle: "Drunk from the *norae-bang*, that one. No good."

These were dad's impromptu size-ups – dissecting people from twenty feet away. It was the discernment he'd need to separate the customer from the shoplifter, and if the rumors were true, drinkers from gamblers, the loan-shark borrower. Downstairs client.

I hung my head, rubbed the side of the file box until three words I'd scrawled in pencil smeared off: *Red Moon District*.

Dad lifted my chin with his palm and motioned over to the sparkling white wines, second aisle. "And look at him, touching, touching, but won't ever buy. He's just here for the cigarettes."

"Cards and cameras can't teach you that," he said with a tap to his temple.

I'd heard it all before, dad's sermons – how "a moving lens was no match for good instincts and a Colt .45," how recorded surveillance was "the pussy machine hovering over a blind shoulder" – I thought a lecture for sure when I clicked open that box a second time. Cards to learn. Instead, dad jerked the box from my hands and stuffed it in a slot beneath the register.

"I'm putting you on the overnight."

***

I stood there, behind the counter; saw dad unplug a grey ATM by the entrance. "It's for your own good, son." The fluorescent lights were flickering above him. "The night goes by, you begin to see with your own eyes," he said with a tap – on a stiff brow this time. I panned across the aisles and froze at the beverage coolers in the back: a Bud can loosened from its six-pack. Then he held it open, the front door still, and turning around one last time: "Invisible, Joel, you just blend in."

Behind a counter, he was teaching his son how to drive; a place where he left me, not a .45 in sight.

That summer, overnight I saw how ten inches of cinder-block platform could sink; the Pak name thinning down to a stack of I-cards in a plastic shell box: *Intimidated, Irrelevant.* Front doors swinging open. Filipino boys play-shoved their way to the potato-chip rack; whispers of *padre* and *puta* by the newspaper trays; and my camera would focus: on magazines missing from stands; six-packs turning into fours; blue bandanas; white napkins falling off their front counters, always by "accident." For six long hours, I stayed invisible inside a *Red Ghost Liquor* store. Squirming. Turning napkin into rope.

But then May stopped bleeding, and the new nights arrived; and men along with them: guarding outside, planning it downstairs. And two weeks later, the red vials, heavy briefcases carried down to a basement floor. I learned the new words during the month of June: *confab, recalibration, diversification*; made steady gains, real progress with my vocabulary: *extortion, trafficking, racketeering, coercion.* Across the known street, a black Lincoln Town Car watched over the store, and I pictured two cranky Chicanos sipping a flat forty and complaining—*Why we gotta watch that pendejo inside?*

16

Things just clicked, boxes shut. I discovered my optimal study routine in July: I swept the floors, shuffled the cards, counted the money; I crushed a line of NoDoz and sniffed, peeled off the porno plastic – to think; and when that Lincoln outside would sleep, so would I. Then on an August night in 1993, a girl tiptoed past her mother to the front of the line, and with her chin on the counter, asked, "Are you that Chinese boy? That crazy *nigga*'s son?"

Come September, I covered up lenses, unplugged plastic vials. I'd tweezer-in a white-pebble promise and breathe, bubble-in the answers until my cinder-block platform floated sixty feet above linoleum floors and Scantron sheets. I dreamt for the first time.

The next morning, dad brought me down to basement earth. He closed the door and walked to his metal desk.

"Here. You passed," he said. "You don't need to work here anymore."

Dad threw a stack of clean twenties at my chest, heavy as a paperback.

I closed the door on my way outside. Walked out of dad's liquor store carrying a 4" x 6" file box and a clear plastic vial. Short sleeves, sprawled out on a bus bench, I rubbed my eyes and squinted past lamp-post rings to sky, and a mail-slot of morning light. Across the empty street, two men stirred drinks in Styrofoam cups, leaning against a black Lincoln Town Car. *Guardians of the Liquor Store* blowing on coffee, whispering mist to the side.

One of the men waved.

I looked down instead, at the open box on my lap. Later, the ground: hundreds of words I needed to learn.

CARTER SCHWONKE

Angelo's Angle

Angelo Jones's expression darkens when they ask him to remember his crime. He sees the day, far off in the distance, but he hesitates to answer. He's taking a hard look at his own conscience and a moment to read the parole board's mood. He's nervously rehearsing the words he practiced and hoping the past will loosen its hold. It's taken thirty years for his story to unravel in slow, unsteady spurts. Yet, he still remembers only pieces: his shame, her prostitution, and their fight. But what Angelo *doesn't* remember, will determine his fate.

He is well groomed and prepared. Waiting and delays are all he knows, but when the skinny parole board lady taps her pen, Angelo remembers that people from the street keep time. Time exists differently for him, in a chunk.

"Mr. Jones. Do you remember thrusting the weapon into your girlfriend?"

"I'm trying, ma'am, I ... I was drunk and high."

"Then you do not remember?"

"We were about to be homeless, ma'am."

Four terrifying board members want to know *exactly* what happened that day: the why, when, and how Dana looked on the floor, kids crying, a bloody knife in his hand. They want to watch Angelo rip the story from his chest, but it's a story he doesn't have. And though confidence is key, his fingers edge towards his hair where each strand is gelled into a style, popular thirty years ago. He doesn't want to muss it; he worked hard to look job worthy, marriage and family worthy, so he quickly drops his nervous hand, determined to hide how many chords they've already struck.

For months, Miss Eleanor, a prison reading volunteer, coached Angelo for this hearing. She told him, "Whatever the board asks you, answer them directly. They aren't determining your guilt. They want to know if you're prepared to re-enter society, and we know you are. Right?"

God, he's so ready to re-enter. Can't they see? With Miss Eleanor's help, he's memorized the words but, now that he's here, time gaps confuse him. Besides, he's of several minds on how to anchor himself in today's reality. Wouldn't a display of emotion show his remorse better than a calmly recited half-story?

Angelo recalls a trick Miss Eleanor taught him; bless her heart. He can endure the drama and tension associated with sitting in this chair, if he pictures himself at a desk in the prison classroom, near her, where he's not hassled or confused. But, after thirty years, confusion is his reality; prison is his real home with church, alcoholics anonymous, and Sunday waffles.

He also has his reading classes in a trailer in the east yard, near the basketball court. Volunteers, like Miss Eleanor, keep workbooks, letter charts, pencils and world maps in a locked cabinet and pass them out, according to level, on Tuesdays and Fridays. Some guys work on GEDs or take correspondence courses; others read about Stevie and his dog, Patches. Week after week, Angelo worked hard on his own story; it's called a man-letter, a written apology to Dana's survivors. It took him years to write his man-letter since Angelo had to learn to read and write first.

Perspiration, under Angelo's blue, buttoned up collar, jolts him back from Miss Eleanor's safe classroom to his hearing. It's his third hearing, and for one-hundred and eight days, since notification, he's anticipated their questions. Why didn't he guess that stray clips of suppressed memories would sidetrack his true, pure intention to be direct and honest? Only by floating sometimes, keeping distance, and creating a different past, has he stayed sane. When it's time to be here and only here, his challenge begins.

When they repeat the question, Angelo remembers more of Miss Eleanor's advice. "Make eye contact with the people who will determine your fate."

"I do not remember," he says, "because I was not there when she died."

The high-haired woman sighs and shuffles papers. Angelo knows most of her papers by heart. He wrote the man-letter, he submitted his Anger-Management course completion certificate, he learned Conflict Resolution skills and How to Fight the Devil. Decades of work went into "Angelo Jones's Packet." If only they'd realize the emotional break-through he made a few summers ago, and then again last fall when his son was shot.

She repositions her reading glasses. "Yes, you left the motel room. We see here, you went to the corner store immediately after the incident. Is that correct? You left your girlfriend, bleeding on the floor, with your two small children?"

Instead of fighting to make a case for himself, Angelo's thoughts escape again. He's the first inmate to arrive at reading class. Eventually, others come. Martin's out of lockdown. Rob, Rick and George were delayed at work, but no Tyrone. Only Angelo knows he won't be back. He got thrown out because he asked Miss Susan to lift up her shirt. Angelo heard him do it. He turned him in, because Miss Susan was a young, shy volunteer, and Angelo feared she'd lift it. No way, would he let Tyrone mess it up for the rest of them. Prison life goes by common sense codes: don't ask personal questions, don't flirt, don't sit too close. Tyrone got weak.

When Miss Eleanor enters the classroom, the first thing she and Angelo work on is trust. Each Tuesday and Friday, he puts her back through it. She has no idea why he asks, this and that, but he's deciding, you know? He's reading her eyes, and deciding if she's the one to trust with revisions to his man-letter. That letter documents his first and last, highest and lowest moments, the beginning and end of his story. It's so damned important; he should just read it to the parole board right now. Let it fly with all the stutters, stops, and gulps that come naturally when he sees his awful story in print.

"Mr. Jones, where did you get the weapon you used?"

The young man wants to know. He's easier to look in the eyes than those women are. Since the board is two men and two women, he's able to look at half. Yet, he knows the other half listens best and tries to work with him. But, his never flirt rule, even with a skinny woman and a high-haired woman, could stop a glance from becoming something else in *their* minds.

There's no way to answer the young man about the weapon. From two previous experiences, he knows the young man won't believe that Angelo cannot remember the weapon. Lying must be best, and Angelo is of several minds again and falls further from his careful plan.

"I don't know," he says. "I was a teenager, in a state of rage and jealousy when I grabbed it. I realize now. But then ... all I knew was what I knew."

"And what was that?" the man asks, leveling his glare.

"She prostituted herself."

Angelo tenses, his parole hearing is a full blown out of body experience. He knows he is still in the chair, but barely. He grabs his collar again. What a mess, how did this happen when he practiced, memorized and role-played? Miss Eleanor, what now? Miss Eleanor, I told you they wouldn't like the truth!

Miss Eleanor was sure they'd see his newly acquired self-awareness, maturity, and deep humility. This hyper-repentant Angelo, with his thick packet of achievements and years of excellent conduct, isn't the same Angelo they saw before. "Tell the truth. Be the *new* Angelo."

Right. With or without embellishments? Fill in hazy details, weapons, and regrets or let the truth lie flat and unsatisfying? Any details he could use blurred years ago; he's never lied about anything, but he could start now. Chill. God, he's lived with a lot worse; he's lived with Dana's death. He murdered her and sat in a cell for thirty years. He can live with an embellishment or two if it means release.

But, he's different now; he learned that doubt, despair, defensiveness and defiance are the devil's fiery arrows. His bigger, immediate problem is how to relate to people from the street. Do these board members want a lie so they can all go home? Do they want a lie so an old guy gets out of prison to make room for the next guy, probably an Iraqi vet? Is Angelo fighting their clock? He understands the power of choices, but there are too many that conflict and cancel each other out. The skinny lady pulls out his psych report.

That report is so damning, he escapes to the classroom again where he scans for Miss Eleanor. He settles into a spring day, when he brought photos of his sister's dog and the backroom she'd cleared for his release. He wants to surprise Miss Eleanor with these photos when she sits next to him, smelling like store-bought shampoo. He calculates where she is in her rotation; three inmates are ahead of him. She'll get to his desk in about thirty minutes.

Now all four board members reach for that psych report. After twenty years of sitting around, five years of painful self-examination, then five more of perfect behavior, it comes down to Angelo's story and his psych report. He's so worried about the report, he reconsiders doubtful choices, like lying through his teeth.

They can't bully or rush him. If lying is the only way out, fine, screw the truth.

"You realize," the high-haired woman, says, "your inability to remember details on the night of August 17, 1982 concerns medical experts. Key suitability factors for release include the extent of your insight, Mr. Jones, and your emotional functioning. With half your story missing, there are concerns about denial, thus, a risk of future violence. Please address this."

Angelo doesn't understand psychiatrists and he especially doesn't understand women; he's drowning in doubt. But he backs off the idea of lying, because he'll have to lie to Miss Eleanor later about how it went. Lies will pile up and he has enough shit in his life. His fresh hair cut, clean nails, politeness, his four-star attendance at AA are all about doing the right thing, feeling the right feelings, knowing your own rightness. The leaps he took over the years to Islam were epoch, considering he began prison life with contraband drugs and weekly fights. Maybe he's not a genius, but he figured out that highs aren't worth lows.

"My daughter is an adult now and I truly believe she will forgive me," Angelo says. "That allows me to move on and think about what comes next. You will see in my packet..."

"Yes, yes, you've learned to read since your last hearing. This psych report mentions better self-reflection and remorse, all good indicators." Our concern is your denial of the weapon and whether your plans for the future are solid enough to deter and distance you from future crimes."

Angelo points. "I've carried those papers around with me, for years. I was scared they'd get lost or stolen, you know, I'm putting together a new life, like it says."

High-Hair sits forward and terrifies him. "It says you have people on the outside ready to help. You've trained in furniture repair and your brother owns a salvage shop. And I'm pleased to note, a half-way house is willing to take you after release."

"Yes, those are my truths and hopes."

They are listening intently; he has their attention, just when he's run out of self-control. The last of it is slipping away. Since lies, clocks, plans, fancy words and tactics aren't his style, and they aren't working, Angelo will have to wing-it. Voice raised, he asks, "You want to know why I didn't call an ambulance when I got back?"

Four heads nod in unison.

"I was too high to call an ambulance because we'd smoked crack cocaine for three days. When I got back from the store, with more vodka, was she still alive? I don't know. I had no sense of time; she was asleep or blacked out. They were all asleep."

Miss Eleanor said they'd listen to the truth, if the new Angelo was direct and ... articulate. She'd used the word, *articulate*. Was that happening now? Papers no longer shuffled, eyes blinked, blue, green, brown. Frightening, but he'd done the right thing. Right?

"I could tell you I bought the knife weeks before. I could tell you I planned to stab her because I hated how she paid for drugs. I could tell you that when I went to the store, I was thinking, boy, I sure showed her. I could say the children made me crazy, and I never wanted them. Any day, I planned to leave and start a better life without all that pressure and crying and disgusting behavior. But I loved her. I've always said, I loved Dana."

The women study Angelo's tears; the men turn towards the small window. As Angelo wipes his cheek, he knows he still hasn't answered their questions. This is the end, this is his usual moment to fail. To delay the inevitable, he glances outside too. Geese preen in the yard, in thick afternoon fog. He's been locked up so long, he hears the ocean lapping the shore through concrete walls.

"Mr. Jones? I can't stress the importance of the question we've posed."

"She was pregnant."

"Yes."

"I would never consciously or soberly kill a woman I loved who was carrying my child. Never."

"Yet, it happened."

"Not consciously or soberly."

Mr. Brown Suit flips pages. "Jealousy is noted by your psychiatrist as a driving force and a potentially unresolved issue for you."

"Yes, Mr. Jones, jealousy will happen again," the skinny lady adds.

Her palms lie flat. She's so concerned, she presses the table. But how can he discuss such things with women? He's a monster. *Miss Eleanor, am I a monster to them?* "No, Angelo, women are no different. Our concerns, our motivations are the same as yours. Don't add gender to your list of worries. Board members are trained officials."

Hope is tricky, and Angelo knows how to manage it. Biting down hard on his tongue works. When it comes to self-preservation, he supposes all humans have little quirks, fears, and secrets. Yes, jealousy is one of his, and there's his other secret too. Reading comprehension—it's poor; but he pretends to understand for Miss Eleanor's sake. Islam and the Brotherhood, he can take or leave, but not classroom time. So these officials are right. His jealousy is quirky, scary, human, and it has no end.

What has time done to curb Angelo's jealousy? Nothing. Time has made Angelo look taller and more handsome to himself, even better qualified to be a provider and father. But time did not teach him how to look in the other direction. He guards that packet with his life—a great example of how a man protects what little he has. Angelo almost smiles. Either he's giving up on his third hearing, or the very idea of a man not protecting what he loves is so unbelievable, he has to react.

The whole room waits to find out if Angelo's heart knows more than it tells. Angelo wants to know too. Are impressions lies? He drops his eyes and hears the ocean lapping, lapping. His final choice is to throw himself at their mercy. His cellmate got out this way. Vic is crazy, but he walks the streets now, probably talking to himself, shuffling, and wondering where the chow line is.

More tears? More remorse? Be a fine, powerful actor on stage or a quivering convict at the end of his rope? These choices stink, and he hears the beat of the clock again. Brown Suit is staring at his watch. He doesn't look annoyed, he looks sad; so does Skinny Lady. High-Hair is re-reading the psych report and Young Guy is unreadable. Angelo's emotional range, limited to variations of fear and hope, has collapsed.

He'll tell Miss Eleanor how he made a strong case for himself and he'll thank her; bless her heart. And while he waits for the parole board's decision, he'll claim respect for the justice system and pretend to read. If he needs the Brotherhood, he knows where to find them.

He has regrets, of course, like how long and unfair his fight with the devil has been. What if he'd been older, educated, or sober? But every inmate Angelo knows regrets drifting in those endless shades of gray before crossing over. Every guy inside has a version of that same blurred-line story. And each story has a carefully crafted curve, reshaped over thousands of nights, so a guy can live with himself. Angelo's doesn't vary, he keeps his angle simple. He never speaks the wrong truths.

RONAN BARBOUR

Crabgrass

It never really
occurred to me
that I could wake up
one day
and not like the way
this story was going,
that I
might not be able to
find the time
to change it.

I guess I always
thought it would end
like a highly
touching and satisfying movie
and when the credits
rolled
I would know all the
names
even those that were
dicks to work with
well now it would all
be over
and what was left of
me in soul
would have to smile
thinking it all
worked out
in the grand shape
in the end.

But now I wake up
sometimes in the
middle of the night
or early morning

and I wonder with
panic
murmuring my heart
how I could suddenly
find myself
trapped in a role
I no longer know,
trapped
in a plot where I
don't trust the author
anymore
after some obscene
twists.

Not that I'm ready to
quit it
just yet
you know
I've worked too hard
to get
this far into the
story
and even if it's
starting to get kind
of slow
the work of this role
is really
all that I know.

And I guess I'm still
blessed to be able to play the part
even if it's not at
all what I expected
it is good to be
working, after all,
while there are so
many replacements
waiting in the
wings.

KEN POYNER

The Torturers

Into my job I pour all of my expectations,
And all of my embarrassments as well.
I steady my work by considering those times
I have come out, yet again, on the short end
Of the public stick: of my being ten points
Shy of the credit score I need when it comes
To the financing option I really want.
I am sure you have felt this way, too:
The smallness in your own clothes,
The need to ride the moment's discourses
Sidesaddle.

This employment
Is only temporary for me.
At the moment, I need the job;
But soon I will be off
To an executive position, moved
To a far better place, in an elevated corner office,
With my own two windows: I will be made
A member of the Order
Of Those Who Have Pleasing Secretaries.
Then I will be able to buy any
Vehicle on the sales lots of the disloyal.
Anyone can see I am wasted at this job.

KEN POYNER

Truth

You will know it when you have it.
Not with the surprise of discovery,
Nor with the conviction of the victim
Exuding facts during torture.
It will have a mathematical ring:
Unaccountable, a simple this or that.
You will not have to question it:
It will fit in. It will need
No preamble, no caterwauling.
It will not stand up to embellishment.
It needs neither reason nor pain.
It does not come with tassels
Or fringe. It has no expiration date.
It does not care that you have
Become dirty to get it; or have idiographic moral
Issues; or equivocate about its actual
Value or cost. None
Of it matters. And if it does not fit
The lilting, faithful narrative,
You can make something up: make something
Flat and algebraic and colorless
And no one will notice, no one, not even
The tin can souls you pry it out of,
Not even you. No, really,
It is only an outline.

STEVEN LOTON

The Ex-Pro

Jack jammed a cigar into his mouth and put a match to the tip. He puffed it six times. It flamed then fell flat. He sat on the bench, puffing and waiting. His team was 2-0 down. Sunday league. Jack was in his football shirt, shorts, socks, no boots. He waited. Then they banged in another. 3-0 down. Christ.

Jack was an ex-pro. 40 now. Finished. But in his day he was pure class. Premier league. Won cups. Everything. Then the drugs took over. Parties. Booze. Women. He blew all of his cash. Now he made guest appearances at parties and small events for some scratch.

Jack heard a voice from the turnstile calling him. He turned. It was a small boy with his father. A fan. Jack waved as the boy spoke.

"Hey Jack, you couldn't score in a brothel, you fat bastard."

Then the manager screamed in Jack's face.

"Jack, warm up. You're going on."

Jack laced his boots, slowly stood up, and did a side stretch. Almost tore a muscle. He took one final pull of the cigar and tossed it.

Jack was subbed on. He jogged a few yards and scratched his gut. The ball came to his feet. He dummied once, moved left, and drilled a low shot that caught some wind and flew into the top corner. 3-1, final score.

The players jogged off at 90 minutes. One came up to Jack, "Hey man you still got it. Just shape up and you could go pro again."

"Yeah, yeah I know, you got a cigarette?"

The player sighed and ran off. As Jack was leaving the pitch, a man in a long coat was standing on the side-lines. He approached. Jack saw his face. It was the sports agent, 'Arry, the bastard.

"What do you want, 'Arry? I paid my debts. I don't owe you shit."

"Firstly, you do still owe us but we don't want it back. Come in for a meeting."

"Meeting, eh? Sounds like business talk for bullshit."

"We been watching you Jack, you still got it."

"Don't waste my time."

"You got better things to do with your 'time', Jack?"

"No."

"Then come in."

"Okay, okay. Hey, lend me a ten."

The next morning Jack woke up with a hangover. Some beard. He scratched his belly and stood. The phone rang. He found it.

"Yeah?"

"Jack, you were supposed to be here at eleven. There's a car out front waiting for you. Get in it."

Jack peeled the curtain back. Was a limo. White, blacked out windows. Class.

Jack dressed and went down. He made sure the neighbours were watching before he climbed in. Jack looked for the booze in the booze cabinet. Drinks cabinet. No luck. The limo took off, drove through town, then pulled up. Jack reached into his pocket to tip the driver. No luck there either. He signed his name on a napkin instead. Grinned, handed it to the driver, then got out. The limo drove off, as the crumpled napkin came flying from the driver's window.

Jack found the office on the third floor. He walked straight in. Johnson's body erected like he was having a heart attack.

"Hell Jack, don't you knock?"

"You're expecting me artchya?"

"Siddown siddown, son."

"'Son', shit we're almost the same age."

Jack sat across from Johnson. Beside him was 'Arry. The office was stuffy. A window needed cracking. Or somebody needed a shower.

"Let's cut to it Jack ...."

"Wait, let's hear some bullshit first. Pour me a drink, light me a cigar, flash some cash, show me some bullshit before you get serious."

"We haven't got time for that now, Jack. Let's talk business. We're in a relegation battle. It's a dog fight. We need at least ten points to stay up. It's never been done before."

"So, sign some young star, from the continent."

"Shit Jack, the transfer window is closed. Do you even keep up with the newspapers anymore?"

Jack looked up at the ceiling. A spider was upside down.

Johnson continued. "We been watching you Jack. You still got it. All you need is to get your fitness back up."

"I don't know man; you got a drink, beer or something?"

"Fraid not Jack, you're off the booze now. Smokes too. No drugs either, you're clean."

Jack rocked back on his chair then stood up, sharply.

"OH AM I HUH? AND I GUESS WOMEN ARE OFF THE MENU TOO HA?"

"Women are fine, Jack."

Jack sat down, "Well okay then."

"You got a woman Jack?"

"No, but I was just checking."

Finally 'Arry spoke from the corner of his mouth.

"We got the contract drawn up. Four thousand per week, Jack. Three months work. You'll be a rich man."

"A millionaire?"

"Not quite."

"Then I want five thousand per week."

"Don't get greedy, Jack."

Jack stood up and walked toward the window, "Now it's six thousand."

"We don't need you that bad Jack. The deal is over. Dead."

Jack spun on his heels. "Don't be hasty now. It's a deal, four thousand per week. Now let's crack out the champagne and celebrate."

Jack did a little dance on the rug.

"Fraid not Jack, you got training now."

There was a training kit waiting for Jack in the changing room. He got changed and jogged out onto the pitch. His teammates were already out there. They were all tall and lean. They seemed excited about something. One with no hair and bushy eyebrows came running up with his hand out.

"Hey Jack, join in, we're running drills. Come on man."

"Yeah, yeah I'm coming."

Jack joined in. But they moved the ball around too fast. They were all fit. For them running was fun. They all had a constant grin on. Jack's heart was busting from his chest. His lungs filled and stayed full. He was knackered. In his mind he was still fit, still a champ. But the mind plays tricks.

Two hours later the team was in the changing room. Jack stepped into the fancy shower. His whole body ached. He turned the tap. Hot water powered down onto his head. It felt great. But odd. The pressure was too much. He stepped out and towelled off.

Saturday arrived and Jack was on the bench. The team was 1-0 down with 15 minutes left. The manager, Robbie Carriage waved Jack over. Jack stood up and jogged over. Robbie spoke into his ear.

"Jack, there are ten thousand fans here. I'm putting you on. I got faith in you Jack. Don't make me look bad, ok?"

"Sure."

"Now get out there and play just behind the front two. Hang in there looking for space. Let a few shots off, okay?"

"Sure."

Jack got subbed on. There were a chorus of boos. Jack waved. The crowd was on his back. They always were. He jogged into the centre circle. The ball was out wide. Then it was in the box. Then it got headed out. Then it was at Jack's feet. He played a little one-two, got it back, stepped over and hit a 30 yard shot with his left. Top corner. Jack raised his arms. He didn't want to waste his energy celebrating. The crowd booed. Jack liked it that way. Final score: 1-1.

A few months passed and Jack was getting into a rhythm. He showed up to training on time. His breathing was easing up. He had scored 9 goals in the league and 2 in cup competitions. They were three points clear from relegation and into the Rumblows cup final. Life was good.

'Arry found Jack in the pub on the corner of Vine Street. Jack had one woman under each arm and an open shirt. He had an unlit cigar in his mouth and a little trilby hat on his head.

"Jack, let's talk."

They sat down on wooden stools.

"Pay the ladies so they can leave."

Tammy stood up and jerked her head back. "Hey we're not prostitutes, ya know."

"Really," said 'Arry, "Can you spell it?"

"No, but what's that got to do with anything?"

"Okay then, just leave."

Nobody moved. Jack flipped his wallet and threw out some notes. Tammy's hand reached out. Each finger nail was painted a different colour. All chipped.

"Let's pick this up later ladies," said Jack.

Tammy and Lyn stood up. Tammy swallowed her cocktail before leaving. Lyn just walked off giggling at nothing.

"How's training going Jack?"

"Shit, we're out of relegation and I'm hot property again. Couldn't be better."

"You haven't scored in five games. You been missing training. You're back on the booze."

"Like shit I am."

The barman laid a pint of lager down in front of Jack.

"That's not mine."

"Don't be an idiot Jack. You got the final next week. It's the biggest game of your career. If you impress in that game you may get another contract for next season."

Jack took a slug of the pint.

"Relax, I got this."

"I hope so."

'Arry walked off into the night. Jack was alone. He felt down. Morose. Depressed. He shook his head and then looked around. Is this what life was? Some small highs and many lows. Jack's mobile rang twice. It was Tammy, the prostitute. He let it ring out. Maybe 'Arry was right. Maybe he should pull it together. He didn't want to be a loser for the rest of his life. Jack thought about his father. A great man, according to his mother, but really he was a huge turd. A total waste of space. Jack's father had been constantly angry at home. Outside of the house he was kind and friendly to the neighbours and to the post man. He even pretended to like animals and small children. But behind closed doors he was a mean son of a bitch. He drank all night and beat Jack regularly.

Jack made it home, lay on the bed, and tried something that he had never tried. He prayed. He prayed for a friend. A good soul in his life. Some kindness, some love. There was a gentle knock on the door. He sat up cautiously. Maybe it was a long lost family member. He opened the door. It wasn't. It was Tammy.

"Jack, you still owe me five hundred. I want my dough."

"Please not tonight Tammy. I paid you already. I have training early tomorrow."

"Training, ha, don't be silly, you're finished. I should find myself a young footballer. One time I made it with Dwayne Pooney. He pays on time and he's class on the pitch."

"He couldn't lace my boots."

"Neither can you old man."

"Watch it Tammy, I've been saving up my sperm for weeks now. It's a boxer's technique. I'm on edge. I can blow."

"You couldn't blow a balloon."

"You certainly can. I can vouch for that."

Tammy slapped Jack across the cheek. Jack smiled.

"Not even in my top ten, baby. Now remove yourself."

Tammy stormed off down the hall. She rang on all of the neighbours' doors and screamed continually until the elevator arrived. She climbed in and the doors closed. It was silent. Jack apologised to the neighbours and went inside. He got into bed and had a good, long, deep sleep. That would be the last time he attempted praying.

Jack spent the next week waking up early and getting a jog in before training. There were some good looking females on his jogging route as well as some not so good looking ones. Jack used to slow down and stretch when he saw a looker and speed up when he saw a non-looker. Training went well that week. His touch was always there but he was building up his cardio once more. Like the old days. Jack was back.

The final arrived. 3pm kick off. The team was in the changing room, before. Nerves were setting in. Jack stood up.

"Listen fellas," he tapped his boots against the wall. "Listen up. I'm the senior player so I should give you kids a pep talk. I know you're nervous."

Jerry looked up, "I'm not."

"Okay," Jack continued, "you may not be, but the others are."

A voice came from the shower room, "We've been in finals before. Nobody's nervous. Hey is there any crap paper out there …?"

Jack strolled around the changing room leisurely. He had no pants on.

"This is the final, lads. We need to show guts and strength. We need to close in on the ball quickly when we lose possession. We need to break quickly when we have the ball and most importantly we need to get the ball to me in and around the area." Jack paused "ARE YOU WITH ME, BOYS? GET THE BALL TO MY FEET."

The manager walked in, "Sit down Jack."

"Wait a minute, I'm giving a captain's team talk."

"You're not the captain."

"Maybe I should be."

"Don't be stupid, Jack, You couldn't captain a rubber dingy boat."

Jack sat down. The manager gave his team talk. Frankly, Jack thought it was pretty useless. But he was starting so he laced up his boots and jogged out with the rest of the team. He did some warm up exercise while sucking on a Lucozade.

The game kicked off. The crowed roared. Jack stayed just behind the top two strikers. He picked up the ball and laid it off. It got intercepted. Some jeers rang out. Few minutes later, he picked it up again and lay off another bad one. Damn. He didn't want to get into a bad rhythm. Football was like that. A few bad passes and your mind wanders. Suddenly the opposing team went up the other end and a cross flew into the box. There was a scramble. The ball rolled into the net. Shit. One down. Half time came and there was another team talk from the manager.

"Well boys that was a terrible half. I don't like to name names but Jack you really were a pile of shit out there."

Jack stood up. "Hey I didn't let that goal in. I'm not a defender."

"It's lucky you're not."

"I can't get into the game. You need to put me up front. Manage me for Christ sakes, man. You have the classiest player this country has ever seen at your disposal and you're letting these two arse holes play up front. No offence Jerry."

Jerry grunted.

"YOU WANNA GO UP FRONT OLD MAN?" screamed the manager.

"If you ask nicely, I may just do that."

"Okay, you got twenty minutes to show me what you got. Don't mess this up."

"Last time I made a *mess* in my pants was when I was five."

The second half kicked off. Jack drifted up front. The ball got sprayed out wide. A cross-swung in. He jumped, got a head to it. The ball flew and rattled off the bar. It got cleared. Son of a bitch. A giant defender ran up to Jack.

"Mate, you're shit."

"That's original."

"You're still shit."

"So's your mum."

The ball was up the other end. It fell to their striker. He hit it. They scored. Holy crap. Jack looked at the manager. He looked at his watch. The game kicked off again. Jack touched it. Put it through the defender's legs. Dropped his shoulder. Took it left and hit a 25 yard shot with his left foot. It fizzed of the grass and flew into the bottom corner. Jack ran off, pulled his shirt over his head.

Somehow that crowd started to chant Jack's name. It had never happened before. It gave him some gas. Made him feel good. The crowd was playing with his emotions. His whole career they had hated him. But sports fans were fickle. All they needed was some reward and they could turn. After all, they paid money for the seats. Why shouldn't they be rewarded?

The ball was drilled low across the middle of the park. It was picked up and swung across toward the corner flag. A cross looped in, got headed out. Jack saw it coming on the edge of the box and as the ball dropped he peppered a half volley straight into the top corner. Jack sprinted off, celebrating. He slid along the grass on his knees and the team jumped all over him. He was hot shit.

The game continued to move at pace. Jacks lungs were fading. He looked up at the clock. 85 minutes. The game was drawn at 2-2. He bent over to inhale and exhale. That felt good. The whistle blew. His team had a corner. Jack jogged into the box. The corner was taken. Jack saw the ball curling into the box. It was just behind him. Jack turned, jumped, and hit a bicycle kick volley. The net rippled. Hat trick. He peeled off and tore his shirt off, swinging it in the air. The final whistle blew. Game over. They won the cup.

The season came to an end. The team survived the relegation battle. It was 2pm and the sun was burning the concrete pavement. Jack was in the pub reading a newspaper. A man entered. He was dressed in a trench coat and beneath that was a pink ironed shirt. He looked around, then sat to Jack's left.

"You Jack Cherkamp?"

"Nope," Jack turned the page. "Got the wrong guy."

The barman put a pint down. "Put that on ya tab, Jack?"

"Sure."

"But are you actually going to pay this tab, Jack?"

Jack looked up into the barman's face. He had these scared little eyes, a rounded head, two day beard and no soul. He had no wife, four children, a mortgage and a second-hand car. He voted labour in hope that there would be some change, but there never was. He kept voting labour.

"Sure," said Jack, "I'll pay it when I leave. You got a problem with that coz I can take my business elsewhere."

The barman nodded and wiped a rag across the bar off into a corner.

"So Jack," said trench coat. "I have a proposition."

"Can you spell it?"

"Yeah. Can you?"

"Nope. Let's hear this proposition then."

"We want to drag you out of retirement again. But this time we want you to play for the champions of the league."

"Can't friend. Retired. Now please exit the pub."

Trench coat pushed a piece of paper across the bar. Held kept his finger pressed down until Jack looked. Then he removed his finger.

"Take a look."

"I don't want your phone number, friend. I'm not that way inclined. But it's two thousand and thirteen. Feel free to act as you will. This isn't Korea."

Trench coat stood up and walked off. He stopped at the door and removed a handkerchief from his inside coat pocket. He covered the door handle and opened the door, slid out.

"That fella is a real arsehole," said the barman. Then he grabbed the piece of paper and balled it up. "I'll throw this in the bin for ya, Jack."

"Put that down."

The barman did just that. Jack unfolded the paper and had a look. Then he removed his wallet and started peeling notes off.

"Hey, Jack you paying your tab, eh, I knew you would, you're a good man Jack."

"There's also a big tip there."

Barman counted up the notes.

"Doesn't seem like a big tip at all. Hey, want another pint, Jack?"

"Can't. Training again."

Then Jack stood up and walked toward the door. He pulled his coat sleeve over his hand and twisted the door handle. His car was parked in the supermarket car park. He found it, got in, and let all four windows down. Then he drove along slowly pissing all the other drivers off.

GEORGE SPARLING

Going the Distance

Sweet Dickie Score lasted one day in vocational school to learn the skills of a tool and die maker. "I'm still a boxer in my mind," he said, eyes tearing up, and I cradled him to my breasts. After seventy-four fights, he couldn't handle tests. We married after he retired.

I saw many of his bouts with his brother Vince. I learned that growing up with Dickie meant Vince was beaten-up a lot. Dickie hated how his brother received accolades for high achievements in academic pursuits. Vince became a tool and die maker, learning computer-controlled ways to make precision instruments, whereas Dickie made his living boxing, that sweet science.

I met Dickie at HiTown, a posh club after he knocked out a top ranked middleweight. He drank too much champagne, hugged too many gold diggers. I loved that Kanye West song, "Gold Digger": "He gon' make it to a Benz out of that Datsun/He got that ambition, baby look in his eyes/This week he's moppin' floors, next it's the fries." I wanted him come to my place, I'd good jazz, and if it was West you wanted, we'd listen to rap.

After losing four fights in a row, the purse getting less and less, I asked him to marry me. He told me he hadn't many scars because the boxing commission switched to fabric gloves which allowed air to pass and had complete leather-backed stitches. In earlier fights his old Mexican-style gloves had padding around the wrists. He said the punching portion of those gloves was thin and compact, and made his punches harder and caused more damage than the old ones. He spoke as a man steeped in professionalism: he loved to explain details of the trade. "I hope I won't inflect damage to you as I had to boxers," he said, and for that tenderness I loved him.

As the years passed, he burrowed into a hole, away from me. As the children grew up, whenever they talked about what they learned in school, he said, "Your mom will listen," and waved them away. They usually beat him in checkers. He watched cable movies, and especially liked westerns and black and white classics. Strangely, he never wanted to watch pay-per-view fights.

"That was work, now I'm retired." He sometimes spoke of Vince, how he, Dickie, should be richer than him after all the bouts, including three championship contests.

Sex was always good. Physically, he was in good shape, jogging two miles four times a week. His hands ached so he soaked them in brine; before each fight, he massaged brine into his face to prevent cuts, too.

"Why don't you get along with Vince?" Or had he addressed the real reason?

"Somebody has to pay for all the pain I went through to make a living."

"Like Vin?" He paused, looked me in the eyes, hard and long, and said, "He bet against me, and won. He bet for me, and won. He told me he did. Cleaned up, he said, many in bouts with you and Vin ringside. Knew bookies, fixers, even my manager was mobbed up, he said. I said, I know, I had to take the count and lose sometimes." The words seemed to hit him below the belt: I saw suffering, more die of that than physical pain. "And you know what, he said he bankrolled Score, Inc. off gambling money from my fights."

"He told me he took out loans and paid them back."

Vince and I were close, though that revolved around Dickie's career.

Dickie showed us old-style gloves he had fixed with barbed wire, sharp barbs staggered, without gaps of smooth wire, fists coiled with hurt.

He threw punches a few feet from our faces, shouting:

"No more Sweet Dickie Score. Hey Vin, here's one for you," and he jabbed the air, cackling with each jab as invisible Vince took barbed blows.

Without a hobby or job, he got fatter, eating pretzels and Doritos, ham and eggs for breakfast, always steak and potatoes for dinner. I tried better diets but he would raise his voice and say:

"This kept me strong. I wasn't a dead man in the ring."

I slept in the children's bedroom, frightened he would attack me in my sleep with those gloves.

"I'll take the kids and live with Vince if you keep those gloves." The choice of Vin the liar opposed to Dickie the vicious was easy.

"No weapons in the house but these," he said, putting them on without lacing up. All he had to do was slap them against my face and I'd be disfigured. Dickie said before our marriage that I looked like Miss Universe.

"I'm leaving," I said and he replied, "You'll be back."

"Will I? I'll have a better and safer life with Vince."

"Lana, somebody will be sorry if you go to him."

Dickie would not see a psychiatrist and take medication. But, he was so nice with the kids, and always kind to me, surprising me with gifts, like framed photographs of him and me I'd never seen, many photos of us making the rounds of clubs, snorkeling off the coast of Yucatan, dancing in fashionable hot spots in Paris, meeting old battlers from foreign countries, posing in Vegas casinos with entertainers .... All that ended when we married.

"I kept them in that locked trunk and gave you back our memories," he said so sweetly, but that hadn't stopped me leaving him. I packed my clothes as well as the children's, grabbed my jewelry, and left. I feared Dickie's sense of justice, maybe he'd lash out at the housecleaner, mail carriers, or solicitors.

I asked Vince whether Dickie had a place at Score, Inc., his tool and die firm. He needed and liked routine. Maybe he'd cool out. Vince paused and said:

"He could be a janitor, though I don't need more, but all he has to do is show up and get a paycheck." I warned him about Dickie's behavior, but Vince laughed it off---he bore a scar on his cheekbone from Dickie's fist. "That was kid stuff way back when."

After settling in with Vince, I still rendezvoused with Dickie in hotels, sometimes even here in Vince's comfy home when he wouldn't be around for a few hours. He had much higher than average sexual skills; Vince's long hours, even weekends at the plant, left him too tired for bed action, or, for that matter, doing anything but slouching around the house, maybe going to the country club for a round of golf and coming back snockered.

According to Dickie, when machinists saw him in the corridors, they often made cruel remarks about him being a dummy. "Vince says you can't beat your kids in checkers," one said to him, but they never asked him about his career or insider secrets of the sport.

Once pegged a dummy, always a dummy.

I suspected Vin was seeing another woman, one who hadn't besieged him every time I recounted my times with Dickie.

Today, Vince called, saying he'd be late, and would get home by eight. Conferencing on Skype held him at work. I told him I'd be here. I always told Vin the truth, only crooked, zigzagy.

Dickie set down his gym bag: he wanted to work out at the gym.

"I thought running was your thing, not weights," I said.

"I need to work off stress."

He drank Cokes mixed with V-8 juice, a concoction that made me nauseated at first, but he insisted I taste it. "Not bad," I said, unwilling to interrupt watching Badlands, about a charismatic serial killer and an underage, reticent, tag-along girlfriend wandering around America the Beautiful as the sociopath killed innocent people. The gorgeous landscape contrasted with ugly deeds of a sociopath killer and a beguiled girl who spouted romantic clichés— this broadened Dickie's usual movie fare.

"It's like when you get belted without seeing the punch coming. That movie knocked me out."

"Vince likes police procedures, just so some lowlifes get the crap pounded out of them in the process of bringing them to justice."

"Some guy told me justice is blind and deaf." He covered his eyes and ears with a pillow, but the joke went stale.

"Vin won't be back till eight, relax," I said as we sat on Vince's latest bauble, an immense $5,000 Italian striped leather sofa. We made love after the movie, and sat naked on the sofa, when Dickie said he wanted to leave before the weight room closed.

Vince came home earlier than expected and Dickie quickly reached into the bag and put on the unlaced, barbed wire gloves. Faster than I thought he could move, he grabbed Vince and slapped him around. Vince's face bloodied.

Lacerations, deep and bleeding, punctured Vince's mug when he gave him right hooks, uppercuts, backhand shots, rabbit punches to the base of the skull, then straight jabs to the nose, a few kidney punches, and many low-blows. He scraped his face around the eyes, cheeks, and mouth. A mutilated maze of rich purplish blood gashed his face.

Benito Mussolini's violent end couldn't have been this bad. Troughs of gouged, oozing, gashes covered his face, blood dripping down as Vince crawled to a corner of the room.

"All that talk about science books," Dickie said, and mashed his jaw. Blood drooled down Vin's face: smashed, ugly fish bait.

"Please, Dickie," I yelled but hadn't the power to pull him off.

Vince on his knees, Dickie crashed a fist to one ear, a right hook to the other. "Dirty fucker," he yelled, and ripped Vince's shirt and T-shirt off, then scraped the barbed wire across both nipples, pushing hard. "Stop," he begged. He pummeled his chest, breasts, stomach, and groin. Shards of flesh clung to the barbs.

Dickie smashed his brother's jugulars until Vince fell backwards, not moving.

Dickie felt his neck.

"Dead. Come back, Lana, we'll make a go of it now. You'll see."

The classy sofa splattered with blood, another man I lost.

I acted rationally when I married Dickie and rationally when I left him for his brother.

Life a toe-to-toe affair, we all go down for the count eventually.

I punched 911 and when the cops arrived, Dickie put his fists up, ready to take them on.

"Give them to me," I said. The cops stood behind me, spectators.

"You take them off."

When one of the detectives said to cook the corpse for five days, making Vince's body disappear, I knew Dickie wouldn't be charged with murder. The other detective objected, not about Dickie murdering his brother; both were glad Vince dead, but Dickie's method of punching him senseless with barbed wire wrapped around boxing gloves bothered him. The mutilation and lacerations surpassed anything Dickie did in the ring during his boxing career. Dickie and Vince's two children would remain with us, our marriage saved thanks to the law.

"Get a 55 gallon barrel and slow-cook the scumbag," the fat dick said.

"I've been to many of Dickie's fights and saw fighters massively cut up. I could've brought my kids and sat at ringside seats for those. Strictly PG-13," the other plainclothes cop said. They left, dropping off their cards.

The wire had pierced Dickie's gloves. From a formidable and expensive medical kit I found in Vince's bathroom, I used cold compresses to clean and cool Dickie's lacerations and cotton swabs soaked in epinephrine, then applied petroleum jelly to cover his hands and fingers. Vince had everything.

"Vince knew what cutmen used in the corners," Dickie said. We lived in Vince's house.

"I'm your cutman," I said.

"Good as Chuck Bodak, Angelo Dundee's cutman. That fat detective, I saw him come and go at Score when I worked there." Score Inc., Vince's start-up company. Where had he gotten the capital?

"Not connected with the business end of tool and die of Vince's?" I said.

"No, I was just a janitor. Saw Vin at lots of my fights. My manager pointed mobsters he was with."

"Gambling and fixes are part of the trade," I said, trying not to sound smug, too knowing. Dickie hated people who thought they were better than him, one reason he killed his brother.

"A few times I saw fat dick carry two suitcases and hand them to Vince in the parking lot. I'd be weeding outside and outta sight." The dicks probably owed money to Vince.

"Maybe he was selling him suitcases," I said. Damn, why the levity? We have a body to dissolve and I had to be jokesy. That big, gluttonous, lardy cop made disposal of Vin's corpse easy. "He reminds me of the grossness of Orson Welles' character in Touch of Evil we saw together after we tucked the kids in for bed." Dickie mulled that over.

"Maybe I'll get in better shape at the health spa's weight room." He pulled flab from his sides, patted his stomach from the cheap foods he loved. I've tried to get him to eat better food, sometimes succeeding.

I felt sorry for the movie allusion but Dickie hadn't been spared from his own corruption, murder the top of the card, the main event. But Vince's death I could live with because I felt closer to his brother Dickie.

"We need to purify ourselves, put distance from the past," I said, Dickie's blood on my brown trousers. He wiped a wet cloth over my face and showed me the blood.

"Yeah, life's messy. I knew that early on when I got head-butted during an amateur fight."

The dicks put the corpse into a zipped body bag, to not bloody the rugs and floors, and dragged it to the basement. We'd cook Vince there. A large drum used for debris was in the corner. The dicks left. Dickie unzipped the bag, pulled him out, stripped him, and stuffed Vince's naked body into the drum. He slid two wooden planks to the stove, making a ramp. Dickie rolled the drum to the stovetop and righted it on two electric coils. I set the temperature at low.

"I'll be here when you get back, just cruising the net," I said. We kissed. I was surprised how his eyes shone brighter. Nothing like boiling the dead to perk one up.

"I'll get a driver's license someday," he said. Dickie packed his gym clothes and walked to the health club. During the boxing years, he, at first, rode in limos, then chauffeured cars. As his career tumbled, taxis.

I read on Google News about a new synthetic drug called 2C-I, how the ingredients were listed online for druggies to make in powdered, pill or liquid form. Users, thinking it purely an amphetamine and psychedelic high, found themselves running into power lines and walls under 2C-I's rule, and died from force of impact. Watching a person's face turn black, black tears sliding down another person's face like death-mascara was a milder effect. As I had seen Dickie pound Vin to shreds, I wondered whether Vin's eyes streamed blackness. Had Dickie's? Human metabolisms generate lightness or darkness, depending on the moods of killers, of victims, of God having a bad day.

"I used lots of machines today," Dickie said, tossing his bag in the closet.

"Going 21st century, uh." He smelled good. "I like your scent."

"Aromatherapy. I rubbed essential oils over my body."

"You shower?"

"Not yet. I used four machines and they smelled like blood. Metallic blood. I feel cleaner, purer though."

"Immaculate. Not like Vince."

"Not like the dicks or Vince."

"Not rotten and cruel?"

"Vince didn't have kindness in his bones, growing up or below boiling."

The kids were doing fine staying with my sister until we could straighten our lives. I told him about 2C-I.

"It's called smiles on the street," I said. He seemed interested, showered, and watched reruns of The Waltons, about three generations living in a big house during the Depression. A poor family in the South struggled to survive; each episode averted catastrophe. Troubles resolved; hope lived another day. Corniness lied. The smell of boiled veal seeped from the basement and made us hungrier than usual.

In bed, we normally talked before sex or sleep, but not that night. "Machines take getting used to," he said before turning over and going to sleep.

Those smells downstairs, how they reminded me of Nell, Vince's kept woman below us in a basement apartment. We raised two kids and had many arguments over that bitch. It made my blood pressure rise and gave me nosebleeds. Every day she jogged an hour then came back to lift ten-pound hand weights. She had been a mobsters' gal until she got shunted to Vince, a "legit" gangster. The chief reason for leaving him was Nell: Who knew where she hung out now that he was steaming?

I never referred to her in conversation. If I had, Dickie would think I was foolish to repress memories better off discussed.

Dickie walked to the health center. After two hours, he returned.

"Nell worked out of machines today. I bought her a power shake."

"What's she up to these days?" I was shocked but concealed it.

"She's marketing her own power shakes, online."

"She's independent now and for that I applaud her." I really wanted her existence lobotomized from my brain.

"We drank shakes in the center's café."

"Did she mention Vince or me?"

"No. But you might like to know I added liquid smiles to her shake."

"Damn. Why? She could get hurt or worse."

"It's the least I could do for you."

"Me?"

"For the pain you suffered."

"Had smiles acted yet?"

"She ripped off her clothes and ran into the weight room. She crashed into one machine after another."

He told me about a huge machine, with a heavy barbell between two massive steel supports on either side of the incline press machine. She bruised herself and gashed her forehead when she smashed her head again and again on the supports.

"She collapsed to the floor. I stopped watching. No one was there."

I jerked myself off the couch, went to the bedroom, and packed all I could into a luggage and one small trunk. After calling a taxi, I said, "I need to get away from you, Dickie. You're on your own."

In the taxi, I thought Dickie might do worse things alone. I pitied a woman living with him in that house. Let him find a grease trap to pour Vince's thin veal soup down. Maybe those detectives would lure him into their unscrupulousness and rot.

Thoughts of Dickie entwined themselves with the movie, *The War of the Worlds*, how the aliens, machines, proved indomitable at first until the earth's viruses and diseases killed them.

His permanence was unacknowledged artificiality and eventually his weakness would be exposed.

MARK DAPONTE

The Survivor

Three policemen holding Thompson machine guns strolled into the warehouse garage through its opened side door and approached seven men playing poker. The policemen were the prototype 1927 Chicago cop: filled with fake bravado and one too many Bratwurst.

Each card player had their personalized way of greeting lawmen. James Clark sniffed and waved his hands before his nose as if the cops had never touched soap. Frank and Peter Gusenberg stared stone faced at their cards. John May disdainfully spit out his frayed toothpick in their direction and placed a new one in his mouth. John Snyder loudly yawned. Albert Weinshank offered the policemen an outstretched hand and a cold stare. Reinhardt Schwimmer wiped away beads of sweat forming on his forehead.

A cop with a grainy voice ordered the men to *immediately* drop their cards, stand, walk away from the table, turn and place their hands flat against the back brick wall.

Albert Weinshank asked the cops if any of them had a warrant. Peter Gusenberg made his brother, Frank, laugh after saying, "I can't figure out what sticks out more. The coppers' stomachs or their gats."

The tallest of the three cops smiled and said, "This must be different, Pete. A big gun 'sticking out' at you instead of you 'sticking out' a bigger gun at someone else. Savvy?"

James Clark asked the cop what was his price for his pals to leave the garage—

"—then leave us alone?"

"You're talking to the only three coppers in Chicago not on Al Capone's payroll. Now slowly remove your weapons and drop them and—oh. And have a happy Valentine's Day."

Six hand guns, three knives, a switchblade and a pair of brass knuckles clattered on the cement floor. The tallest cop approached Reinhardt Schwimmer and guessed that at first glance, it looked like Schwimmer didn't "exactly fit in with his six upstanding 'pals.'" Not only did he not have a weapon to drop, but his friends' eyes seemed to be looking for an excuse to fight while Schwimmer looked like he was dying to avoid one. As the seven men were frisked, a cop with a worn out voice rasped out loud that Schwimmer was giving the appearance that he:

"—hung out with lowlifes for some kind of thrill—like a lot of dumb guys do. Here's some advice: If you want a thrill and live longer, get on a rollercoaster."

"He tried that. It didn't work," Frank Gusenberg said.

"Yeah. Ya ever think some honest guys like guys who work dishonest jobs?" Peter Gusenberg asked.

"Who asked you? Hey sweat-filled thrill-seeker. What's your name and what kind of honest work you do?" the worn out-voiced cop taunted.

"R-R-Reinhardt Schwimmer, optometrist."

The tallest cop placed his nose a foot away from Schimmer's and asked:

"R-R-R-R-R-R-einhardt Schwimmer, optometrist, huh? Are you sure that's not a make believe name and job and you're really Bugs Moran, gangster?"

"No. I *am* Reinhardt Schwimmer. I mean, I've been told I look and dress a lot like Bugs Moran—but I'm not him."

"Actually, you look like Rudolph Valentino, but I don't think you're him either," Frank added. "But maybe I'm wrong ...."

"Shut up, Frank. Nice try, 'Reinhardt.' Just 'cause you don't have a gun, don't mean you don't have Bugs for a name. But I know you're him 'cause I never forget a not-so-pretty face."

The cop walked away but froze when he heard Schwimmer ask:

"Don't take this the wrong way but you look familiar too."

"In what way?"

"Aren't you part of Capone's gang?" Schwimmer asked, then thought, "Why did I just say that? Once again, I don't think of my own safety when I'm with my boys. I think of a way to please them."

"Yeah, Rein. I can tell by the way he and his buddies smell that they're 'Caponers,'" James Clark said as he again waved his hands in the air.

"Shut up you! What makes you think I work for Capone, R-R-einhardt?"

Schwimmer nervously chuckled as he said: "It's funny. I'll forget what I ate for breakfast, but I never forget a mug shot in the

'Tribune'—which is w-where I saw you. But, maybe I'm wrong too."

Schwimmer heard the sound of two footsteps grow in volume. A hand spun Schwimmer around then backhanded him across the chin. Four hands grabbed him by both shoulders and forced him to face the wall.

"One more word about me not being who I am and my open palm turns into a closed fist!"

If Schwimmer's wide eyes could talk, they'd say: "Yeah, I just got slapped by Albert Anselini. You and your cop 'pals' are part of Capone's gang all right. If you were real cops, me and my pals would be in a paddy wagon by now. But—why are you here? I know! Frank said there was a rumor that Capone would send a message to Moran telling Bugs to stop stealing his whiskey. Unfortunately, I'm the one who's taking Bugs Moran's message. Maybe—even taking it with Anselini's bullets?"

Schwimmer thought the wall that he faced hid the tears leaking from his eyes, but it did not hide the sound of him sniffling.

"Having trouble keeping the tears in, Schwimmer?" the gravelly voiced cop guessed.

"It's not tears. It's eye sweat," Schwimmer replied.

As Swimmer's boys and even the cops laughed, Schwimmer thought, "God, I went through my last marriage and my bank account for *this*? All those warnings from Helen … all those times she said, 'One day, your sins are gonna be washed away in a stream of bullets.' Damn if I didn't laugh at the corniness of it and not think of its truth. And now, I'm gonna pay with my life for choosing gangsters as my 'family' instead of the one Helen wanted me to start with her.

"But, that choice was an easy choice; one that I'm surprised *all* guys don't make. What guy wants to hear a woman ask every day: 'How was your day, dear?' and the guy saying, 'The same.'" Ahh, that's the life, for other guys, but not for Reinhardt Schwimmer. No sir! I wanted to hear gossip from John Snyder like who was the latest politician on Bugs' payroll. And see John May assemble and disassemble Ford Model A's and .38 guns. And watch the Gusenberg brothers slap each other on the back as they tell me how many punches a bar owner had to take until he agreed to take Bugs' bootlegged beer.

"And hear them laugh as they recalled acts of carnage.

"Yeah, to the Gusenbergs, violence is a source of amusement; a long running comedy act. A slap to the face is a one-liner. A baseball bat repeatedly to the knees is a comedic scene. And events leading up to a murder is a top notch comedy movie; a movie whose plot and climax they'd eagerly reveal for 'comedy lovers' like themselves …

… and me.

"And to think, I met Frank in a line for 'The Bobs' at Riverview Amusement Park. He confessed that if he wasn't with his wife and five year old son, he wouldn't 'wait in a line to ride a stupid rollercoaster—especially this one. I'd be getting equally bored at Wrigley Field.'

"I ignored my wife and talked to Frank about the Cubs' losing streak and what horse came in first in the third race at Arlington Park.

"Then, we got to the occupation question:

"Hey, Frank. What do you do for a living?"

"I beat up and kill deadbeats for Bugs Moran's gang. How 'bout you, Reinhardt?"

"I-I-I ride rollercoasters," was all I could say.

"Oh sure, Frank and his pals sometimes are intimidating and make me feel like a field mouse in a roomful of feral cats, but experiencing short-lived trepidation is the small price I pay to hear their entertaining 'exploits.'

"Now, standing here in his makeshift 'Death Row,' I-I could kick myself. Kick myself *hard* for never going with any of them on their 'jobs.' God, I never got to go with Peter the three times he used a double barrel shotgun on a double crosser. I never helped John May slip a stick of dynamite in a safe. I never drove a getaway car for Jimmy Clark after he robbed that diamond store at North Clark. I just watched them 'work' from the safety of my own car as if I was some dumb, star-struck theater patron watching actors in a violent play.

Schwimmer looked at the floor and grimaced. He imagined himself falling dead and landing in the splotches of oil by his feet then cursed that he spent a week's wages on his "Oxford Bag" pants and Homburg hat. Soon, both will bloodied and permanently stained. Schwimmer wanly smiled at the absurdity of contemplating his wardrobe's cost and ruination when he was sure he was about to die. He wondered if Marie Antoinette was aghast at the thought of her bodice getting stained with her blood after she spotted her guillotine.

Schwimmer closed his eyes and imagined the "Chicago Tribune's" headline:

"CHICAGO GANGSTERS SLAIN BY FIRING
SQUAD OF RIVALS IN POLICE UNIFORMS!

VICTIMS LINED UP IN ROW!"

—and how he was killed for the crime of looking like a gangster.

"This isn't fair. Was anyone killed in Jesse James' time for looking and dressing like Jesse? Did the Roman soldiers in Calvary crucify those who dressed and looked like Jesus? Just because I watched sins, doesn't mean I should die for sins I did not commit. NOT FAIR!"

"I'm not a real gangster!" Schwimmer shouted. "Don't shoot me!"

"Shhhhh—Relax. No one's going to shoot anyone and you're not a real gangster, Bugs," the tall cop said before he knocked out Schwimmer with one punch. "Because you ain't real, we won't use real bullets. We'll shoot blanks into you, Bugs."

Peter Gusenberg calmly popped a cigarette in his mouth. As Frank fished in his pockets for his cigarette lighter, the deep voiced cop said: "Let me light that for you, Petey."

Suddenly, nine bullets went into Peter Gusenberg, sixteen into James Clark, 31 into John May, 23 into Albert Weinshank, 19 into John Snyder and 18 into Reinhardt Schwimmer.

After fourteen bullets went through Frank Gusenberg, he heard:

"Hey Frankie's ghost. Here's some advice: Never trust a mug, ya mug!"

***

53

Frank heard an ambulance's siren and could feel his clothes becoming soaked by blood; which only served as reminders that yes, he was shot and left for dead. It wasn't a dream.

He tried to shout "Peter" only to discover that bullets and blood had left his voice a gurgled whisper.

The quiet of the garage unnerved Frank, making him wonder, "Am I the only one to survive?"

His head was tilted to his left; giving him a view of six faces and bodies distorted by death. The garage was now a mausoleum holding six men; all lying in an ever widening pool of blood.

Frank wanted to go to sleep to stop the searing pain, but forced his eyelids open because he was afraid that if they closed, he'd never wake up again. The sweat filling his forehead caused watery blood to trickle into his eyes. The pain was so great that Frank couldn't decide if he wanted to be shot with more bullets or with all the morphine in Chicago.

"The hell with dying. I'm living. Because—"

—being alive would not only show that he could take over a dozen bullets, but he wanted to live just to find "and torture those three 'cops' who shot me and my brother and—"

Frank's thoughts were interrupted by a familiar voice gasping, "Oh my God!"

At first, Frank thought the three Caponers in cop's clothes were coming back to make sure everyone was dead. But the voice belonged to a real cop; who stuck his face in front of Frank's. Frank recognized Tom Loftus who had arrested him for an assault in 1925.

"Hey. This one's still alive. Bring the stretcher for—why, it's Frankie G."

As Frank was carried out of the garage on the stretcher, he saw that John May's legs were practically separated from his body. In Frank's gangster world, this was a sign of contempt and a warning to anyone else who might think of hijacking a Capone shipment of whiskey.

"Anselini did what he had to do," he thought.

Loftus asked, "Do you recognize me, Frank?"

"Yeah. You're … Tom … Loftus."

"We're going to take you to Alexian Brothers Hospital. Before we go—ya got anything ya wanna say?"

Frank smiled because in Loftus' police world, Ya got anything ya wanna say?" meant, "You know and I know Capone ordered this hit. So—who did it?"

"Frank. Is there anything ya wanna say?"

"Yeah. Thanks ... for ... the ... ride."

***

Frank's eyes opened and saw pin-hole drywall ceiling boards half-covered by Tom Loftus' face.

"Hi ... Tom," Frank whispered. "What's ... new?"

"You tell me. Tell me how you got into this hospital."

"I ... tried ... its ... food."

"The food didn't put fourteen holes in you. Who did?"

"I took fourteen?! Fourteen and lived!" Frank thought. "Yeah, Capone and Moran and all you other tough guys who would die from one measly bullet. Try taking fourteen?!"

"Who would kill six unarmed men, Frank? We want to bring them to justice. Tell me before you're gone for good."

"Whatever I tell Loftus will be what history records forever," Frank thought. "I can tell them a guy dressed as Charlie Chaplin came in, wiggled his mustache, took his cane and shot us with it. No, I'll take the truth with me to hell. I'll tell Satan: Between you and me, I did it for a woman. Schwimmer's woman. Helen certainly deserved better than Schwimmer who was a watcher, not a doer. Ha, I'd send him out to watch Jimmy Clark rob a diamond store from his car—while I was watching his wife in his bedroom. I'd tell him to watch Johnny May load a gun—while I unloaded on Helen. Ha ha!"

"I see a little smile on your face, Frankie. Something funny on your mind? Tell me."

"Tell Loftus what? That I wanted Schwimmer out of the way so me and Helen could marry without paying a divorce lawyer? Tell him I paid Anselini, Killer Burke and Joey Spinelli—to kill everyone except me and my brother? See, coppers like *you* Loftus will think it was a Capone hit—especially when they saw John May's legs practically off of his body. Instead, Anselini left me to die in that garage with:

"Hey Frankie's ghost. Here's some advice: Never trust a mug, mug!"

"I'll get you Anselini. You dumb, greedy—I told you if you double cross me, I'll hunt you and your two pals down. Guess he didn't think I can hunt him when I'm six feet under. But I got other mugs who'll get the job. Helen knows who they are. She'll see that it gets done. See that Anselini gets killed for killing me and not for killing Reinhardt. That's why I left her the money …. She just better not spend it on expensive clothes like her dead and dumb husband did."

"Talk to me Frankie. Who shot you?"

"God, all those warnings from Helen … all those times she said, 'One day, your sins are gonna be washed away in a stream of bullets.' I said, 'I ain't your weak husband. I make streams; I don't wash in 'em.' Damn if she was right."

"No …… one ……… shot ……………… me," Frank said, then thought, "Listen to me. I can barely talk anymore, barely breathe. Getting weak."

"You're fading out, Frank. You're going. So tell me. Who did it?"

"Sorry, Loftus. You'll never know the truth. Anselini wouldn't rat me out and I'm not about to do the same to him. Let those stupid history books (that I won't be around to read anyway)—let 'em say it was a Capone hit and not because I loved a woman to death … *my* death … and six other guys dead 'cause—"

"Who shot you, Frankie?"

"No … body … I … shot … myself."

Loftus shook his head and put his hat on. Before he left the hospital room, he told the attending nurse:

"Pull the sheet over his head. The mug's gone … too soon and too late."

JAMES BROWN

Instructions on the use of Heroine

I park behind the broken-down Mercury Marquis in the driveway of my drug dealer's house. Ironically he is also my former A.A. sponsor. It's a warm summer night, and as I leave my car a couple of big mangy dogs appear from out of the darkness and begin barking. If I didn't know them I'd be scared, but I do know them because I've been here before, too many times, and they're not biters. The stairs leading to the front door are falling apart, one is missing altogether, and I step over it. The dogs are behind me all the way, sniffing at my legs.

This is not in the ghetto.

This is not the mean streets of San Bernardino, one of the most violent, drug-ridden cities in the nation. This is in the neighboring mountains well above the fray. I live safely removed from the drive-bys, the gangs, and their turf wars. In my community, you can still walk the streets at night. In my community, lakeside homes sell for millions, but even here, among the rich and middle class, there is a darker, subterranean life, and as a user of narcotics I have a special knack, a real sixth sense, for rooting it out wherever I go.

As I reach the landing at the end of the stairs, two powerful sensor lights flash on. I wince at the brightness.

Then I press the button on the intercom and look up at the fake birdhouse mounted in the corner of the sun deck above me. Inside it is a camera, and I want my dealer to see me, so he doesn't panic and stick his 9mm in my face when I come to the door. He's done it before. There's static on the intercom, then the scratchy sound of his voice.

"Who is it?"

"It's me," I say. "Jim."

"Hang on."

On the other side of the door are three iron bars, one at the top, one in the middle, and the third near the bottom. There's also a deadbolt, a chain latch, and the regular lock. Inside I hear the clanking of the bars being removed from their steel brackets, the slam of the deadbolt, the turning of the knob, and finally the door opens a crack. The chain is still latched. He peers out at me.

"You alone?"

"Yeah," I say.

The door closes. A second later it opens again and he lets me in, along with his mangy dogs. Green garbage bags full of dirty clothes, and computer monitors, computer casings, and shells are scattered all over this downstairs area of the house. It smells, too, like urine and shit, because he sometimes forgets to let the dogs out. He's wearing a ratty tank top, but what I notice most at this moment are the syringes hanging from his shoulders, one on each side, the needles sunk into the middle head of the deltoid muscle. On the left, it's loaded with heroin. On the right, it's cocaine. I can tell the difference because one syringe contains a dark colored fluid while the other, the coke, is a milky white.

If he needs a bump up, he depresses the plunger on the milky-white side. If he needs a bump down, something to even him out, to take the edge off the coke, it's the dark side. The idea is to find the perfect balance, but for now he's on the upside, spun on the coke.

To protect his privacy, if only in memory, because he is dead as I make record of this story many years after the fact, I'll give him another name, something common—Eddie. In addition to being a dealer he is also a friend. We met at an Alcoholics Anonymous meeting, and for nearly ten months, before we both relapsed, he'd been my sponsor, taking me through the Big Book several hours every week, page by page. He isn't looking so good lately, little more than skin and bone. We shake hands and I follow him upstairs to the living room.

Eddie gets right down to business.

"What do you want?"

"What do you have?"

"Black," he says. "Crack. Coke. Crystal. Weed. I got Dilaudid. I got methadone too," he says, "Valium, Vicodin, and Oxycontin."

Dilaudid is like pharmaceutical-grade heroin, some junkies think it's even better, and most people already know about Valium, Vicodin, and Oxycontin. Eddie suffers from a serious back injury, and after years of unsuccessful operations, his doctors now more or less prescribe whatever he wants in the line of opioid painkillers. Combine these with his black market dope and you have a walking, talking poster boy for the travails of addiction.

"Some black," I say.

"Any weed?"

In a room upstairs, Eddie has a farm of marijuana thriving under dozens of grow lights, and he's always trying to push some off on me. But I'm scared of weed. It makes me paranoid. It makes me think, and thinking often depresses me, and depression isn't exactly what I look for in the pursuit of getting fucked up. The same goes for psychedelics. I swore them off at the age of seventeen after a bad trip.

"You know I hate that shit."

He laughs.

"Just asking."

"All I want is black."

"No coke either."

"Not tonight."

"How much you want?"

"A gram," I say.

At that, he disappears into another part of the house to retrieve the dope from its hiding spot, his gram scale, and the various other accoutrements of hard-core narcotic use. I sit down on the couch. An old episode of *Gilligan's Island* plays on the TV. The Skipper is chasing Gilligan in circles around a coconut tree, and I watch them, trying to take my mind off the waiting. Soon Eddie returns.

Clearing a spot on the coffee table, which is a mess of empty beer cans and bottles and ashtrays full of butts, he sets up his scale.

"This is good stuff," he says.

This stuff is Mexican Black, most commonly referred to as tar. In its uncooked form, it resembles a lump of brown dirt, but it turns black, like tar, when you heat it up.

From his front pocket Eddie takes out a knife. From his back pocket he removes a plastic baggie and a couple of packaged syringes, small ones, the kind diabetics use. Then he sits down on the couch beside me. I lean forward as he dips the tip of the knife into the baggie, scoops out a chunk of heroin about the size of a dime, and slips it onto the scale. While he weighs it, he glances up at me.

"You in the market for an AK?" he says. "I got a friend who's looking to unload an M-16, fully automatic. He has an Uzi, too, with the Israeli Army stamp on the side. A thousand bucks. And hand grenades; they go for eighty a piece or seventy by the dozen."

I have to think about it. A part of me would like to own an assault rifle or a little Uzi. The other part warns me off. I have no idea where I could even go to fire one. These aren't the kind of weapons you take to your local shooting range. The grenades, they plain scare me.

"It's tempting," I say. "But I'll pass."

I stand up and open my wallet and drop two twenties on the table. Then I go to the kitchen and come back with a glass of water and a spoon. By now Eddie has weighed out my purchase, and from it, before he wraps it up, I pinch off a small chunk. He shakes his head. "You can always put more in," he says, "but you can't take it out. I'd use about half that first and see how it hits you. This batch is stronger than the last." Of course I take his word for it. Eddie has been slamming dope off and on now for over thirty years, and until the last time he shot up, a week after he was released from prison on a possession for distribution charge, the fix that killed him, he'd never before o.d.'d. It's a ritual, from weighing the junk to parceling it out and cooking it; this process heightens the urgency of the act, from the anticipation of the rush to its delivery, the climax of finally shooting up. The procedure is simple: You place a small lump of junk into the spoon along with a piece of cotton, if you have any handy, or just a bit torn from a cigarette filter. Then you add a little water to it. Next you heat it up with a lighter, holding the flame under the spoon. When it begins to bubble and liquefy, you insert the needle into the cotton or the bit of cigarette filter and draw it out into the syringe by slowly pulling back on the plunger. In this way you eliminate many of the impurities and adulterants that might otherwise clog the needle. And for obvious reasons you must always, without exception, make absolutely sure that the syringe comes directly from its sealed package. You must see it done before your very eyes. You must never take anyone's word.

I'm in the process of heating up the heroin when Eddie's girlfriend stumbles out of the bedroom in her flannel pajamas and fuzzy pink slippers. She's barely eighteen, and with her mother's permission, as horrific as that may seem since Eddie is my age at forty and a known dope addict. They've been living together for the last six months. That her mother is also a junkie should help to explain, though by no means justify, her reckless neglect.

I'll call her Crystal, after the drug crystal meth, and she's just woken up, probably having slept through the entire day. Her timing in joining us is, as usual, uncanny. Like me, she has a sixth sense for when dope is near, and Eddie and I know to keep a close eye on her. Things like rings and watches, and especially drugs, often mysteriously disappear in her presence. It's hard to blame her since she couldn't possibly hold down a job in her condition, let alone attend school. She flops down on the couch with us. Her hair is bleached platinum blond, like Eddie's ex-wife, and she's bone-thin from too much heroin, speed, and coke. In the bend of one arm is the swell of a small abscess. Generally they're caused from injecting in or near the same site too often, but sometimes bad junk alone can do it.

"How you doing?" she asks.

"Fine," I say.

"I haven't seen you around in a while."

"Been busy," I say.

Crystal sometimes talks of becoming a cosmetologist.

Eddie sometimes talks of opening his own computer repair shop. For now, however, I'm the only one in the room who has a real job, so I have to be careful about how often I get high. And I'm not implying I think of myself as any better than Eddie and Crystal, because I don't. It's just that I have a family. It's just that I've been strung out before, and it's cost me dearly. I believe, like all those who initially start and stop before becoming full-blown addicts, that I'm the exception—that I can use a little here and there for fun, just to relax, without it ever becoming a problem. I do and do not know that I'm lying to myself.

The heroin is bubbling now, turning black, absorbing into the water. Carefully I set the spoon down on the coffee table, unwrap the syringe, and extract the dark liquid into it. Because it's easy to miss the vein or go right through it, because it can make for a bloody mess, even causing the collapse of that vein, including those in the arms, neck, legs, between fingers and toes, I stick it in the middle deltoid of my shoulder. It feels like a mosquito bite. The needle is so thin you hardly notice it piercing your skin, and over the years I've come to like it, the sting, knowing the promise of euphoria is right at the other end.

Where the high from an intravenous injection is almost instantaneous, the intramuscular shot takes fifteen, maybe twenty seconds to hit and it doesn't come over you quite as powerfully. In this narrow span of time, Crystal reaches across me for the other chunk of heroin I left on the coffee table.

"You mind?" she says.

"Help yourself," I say.

She looks to Eddie for approval.

"Baby," he says, "you really need to slow down."

"And you don't?"

I feel it first in the body, a warming from deep inside, filling my chest, then spreading out into my legs and arms. It comes in waves, this sweeping warmth, and as it seeps into the mind all my worries, all my problems and concerns, immediately disappear. Heroin is the most seductive of the narcotics, bringing calm where there is anguish, ease where there is discomfort, and pain, physical or mental, gives way to peace and serenity. The heart slows. Breathing becomes shallow. The mind, emptied of life's clutter, falls into a state of quiet. I feel it pulling me deeper, pulling me under, as if I'm collapsing into myself. In a minute, when the rush levels off, I'm drifting somewhere between wakefulness and dream.

This is the destination.

This is where the outside world ceases to exist and I am as free of it as the dead.

Crystal has found a vein between her toes, though it's taken her a few sticks, and there's blood running down both sides of her ankle. As the rush hits her, as she falls back onto the couch, Eddie hurries to the kitchen and returns with a roll of paper towels and starts cleaning her up. And he does it tenderly. Like a lover. Like a father. I wonder if it's really about her having nowhere else to go. I wonder if it's because she has no real family. I was told her stepfather repeatedly molested her since the age of nine.

For a while, we all just ride the high. Although I'm stoned, I'm still capable enough of understanding what's going on around me. I'm still capable enough of seeing and hearing clearly, and I watch Crystal sit up. I watch her, as if in slow motion, reach for the pack of Marlboros on the coffee table, shake one out and place it between her lips. Before she can light it, her chin drops to her chest, and then, as if she were about to fall asleep, she jerks awake. This is called The Nods. Remarkably, the unlit cigarette hasn't slipped from her mouth.

"I don't feel so good," she says.

"Don't throw up here," Eddie says.

Rising slowly from the couch, holding her stomach in her hands, she weaves her way across the room. By now, Eddie has worked up a sweat from cleaning up her blood, and to calm himself he depresses the plunger of the syringe hanging from his shoulder, the one containing the dark fluid. Down the hall in the bathroom we hear Crystal retching.

"She gets sick every time," Eddie says. "Never fucking fails."

Even some of the most practiced addicts are cursed with this malady, but it doesn't stop them from using. Once the stomach is emptied, you're clear again to enjoy the heroin high, and further injections, so long as they're not spaced too far apart, don't typically trigger the same loathsome reaction.

She takes her place again on the couch. I can smell the peppermint-flavored toothpaste she used to wash out her mouth.

"How's your wife," she says in a dreamy, faraway kind of voice.

"Good," I say, "though she wouldn't be too happy knowing I'm here."

"I hope you don't get in trouble."

Of course I'll get in trouble if my wife finds out. But she's visiting relatives in Tennessee, and my sons are spending the week with their grandparents in Northern California. Tonight I have no schedule. Tonight I am accountable to no one, and frequently these are the occasions when I mess up, when I'm alone and the bright idea to get wasted suddenly pops into my head.

"She's so pretty," she says in that dream voice again.

By no means is this Crystal's way of flirting with me. She's genuinely interested in my wife. At every A.A. meeting, when we were all still clean and sober, and whenever my wife accompanied me in support, which she did often, Crystal would stare at her from across the room. And there was something desperate about it. Something sad. Something pathetic. It was the way a young girl stares admiringly at a beautiful older woman, the one the girl wishes to be like, the one she might've hoped to have had for a mother. And because she did not, because she lacks the confidence and self-esteem that is every child's birthright, because narcotics steal any fleeting hope of a better life, Crystal trades, as her mother still trades, on her sexuality.

"Can I have a little more?"

Her request for dope is directed at Eddie this time, but he ignores her. He has made a fist of his left hand. Even with the syringes still dangling from his shoulders, he is searching for a vein between his fingers, to mainline, to get the most powerful, immediate rush possible, and he cannot be interrupted. Again and again he misses, extracts the needle, then jabs it back in. Blood fills the crevices between his fingers and curls around his wrist and drips onto the carpet. Crystal reaches for another chunk of heroin, a piece he set aside from the scale, because it tipped the beam over a gram, and soon she too is looking for a vein, again between her toes. Soon she too is bleeding.

I press my hands together.

So they can see better, they kneel on the floor before the table lamp. They search, and in the dim light, heads bowed and blood leaking from their wounds, it looks to me as if we are all engaged in some grotesque act of prayer. Though I've seen worse, junkies stabbing into an oozing abscess or sticking the jugular, even I'm repulsed by all the blood.

"Eddie, man," I say. "Forget it. You're making a big mess."

But he ignores me as he did Crystal; that or he's too obsessed with finding and hitting a vein to hear me. Finally he succeeds. Crystal isn't far behind. Their eyes roll back into their heads and then their lids slowly close. They're faraway now, in a fine place where no one can reach them. Neither will miss me. Neither will notice when I gather up what I came for and leave.

R.C. EDRINGTON

Infected

time nothing more
than a slow throb
of sunlight
that flickers sharp
beneath a bruised
sheath of skin
syringe
after syringe
we soothe our veins
with the false kiss
of forever midnight
& like timid vampires
at the cusp of dawn
failed to chase
hours back
into an oiled blackness
much more darker
than the polluted alleys
from which we slid

CODY BADARACCA

All the drugs in the world

You're 24 and you remember suddenly a friend
telling you something sometime in the past:

"Man, whenever I'm not high, I feel like blowing
my fucking face off with a shotgun."

This is the same friend
you got high with for the first time during school
and successive times after that.

Till you both got caught
and till he eventually moved away
doing various jobs around the country
putting various things up his nose and
in his arm and down his throat and surviving
somehow.

The times have shifted and moved on
and the last you heard from him was months ago
in an e-mail. He was in trouble again.
Blacked out felonies across the board and
the Denver police looking
to nail his ass to a wall with the judge's
sledgehammer of justice.

But the times have shifted and you've moved on.
You don't really do drugs anymore and can't really
empathize. You write him back and tell
him that everything in his life is a decision
and the responsibility is his. And it is.

He probably is fine, you think. Although he probably is
still peering off the pier's edge
into the cold, muddy river of suicide and boredom and madness
which all the drugs in the world won't help you from
eventually sinking into.

And you know because you've been on those
eroding banks before. You've dipped a toe in
and sipped a little of that water, which tastes
like a mixture of gasoline, bourbon and blood.

CODY BADARACCA

Old Country Songs

(1)
I got drunk last night and started thinking
of you. What I remember,
the night played like an old Country song on a dusty record.
A real sentimental classic like "So Lonesome I could Cry" by Hank Williams
or Patsy Cline's "Crazy" or even Merle Haggard's "Silver Wings" –
one of those old Country songs real heavy with feeling and twang.
The sort of song that ropes baler twine around my vital organs
and tugs me towards oblivion through the whine and melancholy warbling.
The type of song enhanced by the static and scratches in the record.
The type of songs that make drinking alone an acceptable pastime activity.

The night browned to the sepia tone-color of bourbon
as the sun slunk behind the earth, ashamed of what it was.
The night came out with its hackles raised and the day diminished in the half-full
bottle of whiskey that I kept coming back to
for inspiration, because it mimics your curvature and full
of that sweet amber liquid and heat that makes me want
to put my lips up to you
and let you drag out whatever is left inside of me.

(2)
I tried writing you, but I got drunk and thought of the bottle in front of me,
that whiskey shimmying like a backwoods nymph
choking me into a sweaty fuck on the kitchen floor
because that heat gripped and kept tugging on me like the welcoming palm
of an old friend.

And the whiskey kept disappearing like water
or the illusion of water in a heat-mirage at the cusp of the road's
edge
out on some poorly maintained highway, where telephone poles
click
by and mingle with wires and grey light and fatigued sagebrush. I
thought of how time
dissipates in the heat and moaned like a train pulling through a
tunnel.
I called for you in the echoes and coughed out heat and smoke and
a menagerie of dark birds escaped my lips.
But I couldn't hear your echo because I was drunk on whiskey and
old Country songs
and my memory is stained with soot and bird shit and bourbon.

(3)
Everything just kept skipping that way. The way a
phonograph needle falls back into a scratch.
I reached out for that bottle
thinking of your curves,
and grasping at the diminishing night,
drinking whiskey and trying
to keep that heat somewhere close in me as
the bottle yanked it out.

When it finally ended, the bottle lay wet and empty
and the sun was mounting the horizon.
I could hear the dry silence of the day
gathering in the early dawn.
Like a dust storm far off on the plains, it was a sibilant wind
blowing through the prairielands
of Kansas or Oklahoma.

THOMAS KEARNES

Nurse

Helen has been in the bathroom for fifteen minutes. Her limit is ten. She knows this. I have the contract in my purse, next to her caddy of anti-depressants and stabilizers. I will show it to her once she returns and say, What did we agree upon last month? I know you like this restaurant, but if I can't trust you here, we can't come anymore. Do you understand? I watch for other women to leave the restroom, to catch the clues not even an accomplished talent like Helen can hide. Older women, their faces pinched sour with disgust and the younger ones, especially in the summer, who bolt from the room with whispers and backward glances. Poor Helen. Like most unfortunates in her position, her hard, impenetrable blindness prevents her from knowing the effect she has on others. In some ways, I prefer our afternoons or mornings in public to the interminable days in which her paranoia keeps us trapped in her home. Aided by the indulgence of others, I can trace her movements and perform my duties more easily.

I check my watch. Twenty minutes. No doubt Helen would implore me in her singsong voice, pale blue eyes darting like goldfish, that time had escaped her. This is nonsense. Those afflicted with her condition, in addition to her myriad other difficulties, have few skills, but they do possess an inborn awareness of where they are in time. This knowledge they rarely apply to their own betterment, but it is a unique gift, a grain of sand's awareness of where the tide will next fall.

Helen's salad sits rearranged, uneaten. One of my coworkers once joked she couldn't understand these women who regurgitated their meals yet never ate them. What were they vomiting? You can tell from this ignorance my coworker is a poor nurse. For unfortunates like Helen, eating, like most intimate activities, was something she only could do alone. Perhaps that is what was taking so long. I believe she was at the point in her illness where she took a perverse pride in the fact she could continue her behavior without anyone trying to stop her. After all, if one makes it her mission to destroy another, someone usually will step in, but if one decides to destroy herself, most will just step aside.

My sister, Carol, the real nurse, travels to a large white building advertised on television instead of crumbling brownstones and ruined, inherited single-frame houses. She put it to me best: We let them go sometimes. It is best. Too much morphine. Fail to report a matching donor. Let the call button go unanswered for a minute, perhaps longer. I knew of the ways. But these means were not available to me. Besides, Carol told me, I was lucky. People like Helen were not truly hopeless, not forsaken by God, merely themselves. They are not lost, she said.

We both remember what it is like to feel the sunken certainty one experiences in the presence of those truly bereft of all hope and time. Our grandfather, so tall and proud, once sipping whiskey and puffing smoke in my direction but never Carol's, lay dying before us. He refused the hospital. All those bitches in white, he said, they don't care. You're not their family, you're not their friends. You're a dollar. The morphine drip stood at his side, not to be controlled by him, we were urged, but of course, grandfather insisted. Technicians, he said, never had the smarts or the money to become a real doctor, but they don't mind giving orders like one.

Carol and I stood around his bed and watched the stunted, ragged breaths struggle to run the length of his lean body. The cancer, the kind that grows back at twice the speed it can be removed, the stomach kind, the kind no one "deserves," had reduced him to one hundred pounds. He was watching the Cowboys game. They were doing well for once, which would happen only two or three times again that season. Our parents insisted he was not aware, but Carol and I knew differently: the truly sick always know.

Helen emerges from the bathroom. Thirty minutes. But for once she does not look away when I hold her in the fierce gaze. Despite myself, I feel relieved. Perhaps she experienced other troubles. When one's diet is as disastrous as Helen's, the menstrual cycle can be affected as well.

She rejoins me at the table and smiles, her wan grin that seems pretty and open in the retouched photos cluttering her parents' walls but in person is a half-hearted appeasement. I'm sorry, she says. I really am. I was having, and she looks around as if someone might hear, as if someone might take an interest in this bony woman-child, barely ninety pounds with limp hair and a floral dress that clings to her. I was having problems, she says. Were you bleeding? When you are in my position, you can inquire about such things without seeming rude.

Helen nods then bows her head, keeps it fixed on her plate as if solace beckons from inside. To feel shame over such a natural occurrence but not over her constant need to rid herself of the very thing keeping her alive, amuses me. Myself, and those in my profession, must be very rational. The occupation demands it. And yet, we are constantly surround by the most irrational society has allowed to survive. I could not help but think Helen would be better off surrounded by those who could follow her pretzel logic, shimmy down its twists without complaint until they arrived at its only true conclusion: *I know they want to hurt me, so I must hurt myself.*

That is when I smell the odor. Rank and vile, like garbage. She had done it. She had done it, and then looked me in the eye. Like I was her doctor. Her mother. Nothing. It is time for us to go, I say. Helen jerks up, startled. Usually, after she vomits and I chastise her and she swears never to do it again and she really, really wants to stop, we talk for a few minutes. This, I have been told, is therapeutic. This, I believe, is to give Helen the illusion of friendship, because all the other people I mentioned who might feel a kinship with this poor woman are, as she is, too terrified to seek it out.

Helen slips into her bulky wool coat, which swallows her, gives her the illusion of normal weight. I wonder if she never bought a smaller size because the experience of a mall would be too much for her or if some dim corner of her mind begged her not to forfeit.

When Helen's parents hired me two years ago, they were frank about their expectations. Our daughter will not get better, her mother said, with the same finality of the doctor who had informed my family of grandfather's cancer. She held me steady with her eyes, pale blue like Helen's, but with the sharpness of a bright, condescending child. She was a former smoker, I could tell. Her right hand erect, resting on her elbow, fingers crooked in position. She knew discipline and knew my only purpose was to, Make sure nothing happens to her, her father explained. He remained behind the couch seating Helen's mother throughout my only visit. She never once looked back at him.

I have been stalling other people's deaths for over twenty years. I could decipher the code. Let nothing happen in public. Already, Helen had run into mid-morning traffic, naked, begging to be hit, screaming in frustration that the street was so congested that she had no hope of death. And there had been other attempts, less dramatic, but just as embarrassing. Like all clients with Helen's predisposition, there were attempts made in sincerity and others made for attention, where the only thing preventing death is the fear of the performance's end. Each time I encountered a patient after one of these escapades, I caught a glimmer of fevered release in her eyes, the thrill from an actor as he watches the audience rise for an ovation.

Helen's parents were busy people, their condo rarely inhabited. Helen would give me my check twice a month, at the end of the last appointment for a particular week. She had never lost the money, spent it, insisted I hadn't earned it, like some others. *You don't need it,* they cry. *You don't deserve this. You don't love me. Nobody loves me.* I grip those checks tightest during my trips to the bank, hand thrust deep in my purse.

Even though I wear an overcoat warmer and more fitted than Helen's, the crisp whispers of winter creep inside my bones, and I imagine Helen shivering in the balmiest of rooms, her own body unable to protect her. It is the scrubs. Not that noxious pink the nurses Helen's age prefer but blue-green. Neutered. I insist on wearing them, and leaving my coat open during the winter months so anyone on the street will not misinterpret my relationship with a patient. Helen is not my daughter, my niece, my mismatched lover. This is not to embarrass those in my care. It is for clarity, order. I cannot abide misunderstanding.

Helen begins to lag behind, gape at the impervious skyscrapers above her that ceased to fascinate me when I was still a child. Grandfather took me on the scaffold while he washed windows and jiggled the platform, harder and harder, heckling me, *Gonna fall, girl, better hold on!* I begged him to stop, cheeks hot and raw from wiping my tears before he noticed. I extend my arm and stretch it around her tiny shoulders, feeling both blades protrude against my coat. Helen starts to curl herself into me, as if I were her childhood plush doll, but I stiffen my arm. What have I told you about that? I remind her, in my pleasant, professional voice I practice when salesmen or my sister call.

She twists her head. This is a familiar routine. Helen will now require a comfort. Despite the catastrophes marking her life, she has a mind for others' routines. She knows my next appointment is not for another two hours. I cannot refuse her.

Will you make me a smoothie? She tilts her head and when I cut my glance to her, I catch those translucent eyes, wet and dirty with need, and I want to gouge them. Twist my hand on her shoulder until the joint snaps like a struck match. Yank that awful coat from her, expose her as a wastrel, a degenerate, shove her into traffic, still steady and lethal before rush hour and shout, *What are you waiting for! Nobody loves you!*

Yes, I say. Calm, smooth. I picture Helen drifting backward, arms overhead, into a pasture of blue and orange silk. Do you have everything I need to make it how you like? Helen nods, proud of herself and no doubt overjoyed to be posed a question she can answer without calculation.

Her apartment is always clean, like the solution of a mathematical equation. All my coworkers complain if it weren't for the patients, the kids, the husbands, the boyfriends, they would clean. Spotless homes, no apologizing for messes. As Helen hustles past me to the plaid couch where I find her at the start of nearly every visit, I let a grim smile widen my lips. So this is how one gets the time to clean.

Helen clicks on her game shows. A whole network devoted to them. Reruns of shows from decades past. I remember them from training in the ward, the electronic beeps, applause and excited screams cranked up to drown the moans filtering from the hall. She watches them, rapt, abbreviated human drama all she can digest.

Do you want your pills separate or mixed in? I turn to her, awaiting a response. The answer is always the same, but I must ask. On the television, an elderly woman seems hardly aware of the camera mere feet away, ogling her bewilderment. Helen croaks out advice to the contestant, urges her to pick the window cleaner. Certainly, that's where the prize hides. I've never seen anyone win this one before, she cries, hands bunched over her puckered mouth. I look back at the screen and the old fool scans the audience for encouragement, helpless amid the battling suggestions, and I imagine Helen there, under the clinical glare of the stage lights, her pale features washed into a white visage, a mask upon which one could rewrite her fate. *Tell me what to pick,* I hear Helen call. *Tell me how to win.*

The old woman clucks the name of a sandwich meat as if her tongue and jaw were not in sync. Helen was right. The host pulls a WIN tag from behind the window cleaner. The old woman allows the host to kiss her cheek while she still gazes into the audience, as if the game were not over. After a nudge, she wanders out of frame.

Put them in the smoothie, Helen says. I break away from the set and take in my charge. Her eyes shock me with a precision I have not seen before. Like always, she says and smiles as if I were silly to ask. I imagine Helen as old as the contestant on television, but she is not the infirm, pitiable creature oblivious to the production taking place. She curls into herself on a heap of soiled and rancid sheets, entranced by her piecemeal wisdom, waiting for comfort. Carol tells me the terminal patients that worry her are not the ones who look away when she injects the syringe, not even the ones who watch the penetration. No, they look her in the eye.

My sister and I had no way of knowing that holding vigil over the bedside of the doomed would become our twin calling. Our parents had exhausted whatever optimism they possessed. As a twelve-year-old girl, I was transfixed by what I knew only then as the "painkiller machine." I had watched the technician show our parents how to operate it, spied my grandfather dope himself when mother and father were gone, his empty gray eyes fixed on me, not worried I'd tell, but curious why I'd bother to watch.

Now the cancer had made even this meek rebellion impossible. Moans like sandpaper over his workbench filled the small, mildewed room in which grandmother had set up his deathbed because, she said, it was all too much, and we need to rest, please, girls, you must rest.

You know how it works, Carol said. The morphine dispenser. Just press the lever and keep your thumb drawn tight, fast as you would against your first boyfriend's hand. With a desperation she had since eliminated from her personality like a childhood stutter, Carol grasped my hand with both of hers. As if I

75

were the synapse between my sister's will and my grandfather's fate, I pushed the lever.

Those old machines were so inefficient, Carol complains. It does not take nearly as long now. Both of us, and it seems so absurd to believe now, were afraid to take his pulse, afraid to touch him, afraid we would not take it correctly and his withered finger, steel gray bristles at the knuckle, would emerge from our closet one night, tapered to a pinpoint: murderers. We waited until the wheezes subsided. Silence filled grandfather's room, the new resident. In the commotion of the following days, no one inquired about the bruise Carol had left on my hand.

My purse stays with me at all times. All those pills, it is simply the responsible thing. I rinse the blender though it has been lying in the sink since my last visit two days ago. Helen has never prepared a meal for herself, but her kitchen bustles with greens, fresh fruit, meat labeled and packed in the freezer, cracker and cereal boxes in the pantry. I suddenly want her check in my fist because that means it is time for my next appointment, an infirmed gentlemen who only requires for me to turn the television from one station to the next at precisely four-thirty. And then home.

I hold the apple cider bottle over the blender, and the thought of home makes me flush. I recall no detail of it. Well, of course I do, but they just—my purse on the counter. Open. I immediately think of Helen but I no doubt would have seen her. The pill bottles rest atop my things. I need to put them back in her bathroom cabinet before I leave. I realize the stupidity of keeping them from her for the duration of my stay when she has whatever access to them any other time. But, like pressing the lever, I never question it. I felt it as surely as my sister's hands cupped over mine.

The insane beeps, the applause, the dumbfounded contestants' yammering continue from the living room. I picture Helen enraptured; life on such a minute scale is tolerable to her. Five minutes a game. Win or lose. Try and succeed. Try and fail. I do not pay attention to which pill bottle I first empty into the blender. They plunk into the cider, zigzag to the bottom, a trail of tiny bubbles wiggling to the surface. I dice up the plums, the bananas, the strawberries. It is her favorite show, and there is a half-hour left. I have enough time. I press the button and the blender roars to life. The traffic outside the second-story window whizzes below me. I imagine how my life might appear to Helen, to all my patients, a figure who appears twice, three times a week, disappears without remnant or complaint—a housecleaner, a home shopper, an exasperated parent, a disinterested spouse.

The sudden bleat of a car horn breaks me from my daydream. I gaze down to the street. Cars stopped, some askew, so it is not a traffic jam. I hear a woman's scream, but not the aimless kind I have heard so often. This was a scream thrust upon its source, not welling up from within. While the blender rumbles, I drift through the kitchen toward the living room.

Surely not during her favorite program.

Gonna fall, girl, better hold on!

On the screen, the silver-haired host tries his best to combat a large-breasted college girl eager for a kiss. Helen would have laughed and applauded. I think she imagines the young, beautiful contestants to be funhouse versions of herself and cheers them on. And now she missed it.

The front door stands open to the hallway; she wanted to make certain I knew. The clarity in her eyes. I will not tell Carol about that. She will say that was my warning. And how she lied to my face about the purging! My breath runs short, my eyes moisten and I blink rapidly, unsure of what to do, unable to blot out the only thought that hurtles through my mind, like the morphine into grandfather's veins as the scaffolding shakes like the very earth even as Carol grips my hand in both of hers: *This wasn't your choice to make! You bitch! You goddamn ungrateful bitch!*

The blender whir softens, having broken up every solid, even the pills. I shut off the television, feel naked, like a caught burglar. I look over to where she sat, last looked into her eyes and realize now I had envied her certainty, even when I had no idea what she had planned, likely had planned all afternoon. The smoothie meant nothing to her. She wanted me gone. Like her mother. Like everyone.

The check lies on the coffee table. I collect it, scan the area around it for a note. Nothing—neat and orderly as always. It occurs to me that once I dump the smoothie and take my check, it will be like neither of us arrived.

I trudge down the hall, purse slung over my shoulder. So no one can see my eyes, I wear the sunglasses I use only for driving. I hope my mood, this unexpected rising, passes before my next appointment. Sunglasses are unprofessional, and I have my duties. The door shut behind me, I hear the faint whir of the running blender as I head for the stairs.

MARY KRIENKE

Things we do

They found Larry in the snow. The town didn't really talk about it. Not in that surprised, shaking their heads, glued to the TV for news way, because this was out of the question, some outside forces must have been acting upon them, and now it was their duty to listen and wait for the outside to be let in.

A man, let's be clear, a man who has lived in a town for all his adult life does not leave his car on the side of a gravel road, five, six miles from anywhere he had any reason to be. A man, let it be said, not too keen on the scenery, a man who, as far as anyone could tell, did not care to note the changes of families moving in and out, farms prospering, expanding, going limp with the lack of rain, sun, attention. He did not—like many men his age—respond to the influx of out-of-towners with annoyance, not in the corner store where he got his morning coffee, not in the teacher's lounge Monday morning where they batted around school politics, their weekends. His job, as he saw it, was to solve the problems that already had answers. He did not have the energy for philosophical debate or issues of social value. He taught the students math, Algebra, and wasn't it enough for a teacher to give such young minds the idea of x?

In just a few short years, a lot had happened to the town. There was the boy who was raped and murdered in the public park restroom, just east of the swimming pool, in the shade of some overgrown trees. He was about to turn ten. It was summer, but the cement of the bathroom was always cool. There were those who admitted to looking at the bloodstains, but it's hard to say if there really was anything left there. Some who went insisted there was no evidence left behind, just the usual smell of park bathroom, a soft trail leading to the doorway.

They found the man that did it—we were lucky for that. Thirty-years old with singed red hair, he wore thick glasses and flannel year-round. He was not well known in town, had moved with his mother from another farm 30 miles west. He did not work, except to maintain the small acreage they rented near the creek, the land flat and dense and in need of little attention. He enjoyed his mother's company, though there is no evidence to suggest he was dependent on her or loved her excessively. He had a last name that sounded like a good man and we believed it, until we didn't anymore. Until he wasn't anymore. Then we thought he looked like a bad man, not one of us. When it came time, no one thought twice about putting him away for life. If he ever left prison, he wasn't coming back here.

The mother moved. She was a ghost in the town before she left. She went to the store, loaded up on groceries, made no motions towards others. She was the type of woman who merged with her background. She matched the gravel roads, the aisles of red meat, poultry, dairy, cereal boxes, a checkout lane lined with lottery scratch cards. The cement leading past the golf course, graveyards, hog farms, farmland, soil without roots left to blow sand.

She moved among them and they did not blame her, did not seek her out. Her farm was left to its own devices, shriveled, browned then died. There was no vandalism, no trespassing, people did not cruise by at night. People didn't exactly feel sorry for her, but no one knew enough to blame her. The father, no one knew where he was; it could've been his fault. But no one pursued this possibility, not with passion, conviction, evidence. The man was an adult, and he moved for escape, from what?

It all made sense to me then. He was a sick man and then a bad man. The sickness had turned, solidified. He had made up his mind that there was nothing that could satisfy him. He chose to try. But when he chose to move—let me repeat, 30 miles away—I still believe he did not know what was to become of him in Benton, Nebraska. Not when they packed the back of their pickup truck, not when he scuttled their things inside, not when he made his room up, placed the few books on his shelves. But when was it then? The first time he laid eyes on Gilmore Park, all the fresh, young flesh darting about, flying down slides, off swings, diving boards. Or was it the moment he saw the boy, the moment they locked eyes, and the man thought, I will end you and we will be as close as two human beings can be. Was it something he just had to do to go on with his life? Would that have been the end of it, had he not made such a goddamn mess? Could he have gone back to his farm, told his mother hello, showered the experience off and gone back to his life of blank thoughts and sound sleep? I like to think he could. I like to think that people can walk back over that line and be born again as people who never cross lines, who clamp down on reality—soil and silence and the tenuous relationships they have left. Let that silence hold everything you have ever done or thought of doing. Let the air hold it and release you from its burden.

But that is not how these things play out. These things— sicknesses, we call them—feed off of the experience, because if you think you can cross back over that line, you want to remember that once you did, and who doesn't want to remember a peak experience? Who doesn't want the ability to experience again and again what they thought would only be once. How many of us look at our husbands, wives, partners, lovers and think, I want to go back with you, but I am done with you. And we find someone somewhere, and even if we don't do it, we think to. But what if you did it, what if you have, because maybe you believe life is to be experienced, and you will deal with what will come, but that is not what you are about to experience, that is down the line, so you do it. Who goes back, safely, after that? Who has a reasonable affair, ends it on good terms, with all parties knowing exactly what is what. Who among us has felt a lasting fullness that has not deteriorated or faltered or been replaced by a quiet awareness of more to come?

As for Larry, he, too, grew up on a farm as a child, but the kind of farm that got no clout. Just a garden, a bit of a sideshow, that happened to be outside of city limits. Larry's father was an animal man—geese, goats, animals of no use really, just enough to give him a reason for space and distance. Larry liked the space for a while, sure, but then there was growing up to do. A woman to marry, children to father, students to teach, because after all he was no dummy at math, and most of those kids hated math as much as English—as much as anything really.

He had his way, as small schools allow, he liked big rings on his stubby fingers, knocking them on the chalkboard to demonstrate his frustration, his Can you believe how fucking stupid you are, because people, you are fucking stupid. Just like that, those rings let him use "fuck" like it was a means of discipline, imparting the importance of the knowledge only he contained. And then there was the way his turtlenecks made his already-retreating neck nearly disappear. A real polished, if repressed, look. He liked giving the students something to talk about.

Though it was no surprise that he'd done what he'd done, no use in going around it, touched some children, the number no one can be sure of, he'd been a teacher—a good teacher—and even a confidante for some of the trailer park kids and the kids with showy and wealthy but distant parents for over twenty-five years. It was only recently that a few of the boys started complaining, or rather stating, that Larry was a bit of a pervert. There wasn't any real alarm in how they said he talked about tits and fucking, the last time his cock got sucked right. It was another couple years before it turned into annoyance, awkwardness, avoidance. It was time for kids to confess.

They all had their stories, not the ones of speculation, just what was said to them, in front of them. There was no hiding that. Parents asked for verbatim, prayed to God that there was no touching, and then Thank God no touching. And then there was a boy who said to anyone and everyone that there had been more than touching, there had been sex, to which people could only respond, "What kind?"

There's really only one way for these things to go. Participation, meetings, Who else? Name names! At school no one admitted anything, except for the one boy, but everyone knew how to get information, reliable or not, complete or not. Who had stayed on the bus after everyone else had already gotten off? Who stayed late at school even though they didn't play sports? Who waited in the lunchroom as the sports kids filed by? Who saw Larry stop in front of those kids and ask, "Ready?" Who saw these kids get into Larry's car?

At the meetings, the parents looked around the room, desperate to find their failed counterparts. After all, they needed a little absolution, too.

It's difficult to know what went through their heads when they got the call. The dialogue was the same down the line, as if all the events led to this one script. The simple statement, "Larry Larsen killed himself," went out across the country, the world, even. Everyone asked How, but it's impossible to say what people meant when they asked Why.

Everything before felt like justice finally coming; after felt like being exposed for what you truly were.

It was winter, a beautiful winter really, but one that didn't seem to want to go away. It was late in March and it was as brutal as ever. Anyone could have killed himself if he'd wanted to. Just go off at night in a car that won't last, that would get you dead soon enough.

Larry was, if anything, attentive to detail. Everything he owned looked just as he wanted. It's not that he had style, because that's not what this was. He did not try new things. He liked the things he owned, and when a pair of pants started to wear out, a slightly updated model would be seen shortly thereafter. The same went for his cars.

This was not the problem. The car did not break down. The gas tank was halfway full, the keys in his pocket. There was not, however, a note.

There were several details people fixated on:
1. When was his court date?
2. What did he last say to his wife?
3. Did she tell him to leave, dare him to finally do it?
4. How many others?
5. My child, if it had been my child, would I have killed him myself?
6. Did he save us the trouble?
7. Did he save us from ourselves?

To a lesser extent, what people did not wonder aloud:
1. Did he think about the boy?
2. Did he stroke himself, thinking of him, others one last time, just to make sure he was sure it would not end?
3. What did he leave in the car? His futile and unsubstantial cum to freeze on the steering wheel? The proof we needed to forget him once and for all.
4. Did he put his filth to his lips as he froze, thought if only it did not exist, if his father's did not exist, had not been writhing with disease, longing?
5. Was he abused?
6. Would that ever excuse it?
7. Did the boy love him back?
8. Was the boy a fag?

All that is left are the people he left behind. Everyone crowded to get closer, to place themselves in context. That is, when they were further away. The ones closest moved. First feet then miles, and years, cars, clothes, faces. There was always an attempt at being someone else, someone who had never been touched, who had never been lured over a line they are sure they should have known was there, and here they were brazenly crossing, choosing to experience, to walk into darkness, the unknown and let happen what had been set out before them.

I began seeking people out, tried to find my way to Larry's son, who had proclaimed his love for me with his father's pen. A detail I wish I could confirm, but I flushed his love letters down the toilet, burned others behind the house after the toilet clogged.

He was a short boy, like his father, but with an athletic body, a kind, if comical, face.

The last time I saw him, he was trying some new seed, said it brought him closer to spiritual transcendence. I wondered then, as I do now, how close he got to transcending all of this.

Several of us got together and held our own personal wake. We flew in, drove up, down, over to the town we had left or were unable to leave.

We drank until we could speak, finding the equation that led each of us to Larry.

One of us, verbose and theatrical, gathered himself, brought himself center stage. The night was still except dogs barking occasionally, cars gently passing by. I wish I could deliver his soliloquy word for word, but we will have to settle for my memory, Sam's story in my voice:

It started for me in 9th grade. If I knew it would happen to my brother, too, I would have stopped it then, but I didn't know that then. I thought, I'm a man and no one is making me do anything. No one is ever going to find out, because who is going to tell them? I was convinced that I was the one who should be scared. I wasn't responding to anything Larry really put in my head. He may have said all of the typical things. I do remember a couple things, but I just laughed them off, because I knew he didn't need to convince me. Just right in the beginning, it's important to know that he's not really doing this as some way of tricking you into outing yourself. One of those: *everyone behind the bus, listening to Larry out this fag* things. How I knew it was okay was that Larry was never in on the joke. He tried talking shit about girls. And he was actually pretty good at that. I'm not sure where he got all his stories, but the guys just used him for material. They never really told him anything. We thought he must not be getting any at home, just needed to talk about pussy to give his life any sort of meaning. But yeah, I could tell it was a front pretty much right away. It's just hard to know if the other person knows it. I mean, I know enough now, as a gay man, to realize how far we've come, but then, that's all there was. Just you in a town that doesn't acknowledge your existence. It felt good to be recognized for what I was, and not in that silent, "you're a freak" kind of way.

The first time anything happened it had rained, so he drove everyone back early in the bus. I didn't drive or have a ride, so I was just going to wait the two hours until my mom came to pick me up. It's not like I was scared of the guy, and I wouldn't say that I wanted anything to happen. It wasn't so straightforward. And it's not like he made it rain. It's not like he made it so I couldn't leave. He may have encouraged me not to call and bother my parents, so we could just waste some time at the high school.

It happened in a pretty obvious way. My jeans were pretty wet, so I changed into my gym shorts. It must have soaked me all the way through because my shorts were clinging to my underwear. And like I said, Larry was pretty obscene, and it wasn't out of the ordinary to comment on each other's cock size, take it out of your pants, slap it around. And it was just boys being boys. But there was no confusing this. Larry just looked at me and his eyes stopped on my shorts. He made some comment about how I must make all the girls scream… if that's really all me under there. I don't know what I did then. I was probably pretty proud of my cock—the one thing I was sure of. And here I had my opportunity to prove myself in some way, even if it was to someone I couldn't care less about impressing. I was pretty amped up I guess, because I grabbed myself, and said something stupid like, "you know it!" I felt like an idiot, but Larry looked thrilled, like I had just told him he never had to work another day in his life. He flat out asked me if he could touch it and something about not ever having been well-endowed, and I can remember he clicked his tongue in the way he always would when he was ready for sex. I remember thinking, I have nothing to be afraid of, and then I dropped my shorts. I didn't really look at what he did to me. I don't know how long he studied me before I felt his hand and then his mouth. And that was the first time anyone had ever done either of those things to me. I was a notorious masturbator, so it wasn't until I felt that warmth and wetness that I knew I was leaving something behind and going into a different world where I never wanted this feeling to go away. Of course I will never be able to capture that feeling again, this would have been the case whether it was a man, a woman, someone my age or not. It was only later that I started to hate him, but by then, the hate I had for him felt like something between lovers, and that was nothing I needed to tell anyone.

There were a few times he came to see me. He'd show up on the door of my fraternity and I would pretend I wasn't home. I wouldn't return his calls. If it wasn't obvious to him, I don't know what, but I knew what I was doing. I was trying to fit in. I had a chance at being normal, and I wasn't going to give that up for a blowjob from a 60-year-old man.

My brother is the one who called me. He said it, and then he told me a story that sounded a little too familiar. For a minute I was confused, almost as if I was watching myself from above and that my brother was narrating my story, but there were details that didn't match up. We were almost off the phone when it finally registered. My brother didn't feel the way I felt. My brother was glad he was dead.

This was the first time I'd heard it out loud. There were always rumors, but to hear him lay it out so precisely, I didn't want it to end. I wanted more. I wanted to live in his body until I could say it happened to me too. I wanted to be on the other side of this, on the side that understood what happens when you don't look back.

Rachel, Sam's best friend, was off in a corner with her cigarette, containing herself. She was quiet while Sam told his story, barely acknowledging it, but eventually risked the price of her voice, "I wish I could still say, 'I wish he were dead.' I want that back."

I knew from Sam that he had once taken a ruler to Rachel's skirt and then stroked it up her leg, under her skirt. She was not confused or afraid and went straight to the principal who said it must have been unintentional, an accident. Never could a child be trusted to know when an adult crossed a line. Adults made the lines, after all.

When it was my turn, I had a feeling of heaviness. I don't remember getting a word out, though I know I must have. I was drowning in my drunkenness, trying to find my way to the surface of a dark and mucked-up lake. I remember feeling like I had no right to be there, with the others who had demons to wash down, bring up. What was there to say, after all? Larry never looked me up and down, made no motion toward my thoroughly-covered body.

That was the last night we talked about it together. We all graduated, moved away, brought it with us wherever we went. We retold the story to new friends, people who did not have Larry Larsen as a part of their vocabulary, did not want to hear stories of murder, rape, suicide. We forced it on them, thought this was the only way to get closer. The story lived outside some of us, and we kept ushering it back in. For others, it sunk into them, took up a lot of room.

It's a strange thing to see people want to change the subject, want to be saved from the horror we relish over and over. I have thoughts about this when I am alone and there is no one around me who wants to listen. I think, I could forget this if I tried, just like everyone back home.

There is a new Algebra teacher who does not curse or insult the students, does not tap oversized rings on the backboard. There was a perfectly appropriate staff—at least for a while—until two teachers were caught late at night—in two separate instances—watching child pornography. They had always been remarkable teachers, with barely any indication that they saw us as anything but thorns in their sides.

They were fired unceremoniously and the school continues to seek cleanness of character. I wonder what is under every new exterior; I wonder what is under my own.

I still haven't found Larry's son, not in the flesh anyway. Someone tells me he's in the army, Afghanistan on a third tour. Sometimes I wake up sure he is dead, wishing I had held him just once, so I could comfort myself with the memory of his weight.

Other times I imagine Larry, lying face down in a field I know. The ground is frozen, but there is a grave, fresh and open. There's only one thing left to do.

LUKE TENNIS

The Secret Coast

Morry Kahn had his pad and pencils and had set up his beach chair on the flattened gravel behind the high fence that blocked the highway. He kept angling his shoulders in such a way so as not to face me. It was only us under the sky just before dark. Holding onto my bike, I didn't like the way he kept angling, so I said, "Morry, kid, let's go over to the pond awhile, you and I."

At first, he didn't answer, then he said I wasn't to call him kid. I kept after him and finally got him to say something.

"Why can't you be more like him?" he asked.

"Who?"

"Gawk. Who else?"

"Who's Gawk?"

"Shut-up," he said. "Don't be a goof."

It was true about his drawings, he was good; he was special, his drawings seemed to say, and he himself believed it. I wanted him to see otherwise, to see that he couldn't ignore me or angle away, because he'd been there that day.

"Let me see your picture," I said.

He pulled it closer to his chest. "You're dismissed."

I wished I'd knocked his pad out of his hands. He'd go for me then and I'd maul him – broad shouldered as he was and one day headed for Yale – I'd kick him on the ground with the fury of my speedy legs.

* * *

Later on I wanted someone to say to me to go to Morry Kahn: look him in the eye and tell him you wish Gawk was still around, tell him nice that he – Morry – had been there that day and that links you two, and so he's not to dismiss you anymore. You tell him and hold out your hand for him to shake, and you say, "Peace, brother."

But there was no one to tell me.

Maybe Mr. Tompkins, a neighbor. One time he'd said if he'd been there, Nickie (Gawk's real name) would never have dove off that rock. Mr. Tompkins held a can of beer at the barbecue and spoke from the heart. His mustache drooped around his mouth. He'd fought in Nam and had a chest the size of a piano. But he and his wife lived on the next block and had no kids and made limited appearances, and, anyway, he wouldn't be the one to tell me.

* * *

Nor Dad, either. He stayed on the sofa chair in his den room that had the dried out plants and the TV on. I didn't know how he could lounge around all the time when he wasn't at work, teaching. I wanted to shake him sometimes and see if he had any stuffing that would come out. I imagined white junk leaking onto the floor. It would drive Mom nuts, though, to have to clean it up.

She stood above us at the dining table. It was walnut, oblong; if you dropped a spill on it, or a splash, she wiped it right away. OCD, Dad called it; a disorder.

"You're not to do that," she said to me at the table, because I liked to cut my meatballs into four exact wedges on the plate.

"Why not?"

Nobody ever answered such questions, and they lingered.

It was as if Gawk was still there, with us, in his seat. Two months, three months, I kept expecting him to come down the stairs or burst through the front door. Mom wiped up more and more: counters, cabinets, even the walls; vacuumed a lot, too.

* * *

Morry Kahn had said how Gawk's white calves stayed on the surface of the water a moment after he splashed into the Merkin pond. You couldn't see him because of the mud fanning out where he'd landed. I was several neighborhoods away, kicking an under-inflated soccer ball against a cinder block wall. Later, in the hospital, standing alone in the florescent hall, I didn't believe a bit of it. Was Gawk behind the door? I pictured him in there eating ice cream, the TV turned up loud. I stared at the door, grainy yellow, refusing to enter.

* * *

One reason I didn't enter was that other kids all had their brothers, so why should it have happened?

Gawk was in the ground somewhere, so I tried not to be home too much. I told my mother about this boarding school in Cumberland, Maryland, that had horses. A boy I knew was being sent there. I didn't give a damn about riding horses. I had never even been on one. But I said I wanted to go to the school with the boy, Tim, and wear the uniform and ride. I wanted to go the very next semester. I begged my mother. For a week I asked. Then she got so mad she threw a glass and broke it against the dinning room wall.

I didn't know why she got mad; I think it was something in the mail, or maybe something happened in the kitchen, she burned herself, or just a slew of things suddenly. But seeing her after, I knew not to ask any longer about the boarding school.

* * *

Sitting on the opposite side of the oblong table, Gawk would sneer at me; he always sneered if I was the one getting the business from our mother. When he was the one getting the business, I didn't know how to sneer.

* * *

Our mom was tall, how Gawk had gotten his height. I was like Dad, short and stocky and pouty. When I won a sprint race at school I got an award as the fastest kid. At home, Mom put her hand on my shoulder. Her face seemed large, her forehead like a blank billboard, brightening for a moment. Then she said the dishwasher needed unloading, which was a job my brother or I was supposed to do. She was always running the dishwasher, and since it was only me now it was hard to keep up. From the dining room, I heard her begin pulling out dishes and silverware and stacking them on the counter for me to put away. I held my gold-faced plaque that they'd given me, studying it for a message what to do.

When she called me, I was in my room upstairs. I heard nastiness in her voice, so I decided I'd cry, to test it out. It seemed okay, though I wouldn't have wanted Gawk to catch me if he'd been in his room, which of course he wasn't. I wanted my mother to come up so that I could tell her it'd been exciting to cross the finish line first, ahead of the famous Blain McGee, super athlete of the eighth grade. She could hug me maybe as I cried, but the thought made me fidget.

If I could show Gawk the plaque, he'd shrug, because he was Mr. Cool. Later, in the backyard, he'd tell me to go long if I was so damn fast. He'd palm the football, then maybe snap me on the chin, and I'd tell him to quit it. Then he'd throw it a mile in the air so that I'd have to run under it.

* * *

There was the rock Gawk dove from: it was jutting. I squeezed my eyes shut and in my head sent a message. *Morry Kahn meet me here.* I sent drawings of my own, too. Me shoving him down the bank; my foot on top of his head, pushing his face into the mud. I waited around awhile, but of course he chickened out of coming.

When I came home, I snuck past my mother back upstairs to my room. I'd left the plaque on my made bed and lay down backwards and held it to my chest. I lifted my bare feet above the pillow and braced my heels against the wall below the United States map I had tacked up.

I sometimes thought of that map as my door, or as a window to open; for instance, Gawk would be there, saying Mom dressed me like a fairy; or maybe, in his room, he'd use his foot to boost me completely off his desk chair, and he'd put me out like I was a dog. I'd have the map to look at then. The colorful states rocked back and forth above my pillow. There were all the capitals to one day visit. At the bottom tip of California, there was a wild strip of yellow that was called Baja and dipped into the ocean like the clip of a pen. This secret coast was a thousand miles long. All would be new when I got there. I'd ride a horse along the trails, up into the hot desert mountains, and I'd squint at the tiny scalloped waves below.

I kept the window open as long as I could.

It got closed the day I told the man smoking the pipe about it. Then, after, I curled upon the bed.

*   *   *

Mom had said I could tell him anything. She sent me to see him, paying good money for me, to help me. I saw him three or four times in his brown walnut office that reminded me of Mom's oblong table. The pipe in his mouth leaked a cherry smell. I couldn't see his face behind it or, rather, I wasn't interested in looking. His cracked green leather chair that he had me sit in had buttons in it. The first time I didn't say anything for a half hour. Finally I said about the map. After, when I went home, I couldn't look at the map and not think of the man without a face, only a pipe, only because Mom had said I could tell him.

Another time he said the map was because it was hard to think about my brother, and if I could think about him, what would that thought be? I told him it would be that my brother was dead, deader than dead. He asked did I have any nice thoughts about him, and I said I did. *He could throw a football high and far.* Then the man's pipe shifted from his left to his right, and he asked why I thought my mom had sent me to see him. I fidgeted, wondering if maybe I should begin to cry, then the man would stop asking me things.

"I don't know why," I said.

*   *   *

All that happened was that my mother got more and more pale, or maybe it was the kitchen light. She spoke of her own private room. It was a reading room she wanted away from my father and me. She could paint the walls a fancy cinnamon color and put in books and an antique couch and delicate things. Of course there was Gawk's room, sitting empty.

I wondered if when I moved out, say, when I went to college, if I'd tell my roommate and friends about Gawk. Maybe I'd have a girlfriend I'd bring home for visits and show her his old room if my mother hadn't transformed it. She'd ask if I missed him, and I'd tell her how we used to play football out back, and if we were on the same team we'd kick ass. I'd tell her it seemed unfair and, yeah, I missed him, and maybe even I'd have a tear, and it would make me special.

"Kiss me," she'd say.

On my bed, I felt myself.

* * *

To reign myself in, I answered a question when asked at dinner and cleared the table as I was supposed to, and I got passable grades in school. I didn't ever go into Dad's den room. I avoided the Merkin's shallow pond, and I avoided Morry Kahn because he'd been there. I took up reading in my room to pass the time, books that weren't a part of school. Spy novels, mysteries. I hoarded candy in my bottom drawer, and I found Gawk's old skin magazines. I tried cigarettes with a new friend in an alcove somewhere just off the middle school grounds. I wasn't sprinting anymore, and in the spring I didn't run track. I got acne from the candy and my hair was oily. I smoked Marlboro Red, and the new friend, Brooks, developed a scheme for us to shoplift games and CDs.

When we got caught, my mother came to the store in the mall to speak to the manager. A draft chilled me in the hall outside the office while she talked to the manager inside and signed the papers. I hadn't even wanted the games and CDs; it'd been Brooks' idea. And worse was a special insight at that moment – that Gawk's eyes would be shut forever. That he would fade in my mind until the day I could only recall him as something long-ago.

* * *

One year after he dove, I cornered Morry Kahn in his beach chair, called him chicken for not meeting me at the pond, to which he gave me his severe look. Low eyebrows, that look. He said something right to my face:

"If there's a family, and there's two boys, one is always the good one and one is the bad one, and in your family Gawk was the good one, so what's that make you?"

But he didn't angle away this time. I said, "Your drawings aren't even that good."

Now he did angle.

"Your drawings suck."

He put his feet down on the gravel and leaned forward, getting ready to stand.

"C'mon, Morry, kid. Dismiss me."

"You're embarrassing yourself, squirt."

"You didn't do shit, did you? Just watched Nickie dive. Or maybe you pushed him."

He had those big shoulders. The ripples on his forearms were tan, the hair blond; he was beautiful and gifted. He didn't stand, though he kept the low eyebrow look. But he had a slight smile, too, a smirk that said that no one, and certainly not me, could say those things I'd just said to him.

"This is not the way, squirt," he said. "Think of your brother. Would he want to see you like this?"

"Don't mention my brother."

"What do you want from me, a beating? Would that do it?"

I felt my eyes tear up, but I resisted wiping them.

"Why don't you just go your way and I'll go mine?"

"Because," I said.

"Because what?"

But I wouldn't answer. Riding back home on my bike, I decided not to go upstairs to my bed this time. In the backyard, where once we held our football games, I hid in a tiny cave the bushes by the house made. I curled in there and made a last-ditch vow to always feel this crummy, to always do bad.

OLYN OZBICK

And in the End

The worst is this leaning over and looking at that mouth. A sticky, unforgiving place: not deep, not pooling, not significant in its subtleties; only stuck with globs and spit not swallowed; crusted at the corners and moving slightly; cracking open and trying to tell me things. The lips are dry all the way to the inside, under the gums and beneath the teeth; surprisingly crooked teeth, and pointy, little sharp things veering off in all directions. The face no longer moves. Only the mouth, edging almost imperceptibly more open, then less, then more. This means something. This needs to be watched. Not the eyes, that's for sure. Sometimes they open, half, or less than that, to see I'm there. They tell me nothing. I would have thought, before, that they would be what I should watch, look into, gaze into even. That's foolish. That's what you think until you know. In death, it's about the mouth. And now a sound.

"What? What are you saying Dragan? Say it again. Do you need some water?"

No. The mouth says no. It stops moving which tells me no.

"Do you have pain? Is there pain?"

The bottom lip tightens.

Yes. Yes, there's pain.

"What can I do for it? Do you need to be moved?"

I know that he's dying. I knew as soon as the rail hit the car. Tossed him onto this empty road. But he didn't know then so I didn't believe either, not entirely. Now I do. I understand completely.

And the mouth. That maw. Ah when it screamed it was awful. It wasn't the screaming itself really: the sounds of pain, they were sounds. They meant he was tortured, but I knew that. It was the mouth that was grotesque. It opened and the lips were thin and the inside yellow with a tongue gone white, though there was also blood in there, streaks I saw when he opened wide enough to make large sounds. But already he can't open like that anymore, for which I would be grateful except this is worse. Now I can't decipher his needs, can't do anything for him. Well, for me, to be truthful; he is beyond help now. My help helps only me.

All I can do now is call out for others. I don't, though. It wouldn't change anything. That is apparent to me, and also to him now, though he can barely say, can only lie there, eyes closed, mouth breathing, blood in his beard that I tried to clean out with a tissue but couldn't. A deep rumbling comes from inside him.

He grabbed me earlier, when he could still move. I was leaning over to hear his watery whisper. Well, not a whisper at all. A semblance of words that came from his throat or deeper. A guttural sound, an animal noise, a moan. "Iiiiisss kiiiiih heeee." That's what he said. "Iiiiiissss kiiiiihh heeeee." I didn't know what it meant. You couldn't.

"I don't know," I said and jiggered my head, thinking maybe I could grasp his words with my ears; catch them like bubbles out of the air.

"I don't know Dragan. What do you need, what are you saying?"

I looked at his mouth. The guck drying in the corners trembled. I leaned in and put my ear to his mouth.

"What do you need?" I said. "What do you need?"

His arms could still move then, and he reached one up and wrenched it around my head. He was still strong, I hadn't expected that. His arm held me shockingly tightly and I thought, Oh, he is still the hunter. He had my head and yanked it toward his chest. I struggled and he struggled back, wrestling my head and pulling me in. I could have got away, if I'd fought him, but I was surprised and feeling tender. So he forced my head. The old bugger: I wondered if he wanted to kill me too, strangle me maybe, and then I softened. It's a hug, he wants a hug. I held his shoulders while he held my head, but the tug got harder. It wasn't hugs. Not ever, not now. It was this: "Iiiiiissss kiiiiihhl mheeeee." My head was flattened to his chest, the rough wool of his jacket pricking my face. Through the warm pile of it, a sound emanated, dim and echoing as if rising from a distant place. Muted. Terrible. A vicious reveille. This time I understood. It was the call of his death; he had heard it and wanted me to know.

"Yes, Dragan," I said. "It's killing you." I felt relieved. Not relieved that it was true, but that it was out, said, and also, that I knew what he was saying.

KHANH HA

Thy Name is Death

The moon over the Delaware U.S. 13 Dragway hazed in billowy white, smokes from spinning tires during a burnout. The long, violent, extra burnout by a canary-yellow Camaro brought cheers from the crowd in the bleachers. The driver, last-year 1982 champion, pumped his fist. Drivers in the pits, in the staging lanes could smell the tang of burning rubber. The gasoline fumes dampened the crisp, chilly air in early February.

His staging lane was called. Vinh Hoàng drove his '68 candy apple-red Mustang to the lane and lined up. The dragster's V-6 idled in a deep throated rumble, as husky as a small V-8. Back in the pits Richard Wolcott was sitting on the hood of his '70 Nova, eating popcorn. The glare in the parking lot shone on the Nova's deep black paint. Vinh felt butterflies in his stomach. Three months before, during the first round of eliminations, he bent the car's chassis in its launch. The front end of his Mustang leaped two feet off the ground, the car stood on its rear bumper then banged down, hooking left. He overcorrected the wheels and struck the retaining wall. He aborted the race.

Now this was the trial run. His quarter mile elapsed time was 15.45 seconds at 90 mph before the accident. That was like ten years ago. Wolcott's Nova ran 11.2 at 115 mph in a quarter mile. It launched like a rocket. "You can do the same thing for your Stang, Vinh," Wolcott told him. He found a cure.

The mechanic Wolcott recommended was a retired American Indian in his sixties. His black hair was knotted in a ponytail. He was toothless, his upper lip bulged from dentures. Wrecked Mustangs littered his backyard, an elephant graveyard where weeds grew wild drooping against the car windows. The Indian filled the doorway with his bearlike frame.

"What do I call you?" Vinh asked. The handshake hurt his fingers.

"You really want to know?" The Indian said, looking up and down the road behind Vinh. "Anyone ever told you how the Indians name their newborn babies? Awright. They have names like White Thunderbolt, Running Deer. Things that their mothers see outside the wigwam after the baby is born. So one day I asked my Dad, What'd Mom see when I was born? And he said, Why'd you want to know, Two Dogs Fucking?"

The Indian liked Vinh's souped-up dragster, which Vinh bought last year from a family in North Carolina through a newspaper ad. It had a roll cage around a fiberglass racing seat secured by 5-point harness.

"Fix the frame," Vinh said. "And do something to make it go faster."

"How much faster?"

"I'm not an engineer, but I think if I install a super heavy flywheel, I might crank up enough juice for the launch. Problem is I could burn the clutch in a hurry. The transaxle would take a pounding and might break too. What d'you think?"

"You fucking nuts," the Indian said. "Okay, here's what I'll do. I'll soak the clutch in rubbing alcohol. You know what that will do? It'll grab like a bitch. I'll pull the engine for you after every race. No fucking small job. I'll replace the bearings, too, at no fucking cost." He popped his plastic teeth out of his mouth and gripped them in his hands. He bared his dark gums. "How's that sound to you, mister? Heh, heh, heh."

The Indian built Vinh a 70-pound flywheel, made a model of it, and had it cast at a foundry. To get the ring gear on, he cooled the flywheel with dry ice. It shrank, and he slipped the ring gear over it. When the flywheel expanded, it grabbed the gear tight.

"You'll go off like a slingshot, mister," the Indian said. "Fucking problem is the rear tires will be pounded so bad you might spin all the way through first gear. You'll need bad-assed tires, mister. Real bad."

The Indian fitted the car with a set of 29-inch tall slicks— treadless tires—and changed to 10-inch rims. The tires were stretched badly but assured a maximum footprint.

"You ready, Mister?" the Indian said. "This Stang of yours now has some oats. I did sometin like this five years ago for a street racer. In one race the flywheel flew out the back end of his car like a hand grenade. Hit the starter guy when it flew by. Zapped him. The guy still held the light switch in his hand when he died. It cut the fuel line and the car was a ball of fire. My guy got burned, but lived. Some thrill. Heh, heh, heh."

Vinh tried to smile. "Then why did you do the same thing for me?"

"You gave me an opinion. That guy gave me specs on how to build a flywheel. I told him he needed a seventy-pound flywheel, but he fucking insisted on a one-hundred pounder. Heh, heh, heh. I'm no engineer but I knew more about Stangs than I knew my fucking body. I used to drag race, build my own go-karts. I have car parts as old as you." He pointed at the new slicks. "Don't do long burnouts. You'll kill the slicks that way. And no extra burnouts."

Now the burnout-box man waved at Vinh to move up to the water strip.

Vinh set the line-loc to lock the front wheels and revved the engine in second gear. Water sprayed, then smoke rose from the rear end. The slicks were now heated. The hot acrid smell got into the compartment.

It was time. He nudged up to the pre-stage beam, kept the engine revving steadily. He had never tested his rebuilt car after he left Toothless' garage. Too dangerous anywhere but on the dragstrip. All the time he could feel that tightness the car held, that raw power packed under the hood. And the monstrous flywheel. He staged, revved hard. His heart throbbed with the motor. The crowd in the bleachers blurred. He glanced at the starter's thumb on the switch. If he guessed right, he would floor the gas pedal, let go the clutch at the flick of the starter's thumb. If the starter tricked him, he might jump before the green light and be disqualified. He focused his eyes on the signal tree ahead of him. Then the top bulb on the tree flashed.

The second he dumped the clutch, the car shot forward, the front lifted up then banged down. The force snapped his head back, the floor seat-fastening bolts broke, the seat skidded back. He braced himself with one hand on the steering wheel, the other on the shifter. He threw it into second, then third and fourth. The RPM dropped, the flywheel slowed down, the car hurled through the traps and the board flashed his elapsed time. It was too fast as he flew by. 11.11 or 11.1? He would be damned happy to have 11.11.

He followed the turnoff lane and cruised by the timeslip booth. The man handed him the slip. His elapsed time was 11.1 at 115 mph.

Toothless was waiting in the pits. He pumped his fist as if with an imagined tomahawk.

"Good as sex, heh?" the Indian said. "This is one bad boy. I fucking flipped over in the bleachers. The front didn't kick up that high. One foot, maybe. Fucking good launch."

Toothless welded the seat back into the floor, then walked to the bleachers. "I'm gonna get fucking drunk when you get to the quarter finals," he said.

Vinh met Wolcott in the crowded pits. Over 100 competitors entered tonight's race. The air was dry, sharp and smelled of buttered popcorn.

Wolcott looked at the timeslip. "I'll be thrilled to race against you if they pair us up," he said. "The chief really did it."

"Thanks, he didn't get me killed," Vinh said. "Until I went through the last light, I've had dreams about the flywheel." He looked over the rear slicks. "Only a thin line between getting thrilled and getting killed by his standards."

Wolcott leaned against the Mustang's door. "We need to talk."

Vinh stopped writing on the car window. He was chalking his elapsed time in white shoe polish.

"I want to go ahead with your nomination," Wolcott said. "Soon. But there's a monkey wrench."

"Fitch's still in it for his boy?"

"No. From the Hill." Wolcott jangled the coins in his pants pocket. "Congressman Byrd asked me a few questions about you that got me thinking. You know how politics works. If you can defend yourself, you win."

"Level with me, Dick. Stop beating around the bush."

"I want to know everything. Remember we're in this together. This thing doesn't have to be dragged out and up the Hill. I want no surprises. Let's have it now rather than later in front of the committee."

Robert Fitch, the director of the Bureau of Refugee Programs at the State Department, had two deputy assistant secretaries: Vinh Hoàng and Gene Jensen, Fitch's right-hand man. Wolcott was Vinh's age, 48, but had a billowy cloud of white hair. He happened to be Fitch's boss and Vinh's mentor. The two of them had been friends back in the early sixties in South Vietnam when Wolcott was an advisor to the Saigon mayor.

Vinh put away the shoe polish can. He wiped his hands with a paper napkin, then from his jacket's pocket took out a small bottle of cognac. He threw his head back for a swig.

"I'll be honest with you, Dick," Vinh said, exhaling. "I'll tell you everything you want to know. I don't know a lot, but I know a lot of what people said about me isn't true. Unfounded, cooked-up facts are the fabric of politics."

"Ain't that a bitch?" Wolcott took the bottle from Vinh. "But Byrd happens to be sitting on the committee that reviews the nomination." Wolcott wiped the mouth of the bottle, wetting his lips. "You know, Byrd was a friend of Jensen's dad. Senator Jensen knew you well before he died."

"Byrd said that? Well, I entertained Jensen's father when he paid our President a visit. I hardly knew the man. Dick, get on with it, will you?"

"Byrd said you had a communist affiliation."

"True or false?"

Wolcott sipped the cognac. "In sixty-seven, you let Reuters in on a story of the American atrocities. Remember, you were working for the President of the Republic of South Vietnam, so it made this case even more special. It took place during the transport of sixteen Vietnamese prisoners from Rach Già to Saigon. Yes or no?"

"Yes."

"Why?"

"Did Byrd tell you the whole story?"

"I know what happened."

"No, you don't." Vinh drank from the bottle.

"Well, I don't know all the details and I know you were in one of the three helicopters which brought back the prisoners. Your story could be different, but that's not the point. What Byrd questioned about is your intention behind it."

"It's hard for me to explain something like this without being able to share the emotion connected with what happened."

Wolcott removed his hand from his pants pocket. He counted the change in his palm with his finger, closed his hand, opened it and counted his change again. He said without looking up, "What's your version of the story?"

"I used to monitor the work of the Psychological Warfare Civic Action Operation. That time I was in Rach Già in the Mekong Delta. The American Fifth Special Forces were bringing back a dozen captured Việt Cong" Vinh stopped. Wolcott was still feigning interest in counting the coins. "We landed in Saigon and there was a party waiting for us—an American colonel and several field grade officers. I got off the helicopter.

"There were only three prisoners left in one helicopter, and one in the other. I asked the American door gunner in one of the helicopters, 'What happened?' The guy said they had pushed them out over the Mekong Delta. Then he pointed toward the doorway." Vinh took another swig of cognac, then handed it to Wolcott who shook his head without looking up. "Those double-rotor helicopters, the H-121, had only open doorways. When I got near the doorways I stopped. There was torn flesh stuck to the doorjambs. Flesh from the prisoners' hands when they were pushed out. There was blood all over the floor where they were beaten. I walked up to the colonel just when he asked one of the pilots, 'What the hell happened to the other eight?' The pilot said, 'They tried to escape, sir.'"

Wolcott clamped shut his hand. "I understand how you must've felt. But there was a war going on and we were trying to do our best to win it. Any efforts to flaw our image are sabotage to our psychological warfare. That's aiding the enemy. I'm only putting it to you mildly, Vinh. Byrd and the committee are more of the hardcore."

"It's a matter of conscience. Whether you can live with yourself after witnessing such atrocity. There're hawks on the Hill, hawks during the war. I was only a pacifist. There's a difference between being a pacifist and being a communist sympathizer."

"That conscience stuff won't fly by the committee. You can't afford to leave those guys with any ammunition to shoot back at you."

"I oversaw the Civic Affairs, the Psy-Op, and how could we win the hearts and minds of our people when the U.S. government tolerated such atrocities?"

"Then tell Byrd why you protested against the bombing of villages in the Quang Ngai province. Byrd said our intelligence had proof that those village hospitals were run by the Viêt Cong for their wounded. But you were against it."

"Yes, I protested against the U.S. war policy, the American indiscriminate destruction of the Vietnamese villages." Vinh screwed shut the cap of his cognac bottle, then slowly untwisted it. "I read a report filed by a Quaker worker in Quang Ngai in February of sixty-nine. She witnessed an AC-47 mowing down a village the Americans believed controlled by the Viêt Cong. That gunship spewed out five-thousand machine-gun bullets per minute. She said she and her coworkers survived, but many Quang Ngai people didn't. She said, 'The beating the civilians are taking in this war is beyond adequate description. Man's inhumanity to man has reached its climax in Vietnam.' But the Americans believed that in order to save a village they had to level it. It's damned hard to win the war without the people's support. That's my point."

Wolcott bit his lips. "If you say you're innocent, so be it. I'll deal with Byrd." He turned and leaned back against the Mustang's door. Dragsters were returning to the pits from the elimination race. It had just begun. "I know where you're coming from," he said. Took me a long time to admit our mistake in Vietnam. I thought we did right in Nam until I came home. I had time to look back. I wish we could use every eight-hundred-dollars per second we spent on war to come up with a cure for cancer."

Vinh spat out the chewing gum into his hand. Wolcott's wife had breast cancer in remission.

"A lot of us who returned from Nam don't feel like whole human beings," Wolcott said. "War is a continuation of politics by other means. Who said that?"

"Võ Nguyên Giáp?"

"Baron von Clauswitz, master strategist of war." Then Wolcott sighed. "A bunch of us came home with self-doubt, self-hatred, social paranoia. I came home with one hundred and some GIs on a plane. My American fellows. The rowdy, chatty, friendly Americans. But during that flight no one had anything to say to anyone. If there had been a stripper shaking her boobs down the aisle, they'd probably tell her to bug off. We have some seven thousand Vietnam vets checking into VA hospitals. Half of them have suicidal thoughts, the other half have tried suicide at least once."

"Dick, you're not alone," Vinh said. "The U.S. government never explained to you why they decided to enter Vietnam. You were urged to kill like the primitives, and that was okay by your military racism."

Wolcott folded his arms and spoke into his chest. "I didn't look at the Vietnamese that way, honestly. The truth is, racism will surface when you move from an affluent country to a poor country like Vietnam. I admit that. But you know many American GIs fell in love with Vietnamese girls. My sweetheart was Tuyêt Mai, whom I still love."

Vinh met Wolcott's girl many times at the French Cercle Sportif in Saigon. The girl was still in high school, the French boarding school Lycée Marie Curie. Vinh never forgot her navy-blue skirt and white blouse—her school uniform—when he thought of her pretty face. Wolcott lost her when her family, anti-American and anti-interracial marriage, forbade their relationship.

"You might think I met Tuyêt Mai at the Cercle Sportif," Wolcott said. "I met her at a hospital in Saigon. She was a volunteer there." Wolcott unwrapped another stick of gum, chewed, rolling the green wrapper slowly between his fingers. "A few days before I was down in the U Minh forest in the deep south. We were on a patrol boat in the swamp when we saw a sampan drift by. There was a woman in it. She was lying facedown with a conical hat covering the back of her head. Next to her was a little girl. A lovely girl about eight. Blood was all over their bodies. One of the girl's leg was half gone. Shrapnel had cut through her thigh. She saw me and pulled at the woman's arm. 'Mommy, *ông Mỹ!*' she said. *Mister American*. But Mommy was dead. The back of her head got blown away." Wolcott spat, then sucked in his lower lip. "In those remote areas medicine was gold. You might die from a tooth abscess because you couldn't stop the infection. The Viêt Cong were short on medical supplies. So they saved them for their own people. They put wounded villagers in a sampan, shoved it downstream. If these folks were lucky, they might get picked up by a South Vietnamese patrol boat."

"You saved her?"

"Sort of. When I picked her up, she smiled. God only knows how. Here I was in a flak jacket, cradling her in my bare hairy arms and she smiled. To this day I still don't know how she could smile. But the medic gave her enough morphine so we could fly her back to Saigon. There she was put to sleep while they amputated her leg. The Vietnamese doctor said he had no choice." Wolcott lifted his face skyward and spoke as if to the stars, "When she woke up she saw *ông Mỹ* by her side. She smiled and reached down to feel her leg. The fright in her eyes sickened me. If I were a ghost, I would've probably felt more human. I don't know how I could ever express that feeling. I just don't know, Vinh. You feel the absurdity of it all. You feel as if God plays trick on you." Wolcott took out some change from his pants pocket, tossed up a quarter and caught it with the other hand. "I don't deny racism," he said, "and savagery. When a friend of mine, a pilot, asked me about Tuyêt Mai, he said, 'What's her name?' I told him and he said, 'I knew a whore who worked in a massage parlor on Tu Do Boulevard, is that her?'"

Wolcott stopped as a dragster rumbled by. The canary-yellow Camaro was heading toward the staging lane. Vinh wished he could race against its driver—the current champion. His elapsed time, 10.95, was displayed in white shoe polish on the window. *Try to beat that.*

The Camaro was snaking around parked cars. The champion, a welder by profession, got out and hollered at a Dodge Dart. "Move over," he said. "Piece of junk. Is he taking a crap?"

Other drivers surrounded the Dart and pushed it to one side.

Within fifteen minutes Wolcott's and Vinh's numbers were called. With shock in his eyes, Wolcott shook Vinh's hand. "May the best man win," he said.

They drove up in the staging lanes and waited. Paired up, Vinh was on the left lane because of his better elapsed time. Ahead, dragsters, two by two, were rolling up to the starting line. The engines roared, the amber lights flashed, the cars lunged forward. Tires squealed, fumes and smoke drifted back in the staging lanes.

Vinh sipped his cognac. The bottle was near empty. The last time while out here in Delaware for drag racing—the second time this year after a long layoff—he got drunk with Wolcott, both lying on the bare floor of his Mustang with nothing else but a driver's seat, windows with no glass but the fluttering fishnets tied to them. They reminisced about ancient times in an opium den in Cholon. He had fished Wolcott out of there before Wolcott made it his permanent home—a dark second-story room whose wooden floor sagged and creaked, where cot after cot filled the room with barely a gap between them to put your feet down, cots never dusted, each a sanctuary for lice. He had sat there convincing Wolcott to leave until his English ran out. Wolcott looked like a caveman with a full beard, hollow eyes, and smelled like dried mulch. Vinh watched him scrape out the residue from a pipe, mix it with a few drops of liquor, and roll it into pea-sized pellets. The man was scavenging the remains of the sticky brown wax to keep his addiction alive. Only the bums cleaned out pipes and lamps, but such was the skid mark of the man's downfall. It hit him. Hard. In front of his eyes lay a brownish body, gaunt, glistening with sweat in the dark room, eyes glazed over. Without a word, he reached over and snuffed out the lamp.

Now, he'd better keep his mind on the race.

Their turns came. They positioned their rear tires in the water and did their burnouts. Vinh had goose bumps when the burning rubber stung his nose. Somewhere in the bleachers the Indian was watching him.

Watch me, Two Dogs Fucking.

They staged. Vinh brought up the rev. Hard. Redlining at 6500 rpm. The fumes made him drunk. He glanced at Wolcott as if at a stranger, glanced back just as the three amber lights flashed. Then the green lit. He dumped the clutch, felt the shock knock him back against the seat, the front of the Mustang reared, the slicks spun, hissed. He muscled the steering wheel to keep the wheels straight as they thundered down. Second, third. He overtook Wolcott by a nose when he lost the road feel through the steering wheel. The car shot left then right, the steering wheel now a toy, disconnected from the wheels. He felt the car step sideways. He lifted off the throttle. The car tipped. Panic, he bopped the accelerator, the car righted itself, tipped to the right, then slammed against the guardrail and overleaped it, spinning in the air, lights swirling, a black sky tumbling, the bleachers full of people hung upside down, voices shrieking, as he felt shock after shock shooting through the car frame through the seat of his pants, the steering column. The crashing noise seemed to tear his eardrums.

He knew he was alive. He could see the bleacher seats beneath him, where his car was suspended. Dazed, numbed, he slumped over the wheel. "Ambulance!" someone shouted. "Git over'ere!" Blood was trickling down the front of his shirt. He felt his face, his brow. The cut was somewhere above his forehead at the hairline. His muscles ached, his joints hurt. Yet the roll cage had saved him.

The rescue squad ran up from the pits, the ambulance was nearby, its dome lights spinning. He was disoriented when the workers pulled him out. A few seats down someone was being attended to. He strained his eyes to look. Everything was blurred, the voices around dinged his ears. He saw a man. First it was just a face in the crowd, then it became familiar. He recognized Wolcott.

"Jesus!" Wolcott said, grabbing his arm. "What the hell happened, man?"

"Don't know," Vinh said. Then he focused his eyes on the victim surrounded by the rescue workers.

The moment he saw the face, his knees shook.

"Oh Lord!" Wolcott said.

The Indian's eyes were knocked out of their sockets. His dentures had popped out of his mouth. Blood was oozing from his mouth and his nose. The tires probably got him. The impact took his life.

The workers pulled the white sheet over him. The crowd peeled back to make room for the stretcher. Wolcott gave Vinh his own handkerchief to wipe the blood on Vinh's forehead. Vinh took a deep breath, closing his eyes.

The air felt sharp in his nostrils. It held a tang of buttered popcorn.

ZACHARY AMENDT

Chalino

He likened moving drugs to human steeplechase: evading checkpoints, midnight runs revved up on Bustelo. Miles became kilometers at the Mexico border. Vaporizer straws and Quaaludes, scurrilous cops, worn-out treads. Small victories in illustrious lives.

Life was fodder and women came to him like farm animals. His songs were road candy. Chalino didn't sing, he barked. I hadn't seen him in six months. He was onstage at Arandas amid a serpentine of cords. Cesar Chavez had spoken there, along with that other great Mexican, Geraldo Rivera. Chalino sported a gold rush around his neck, in a tuxedo and frilly shirt and cummerbund, as if he had just stepped out of a brown limousine in a telenovela.

His canonization of drug smugglers was a disconcertingly insistent motif in my orbit. At soundcheck he played the first four bars of the Micheltorena and cursed. It was the mixer or else he was fighting a mild VD and didn't care who was looking. He tapped the microphone one-two. At three his pistol fell from his belt onto the hardwood and bounced.

Somewhere he had switched his allegiance from revolvers to Lugers. I didn't flinch. It was necessary. His gat was his pulse, his reassurance. Guns were commonplace. In Coachella, one was always going off. In high school we played spin the barrel.

"Chalino," I said.

He squinted to see who it was.

"Pager boy."

He emptied his clip by some sleight-of-hand, motioning for the band to break. Hopeful groupies had gathered near the bar, parting like a school of minnows when he approached. We hugged. His suit was polyester and stiff. I panned the shoreline of his hairline, where he was balding. He saw me watching him balding. My imagination was making it worse, bigger.

I asked, "How's the karaoke circuit treating you?"

He didn't laugh. One had to pull his mouth up at the ends to make him laugh. I bought him a Victoria, cheering to his new success. We weren't family, but anyone else named Sanchez he treated like a cousin.

Coachella textured in the fall. Fronds fell. Our black market was small things: dime packets traded after church, Social Security numbers stolen from resort guests in La Quinta. Diesels and stolen cars clogged up Harrison and Jefferson and Monroe, bisecting town. My people drove like illegal immigrants, unaware of whose founding fathers these were.

Chalino finished his beer in three pulls. As a chaser we shot back La Reserva. It sublimely took the edge off. He had seen the handbills posted around town depicting him with round effeminate features, enshrouded in pastels and halos, as if he ran an ashram instead of meth. It was not a carefully cultivated image, but as a rule he was never photographed unarmed or untangled in ammunition belts.

"It was Florian, that Carranza tagger," I said. "Want me to fuck with his pager?"

"Juan Carlos, don't," he said. "They'll chop your dick off."

Chalino was right. What did I know? I liked libraries, and in his calculus, libraries breeded undesirables.

"How's Adan?"

"He doesn't cry much. He likes bread."

"Growing up to be like Dad?"

"He'd better not," Chalino said.

"And your old lady?"

Chalino shrugged.

"And Ana?" I asked.

Famous people have sisters, just like us peons. Ana had ham legs, haunches, fifty gallon drums. Her skin was sweet espresso and our nights, in high school years before, amid perfect bodies, were menudo and lime salt on wrists. Her moods were elliptical and she was a prophet of ailment. *This was my headache week*, she'd say to excuse herself from P.E. *This week I experience lady time*. It was on her day planner in pink highlighter.

"She's good. She's here," Chalino said. "How's Gil?"

Gil, the Third Caballero, who was so thrilled for Chalino's homecoming – a feeling we rarely registered.

"Gil's good," I said. "He wants you to write a *corrido* celebrating his weight loss."

*

Chalino and Ana moved from Culiacan in '77, my junior year of high school. I was an anomaly of friendlessness before they arrived. Soon we were a segregation of three. We adopted Gil, the fourth wheel. The school mascot was the Arab and our senior yearbook was a roulette of low hopes, gang affiliations, mothers-to-be, armchair welterweights. We did not go away to college. Family kept us on short, guilty tethers. Fifteen years later our problems were small (gangs) and Chalino's were big (cartels). He hollowed out surfboards, the lining of spare tires, for cocaine. He broke a rotation of limbs whose casts were cocaine. He was privy to secrets. He knew worldly things. San Diego had the laxest customs office. Banning police never searched the glove compartment.

*

It was an affection at first, then an attachment, then a full-fledged allegiance. "A fine bromance," Ana observed, "with no kisses." For Halloween senior year we went as masked Mexican wrestlers. (I as Santos, Chalino as the Blue Demon. I couldn't believe no one took photos.) We were products of our generation, meat-and-potatoes Mexicans, enchanted by industry, lording our nympholepsy and immune systems over everyone.

Given his machismo, it was no surprise that next summer Chalino got in my face about my College of the Desert ID card.

"Juan Carlos, what's this shit?" he said. "Who's Carl Sanchez?"

"That's my name," I said. "Carl."

He looked at me reversing my heritage, and at my overexposed photo, and again at me, vacantly.

"It's a typo," I backtracked.

"It suits you," he decided. "*Huero* Sanchez."

Caucasian Sanchez.

*

I thought my nationality was a skin to be shed, a vogue exodermis, a tilde over an *n* in a surname, a strategically placed accent that turned Hector into *Ecktor*. I didn't apologize and he didn't. We followed the rift. The face of the earth was fallen off of. In my senior year at COD, Chalino joined Ana in L.A. He was in his depth and I was in mine. College was an agog naïve me submerged in a rolling tide of intellectual juggernauts. Inglewood was vagrants trying to wrest pints of vodka from Chalino's inviting, porous hold. It was a mutual envy. Birthdays were missed, and holidays, and *quincineras*. He started guitar-slinging. At first he sang whorehouse music. Then, suddenly, he was Irving Berlin. His *corrido* was mercurial ragtime, an economics of the bullet and guitar strings, a gentrification of music for losers. Short verses, long choruses. Hard to sing, hard to say, unforgettable.

"You have to understand," Ana once said to me over the phone. "In L.A. he can't go anywhere. Sometimes he's followed."

Someone's mother or aunt would approach Chalino after Mass, clutching beads and a cigar box with the family savings. Her son or nephew – he was a good boy – in trouble with the law, sure, but always good to his family – he didn't narc on anyone – it wasn't a stolen car, it belonged to a friend – it wasn't unusual that a screwdriver was jammed in the ignition – he wasn't reaching in his pants when they capped him. Details were nothing that immortality wouldn't cure. Chalino had no flat commission fee. (Once, he was paid in poultry.) He used pencil. The word processor was lucid, but it wasn't subtle. Soon he'd written dozens. It took some persuading to get him into the studio to record. His coercion was the prospect of becoming what he glorified in verse. Then it was more music, less quietude, less repose, more eminence in the gangland, thicker bars on the windows, Los Angeles as the nucleus of the world, the San Gabriels, the Topangas, mountains he could switchback into, the assurance of the aqueduct, faith in the trend that was all his.

He did everything hard. Brushed his teeth hard. Americans would never lay their flesh on the line. Heroism was a calculus they refrained from. I had hoped Chalino could parlay his fame into a recurring role on TV, or a Latin Grammy. Things in soap operas came easy. There was a God in those machines.

*

"*Huero*. Take Ana out, will you?" Chalino asked me this after rehearsal. He had autographs to sign, phone numbers to fetch. "You're not doing anything."

Sunday was her favorite night. She ran amok. I drove her around in Chalino's F-150 with the nitrous and the gun rack, hauling caches of shrink-wrapped powders, prisms of pills, Colt pistols whose grips he gold-plated, a spare guitar embroidered with roses. By day, Ana dressed like human resources, in grays and navys, no flesh showing, reserving her flamenco colors for dusk.

There were actual tumbleweeds then. Ana popped in one of her brother's tapes and jacked up the volume. The recordings had a homemade quality to them, like the anti-tobacco cassettes of Allen Ginsberg my COD professors had cherished ("Don't smoke/don't smoke/don't smoke/suck cock").

"Chalino's voice is ok," I conceded. I wanted to tap my foot, implode with verve. I liked a bilingual jukebox. Good tunes wasn't Iglesias.

"We're not all refried beans and gardeners," Ana said. "It's not a voice, it's a movement."

"Sorry I got it wrong. Also, where the fuck have you been?"

She gazed out. "Nothing changes here."

"This isn't Culiacan," I said. "They just opened up a Sizzler."

In high school she was bawdy, crass. On spring break she lost her whiteness, which she prized. High school was a painful thing to her, writing papers, making friends. It was grades she feared. Money was easier, less work. Work was writing Spanish captions for silent American films under restoration, or explaining to disinfectant executives how no Mexican wants a muscular *huero* wiping down her kitchen with disposable rags. Money was easier and less work but she wanted more, a ubiquitous 'more' spoken without conviction, suggesting a restlessness curable by moving around furniture.

"Still selling pagers?" she asked me.

"For now," I said, maudlin.

I drove her to Costas at the Desert Marriott. A demolition derby of old cars filled the parking lot. We found the quietest corner pocket. I didn't want to talk about me, but that's where the conversation went.

"You know how I feel about school," she said.

I knew. Senior year in civics she wrote I *hate school* 1978 on my Converses. In felt pen.

"I had hoped more for you," she said. "I thought you'd wake up each morning and do something important. But you didn't."

"You're so wrong," I said.

"You didn't learn anything about women," she said.

She was tea. She was to be steeped. Her contemporariness. She was a 'goer:' concertgoer, moviegoer, a voter if she could get her citizenship. She was reverent of pheasant and wished Chalino and Gil and I the worst of hunting back when I used to feel safe around guns. She found white men exotic, and was confused by their standoffishness. She thought one was staring at her at Costas, but his eyes were elevated: it was the football game on the TV overhead. Not her.

"It could be a conquest thing," I said.

Her eyes rolled, glazed. She was at that sober/drunk threshold.

"That *huero* might think you only date within your race," I added.

"Mexican isn't a race," she said.

At a touchdown, the uninitiated Raiders' fans around us flailed at air.

"Also, you're not the warmest of people," I said.

I knew her warmer currents ran under the surface. She plumbed waters, tested baths with her toes. Her aesthetic was branding and billboards were beautiful things. She had sorrows, it was clear, buoyant sorrows she couldn't drown in warm beer and Clamato. Losing her virginity was a slimy sacrament. At fourteen she was raped and at fifteen Chalino wouldn't say he didn't kill who did it. It was tragic, but the outcome was not. She wanted children, she said it every time we were together. I was fluent in nuance. I still am.

When the bartender came over with two ice waters, she declined. It would kill her buzz, she said. Plus she was watching her weight.

*

That week was sulfuric: the Salton Sea tilapia were dying in droves. I worked as little as possible, except for a "State of the Pager in the Coachella Valley." I delivered to conventioneers at the McCallum in Palm Desert. Nights with Chalino were sacred cows. Bills were due and I was robbing Pedro to pay Sol. I was a morning person then, even if I woke up in the afternoon, asking myself: how many guitars was he going to smash? How many autographs? I couldn't put a finger on his impulse. It was jumping off a Ferris wheel in Cabo or it was a xylophone that didn't belong in the rhythm section in San Gaspar or it was Mexican roulette in the alfalfa fields and everyone dying except him.

We drank at The Tack Room with Gil, rolled blunts, piñatas tastelessly dangling behind the bar. Gil sported new Nikes. Jordans. A train had derailed outside Thermal, spilling boxcars of the coveted footwear. In the booths and on the stools were white kids in Clippers jerseys, cholos, derivatives of the punk scene. I needed these nights, these people, antidotes to my formal education.

Gil was concerned about the concert. Chalino said it was nothing to worry about. He didn't need a bodyguard. He had me, Carl, the sharpshooter. Carl could hit anything with both of his eyes closed.

"Just protect yourself," Gil said, pounding his chest. "Nortenos got your back."

Chalino declined – it was music, not a street fight – and when Gil registered confusion, Chalino lifted his shirt, revealing two pistols tucked in his belt. And Gil lifted his, revealing his own handiwork: the nascent muscles of a six-pack.

"It's appreciated," Chalino said, fatalistically.

"Give me your playlist afterward," Gil said. "Or something."

Chalino was Gershwin incarnate, stingy with himself. Jorge Gershwin. S'wonderful he did most of his songwriting, like most everything, in bed, the duvet tangled, up late. S'marvelous his English was broken English, a half-English, a thing force-fed to him, a charade of slang cliché. We loved him until he upset us and were about to write him off – until with some obscene kindness he would surge back into our lives.

Obscene, like a ditty for the 50 lbs. Gil shed running track. I pulled the plug on the jukebox and Gil silenced the grumblers as Chalino fetched his bedazzled Fender and barked:

Brave Gilberto of the Valley/
Lo-Cal Celebrity/
Melting Away in the Mid-section/
Finally Earning his Pussy

Gil indicated he didn't understand what it meant. "Is that me? That's awesome."

It was over his head. He was five-foot-four.

"Ask Carl," Chalino said.

I told him. I wanted to say it for a long time. He's 30, he's 32. Emotionally he was menstruating. How he did not like revealing his humanity, which he had in spades but kept to his vest. How the things he left unsaid he sung. How we were not as synchronized spiritually as we thought. The frustration of his ire because I thought school was the viable third option. How hard it was to start with plans and scrap them. Family are against school. Loans are confusing. Merit grants more so. Selling pagers wasn't life. Indio melted into Coachella. Thermal fell into the sea. The best friends of La Quinta heiresses were the help.

"You both speak the same language," Gil said, "whatever that is."

Except Chalino was a coiled snake, his aim sure. The Nortenos would not show, but the Carranzas would, he could be sure of that. I would perch myself in the wings, a flaccid snake, on lookout. Who knew if I'd be called upon to do some heroism.

*

The day of his concert the temperature gauge read 107 Fahrenheit. Ana's jewelry burned her clavicle and wrists. People stopped saying hello in the market, or gesundheit. By 4 p.m. they had already queued up outside of Arandas, tailgating. Inside they lined up seventeen bodies deep. One girl asked me for a lighter, thanked me and unselfconsciously singed the tips of her dreads. It was a fanship akin to neighborliness, not adoration. Growing their beards out in solidarity. Connoisseurs of our brother. For most of them Chalino wasn't their savior; he was their main event.

A wave and a hither from Ana was my backstage pass. My lateness was immaterial, she said. I was here. What she said breathlessly melded into the bass. She was drunk and Chalino was in strobe, in silhouette, frontloading his set with his best songs. Sidelong glances at Ana and I. Ana leaned in, scared of loud noises. Disdainful, Chalino said nothing to the crowd. He sang them into frenzies, meriting furious, profuse applause. They clapped until their hands bled. Ana pulled me in because I was closest. Too close for Chalino not to notice. She was marginally thinner and her face had cleared up. In the on-and-off dark I could only feel her and the reverb. She fell into the kiss before I offered it. I didn't want it. She could keep it. But we ignited each other. She could've been anyone in her brother's viewshed. It'd have been the same. If I saw me with Ana I'd want to kill me. Or at least maim. It was everything happening. It was the Salton Sea desalinated, and parking a boat at the yacht club, the modernistic one, designed by Frey. I would shower there and write my mail and take meals. Waterskiers instead of floating fish. We would enter in my cabin, ostensibly to play rummy. I'd start taking off Ana's bra and say to her, *I need you to be judicious*, and have her say, *let's go to your stateroom*, and fumble with the clasp, and have her laugh and ask *what's the name of this ship*, and I'd say *it's not a ship, it's a boat*, and that it's named the Elusive, just like her bra. I thought our lips weren't accidents of clamato and Tecate. I thought Ana wanted me to come back to her people, to her. I couldn't in that moment have possibly fathomed our future: an unmarried couple buying a house together without any collateral in the relationship: no ring, no child, no Chalino: only a 6 lb. dog with a 60 lb. bark.

Chalino: Unplugged at Arandas was his national news debut. A Carranza elbowed his way to the front during the encore. Carranza was tattooed all over him. A beeper was clipped to his belt. Florian leapt onstage and his first shot only grazed Chalino, who didn't stop singing, who never missed. Except his first few rounds went astray of Florian, waylaid warning shots, Florian also firing strays, pumping bullets into the curtains and backdrop, until Chalino sighted on me as Ana clung and screamed and finally found flesh and felled Florian, and melee.

I was not surprised and I was not prepared. In the commotion at Arandas I remembered my textbook errata. Saliva was a natural coagulant. All Sanchez were family. Chalino survived that night – the lead in his ribs amounted to nothing – but in six months they evened the score.

Whoever they are.

JOSE HERNANDEZ DIAZ

In My Barrio (An Improvised Tune)

In my Barrio
An abuelita
Sits on a
Breezy porch
Knitting
An elaborate sweater
For a weekend
Baby shower

In my Barrio
A mural of
La Virgen de Guadalupe
Adorns a
Liquor store's
Outside wall
Where even
Gang graffiti
Doesn't dare
Disrespect

In my Barrio
A Chevy lowrider
Cruises
The avenues
Equipped with
Shiny rims
And a
Stereo system
That rattles
Every window
It slowly passes

In my Barrio
Primos play
A game of

Futbol in the park
Pausing only
To buy an
Ice cream
From the local
Palatero

In my Barrio
A mother pushes
A loaded
Shopping cart
Home
As her
Daughter
Hums an
Improvised tune
And tightly holds
Onto a balloon string

In my Barrio
You do not
Need to know
A single word
Of English
To survive
But it helps
To roll your
R's with stilo.

JOSE HERNANDEZ DIAZ

We call it work

Some of us
Immigrants
Take the bus
To work in the
Misty morning
And never complain
Of the minimum wage

We lift and pull and shift
Our hands
Like rapid waves
To and fro
Tedious thankless

But yes
We call it work

We endure overtime
Everyday
For half of what
You earn
We twist and bend and break
Our backs
Six days a week
For a third of what
You earn

But yes
We call it work

And still they insist
On conservative radio
They shout
It on FOX NEWS

That we will take over
Their country
We will pollute
Their culture
We will constrict
Their language

It's absurd absurd
The only
True conqueror
If you haven't heard
It's *peace* and *love*
It's *love* and *peace*.

MITCHELL GRABOIS

Moral

We were driving home from the theater
I was in the back seat of my father's VW Bug
and he asked me:
What was the moral of that movie?

We'd just seen *West Side Story*
I was only five
but I knew what a moral was
the lesson to be taken

I wracked my brain
but all I had in it
was a lyric from the most comic song:
Office Krupke, we're very upset
We never got the love that every kid oughta get

So I almost said: *Love your kid*
but knew that was the wrong thing
to say
My father putted on a cigarette
then crushed it into the ashtray

and after a while revealed the answer:
Stick to your own kind

When I became a teenager I began to ridicule
my father for all kinds of things
including that message
and when I married
it was to a non-Jew
a swarthy Sicilian
who sometimes reverted
to objectionable table manners

Now my son has brought home
a woman for Thanksgiving
a Roma, also known as Gypsy
The Roma, I understand, stick to their own kind
but not her

I feel in my bones that she will steal from my son
and break his heart
I want to say: *Stick to your own kind*
but no longer know what kind that is

DAVID LUNTZ

Roadkill

Roger is skeptical, because last time he and Sollie drove down to the Cape from Joburg, Sollie flipped his pickup, a brand new Datsun, almost off a mile-high cliff. After that, they had gotten smashed out of their minds at some shebeen and had to hitch their way home. But now Sollie's waving his hands "no, no, no" at the dismissive smirk curled on Roger's lips, telling him "it's all safe mate," and "so what if it's the middle of Friday night, there'll be loads of time to get back to Joeys before Monday morning."

Still, Roger's not buying it yet, or maybe he just likes to wag Sollie's tail, and says, "Ag man, come off it, you just want to see that Tulbagh witchdoctor so she can spray snake piss on your cards, like she's gonna juice them with voodoo and spice up your luck."

Sollie laughs, punches Roger in the shoulder and shoots him his best "Ja, how-did-you-guess?" smile, even if he wasn't thinking about that toothless hag. But now that Roger's mentioned it, a check-up with that poofie granny might be just the medicine, because the cards and dice have been total crap these days, like his luck's been hexed, or even worse, his joss burnt through all its sticks. Still, he's not sweating it about Roger's coming along, because he knows Roger can't get enough of the glinting, calico shacks of the Karoo; the power lines drooping like downed telegraph wires; the expectant hills of the Swartland (so swollen this time of year their water's about to break); the regal light and pounding surf of the Cape. And, true to form, Roger stomps out his Lucky Strike, burps, and says, "Sure, my man, why not?"

They've done this trip so many times they could do it in their sleep. They'll take turns driving. Roger will drown himself in the desert's emptiness, wash away his memories in its open, hungry spaces, become a child again. Then, floating off on his temporary amnesia, he will count the stars and go on about how they are not gas and clouds and all that science shit, because, you know, they're really nothing more than flares the angels shoot off to guide our souls when we pass into the long night: as if he can't wait to get there.

But Sollie doesn't have Roger's gift of forgetting. Mostly, he just tries to suppress the acid reflux that scorches his throat every time he thinks about his ex-wife and the other parts of his wrecked life – at least until the first shafts of sunlight ignite the silica and feldspar in the earth around him – as if an errant spark from one of Roger's angel's flares had drifted down and touched a hidden reservoir of kerosene. Because, in those rippling sheets of flame, he sees it's the world's heart, not his, that's cracked and broke and doesn't ring true. At such moments, he feels uplifted, like he's sitting at the right hand of God. He looks down on his rainbow nation's shattered prism with an alien tenderness, a delusory compassion. He swears to do better when he gets home; call up his ex-wife; cure himself; spend more time with his children; learn to love his ailing country. The feeling never lasts, the vow is always broken. But this time he knows it will be different.

He gets behind the wheel and puts the Glock in his lap. Roger looks at the weapon and nods sagely, because last time they did this they almost got necklaced by some drifters overdosed on tik. But gun or not, Sollie's terrified out of his mind. Can't stop thinking about that letter from the hospital lying on Roger's desk. The one he had filched without thinking, because that's what he has done his whole life: lied, cheated, gambled, and stolen – all without thinking. Given up donkey's years ago trying to figure out why – accepted it's just how he's wired, no matter how hard he's tried to change, no matter how many drives he's done with Roger. But through it all, the only thing that's kept a part of him pure, like some hidden flame, is Roger. This riddle he hasn't quite cracked either. But he suspects the solution may have to do with his fidelity; that he's never cheated on or lied to Roger: never, not once, because Rog is tops, real class, best man at his wedding, best mate since school.

Then later, at his flat, when he opened the letter, he felt his knees go numb, his throat clamp shut. He dropped to the floor groaning; pissed his eyes dry; writhed like a butterfly being pinned to the back of a picture frame, struggling to fly away. But the next morning, he understood. It's better this way, as though his whole life suddenly made sense to him: why he was born to lie and cheat. He sees the spot where he's taking Roger: a grassy donga below a kopje that he could find blindfolded. He's worked it out so they'll pull in right as the sun rises. He touches the gun to make sure it's still there. He just wonders if he will have the strength to do it, have the courage of his love, when the time comes. No, he will be true to the end. He will laugh and smile and lie and fake it so frigging good that Roger will feel the cold surf on his shoulders, the sand between his toes, the salt in his lungs, and never see it coming. After that, he will make sure Roger doesn't feel a thing.

TED JEAN

Ballam's Ass

Jack Ballam is a loony cracker
who lives in a tar-paper shed
on what used to be a farm
out past the dump on River Road.

Kids off the school bus have learned
to ignore Jack's crass revilements.
Possibly dangerous, he is known,
in town, as an angry psycho, whose
wife and kids ran off, abhorrent.
Humorous rumors still circulate
about his gifts as a witch, a charmer.

Well, Ballam has a black mule,
bony, sly, and scrofulous.
There is no longer work to be done
on the erstwhile farm, but Jack
means to maintain discipline,
so he beats Blackie regularly.

One day, in a specially tenebrous
funk, the master administers
a two-by-four to Blackie's head,
and brings the old beast to its knees.
Jack curses, challenges the brute,
"Tell me you're whipped, you devil!"
and Blackie relents, "I beat, boss."

Now it's Ballam who is stunned,
and takes his turn genuflecting
in the stable mud.
As the mule struggles to its feet,
it grunts in pain, and mutters,
"I make it a practice
not to smoke while I'm sleeping."

Jack retreats to the shack,
returns with the shotgun.
Blackie slouches by the fence,
staring off into the woods,
his floppy grey lips quivering
as he quotes random passages
from Thomas a Becket's
"Imitation of Christ." Jack fires.

Digging the burial trench,
Jack tweaks his left knee.
Levering the mule carcass
into the hole, he wrenches it worse.
All night, wracked with pain,
Ballam is tormented with his gift.
Now that he knows
he can work wonders, he will.

Except that, at midnight,
as he hobbles from bed
to empty his bladder,
an abundance of bile squirts
into his little black heart,
and drops him, stubbornly dead,
just short of the toilet.

FREDERICK POLLACK

Visitor's Pass

The photo ages as I age. The face
is never one I'd trust.
The plastic frays; the print below it
never convincingly explains.
So I'm often stopped, and questioned
in rooms not much inferior
to those for visitors.
When I'm released, the view
beyond the window-wall beyond
each corridor, though impressive as before,
also seems yellowed.

When I'm released, my notes
are pleasantly returned.
With claims not to have read them,
that technology has passed me by,
that I could be helped to move them
to a laptop, an iPad – something
smaller, swifter, and vaster
each time. Till, reduced
to one hermetic symbol,
they could be safely lost, and I could leave.

I like the service staff. They answer
questions with no doubt compelled
and rehearsed clowning,
rebellious murmurs that go nowhere. Women
run the place and are run by it. Executives
are always between meetings,
endlessly discuss themselves, and –
without having been told to –
never meet my eye.
They have made it very clear
I must always wear the pass
or risk belonging.

FREDERICK POLLACK

It's My Party

Everyone of course is in the kitchen. Wives,
girlfriends collaborate
on salads, nostalgic casseroles;
complain of being squeezed and are
apologized to, but nothing changes;
discuss carbs, yoga, the right knife
to slice cucumber. The men
are 1) Bigbellied thicknecks,
whose hostility flows
into any social container
provided, but at my party is constrained;
that's the fun of inviting them.
2) Suits, who are not, however, suits
enough to be fully automatic;
they improvise, get angry. 3)
Creative and scholarly/squalid,
who hover as the others flex.
Tics, affectations, vast personal losses
pass as ideas. One begs me in confidence
to make him invisible, or at least faceless;
I refuse. A girl, not cooking,
entertains the cooks
by satirizing her dear professor,
me. The lone gay tells a story
about Paul Goodman, who, during the Fifties,
went to a party, having been promised other gays;
and finding none, spent an hour
exchanging kisses with an Irish setter.
I always rather admired that gesture,
I yell from the bar, where I'm trying
to recreate the Pink Iguana
that caused my triumph on Aruba
one distant karaoke night.
Daylight come and I wanna go home.

DENNIS KENNEDY

Casualty Report

In those days there was a fake German pub on the Waikiki strip. I think it was called the Bierstube, though it could have been the Hofbrauhaus or the Rathskeller, filled with fake Biedermeier furniture. A piano player had a repertoire of safe German songs, Broadway show tunes, and low comic patter. He called himself Franz and his accent sounded authentic, but after all those war movies that's also easy to fake.

I was a fake myself, halfway through four years pretending to be a Naval officer, sent a month before from my ship to the Commander of the Service Force of the Pacific and given a tedious desk job, keeping track of the readiness of the oilers and reefers and ammo ships that kept the fighting ships fighting in Vietnam. I summarized their mechanical problems onto a display board for the admiral's morning briefing at his HQ in Pearl Harbor. The job could have been done by a reasonably bright idiot; it certainly didn't require a university degree and a commission signed by the Secretary of the Navy. Today it would occupy about three seconds on your smart phone. The rest of the day I searched for occupation. The job was meaningless to me and didn't seem to mean much to anybody else either.

I'd moved out of the BOQ in Pearl, that's the Bachelor Officers' Quarters, into a garage apartment in Manoa Valley, the rainiest part of Honolulu, in the shadow of steep mountains and imposing waterfalls. My shoes grew mold and in the mornings I had to check them for scorpions. At night I'd watch pale geckoes feeding on the outside of the plate-glass window. The street light made them transparent and you could see the insects go down their gullets, little black peristaltic dots disappearing one by one.

It was Thanksgiving. I'd spent the afternoon at the zoo, squawking back at tropical birds, feeling just as caged and dislocated. Maybe that's why I wandered into that bar, maybe I heard Franz singing a vaguely familiar beer-hall song, I don't remember. I was lonely, though didn't know how much. I can't say I was ever very self-aware, and in those days I wasn't thinking of past or future, I was thinking of tits and ass, and there was plenty of

131

that around. So much, in fact, that in the month I'd been there I could have been arrested for Conduct Unbecoming. Oahu, desperate island, the last stop on the wagon train. If you were a woman escaping something back in the Forty-Eight, this was as far as you'd get, and there's no better cure for desperation than sex. I hadn't made good friends, was missing my parents back in California, and wound up alone for that self-satisfied turkey of a holiday, crying in my Bierstube beer. Then someone began to sing.

She was standing next to Franz and filled the place with a shocking crystal soprano. I had studied music in college and still played the violin. I'd been to the opera a number of times, but I'd never been so close to anything like this. In the warm Honolulu night it felt like dropping into a cold well of sorrow. Whatever I thought about Bavaria on the beach, her voice, even though she sang in German, didn't seem out of place at all, and the crowd loved her. Her dress was long, pale beige, tight fitting; her voice was trained; she had long, thick, dark-red hair, was tall, elegant, voluptuous, and moved on without effort to "Some Day He'll Come Along, the Man I Love." Despite the upbeat piano and hopeful lyrics, her voice dropped down to deep regions of loss.

Over the applause Franz called her Aisling. I asked at the bar for a table and had Wiener schnitzel for Thanksgiving dinner. A young girl in a figured white blouse took my order – I was sitting at the end of a long beer hall table crowded with tourists, close to the kitchen, at the far end of the room from the piano. Aisling finished but soon reappeared serving meals, now wearing one of those German apron things with a starched bib as she set down my plate, covered with sauerkraut and potatoes with mustard seeds. As she moved on she left behind a vanilla scent, something I'd smelled once before. Shalimar, I think it was called. The sauerkraut was acid, the schnitzel was leather.

When she next passed I asked if she would sing again. "Busy now," she said, and moved off quickly. I was surprised by her Irish accent, which hadn't been apparent when she sang in German or English. She looked at least a dozen years older than me.

I lingered over the meal, got dessert from the other waitress, dry Black Forest cake; had coffee worse than the Navy's and some kind of schnapps, passing time until the diners had thinned. She sang once more; I think it was "Some Day My Prince Will Come." Franz took a break; when he stood he was short and walked with a stick. Aisling arrived with the bill, apron discarded. "You didn't finish your dinner," she said, slightly mocking.

"I dined on your perfume," I said. Corny as Kansas in August; but she smiled. "Why don't you sing more?"

"They hired me as a waitress. Franz lets me sing now and then."

"Everybody likes your voice."

"You think so? I tried to be a singer back in Dublin, never made it there, or in London." The last three words with a bitter burr.

"That was Mozart a while ago?"

"Last act of The *Marriage of Figaro*, the Countess trying to get her husband back." She closed her eyes and spoke rapidly. "LaNozze DiFigaro Ossia LaFolle Giornata OperaBufa TwoActs Vienna1786 Libretto DaPonte From Beaumarchais." I thought she was making a joke with a schoolmarm recitation, but she wasn't. She opened her eyes and looked straight at me. In the reflected light they looked as green as the water off the coral reef in a rain shower. "You know it?"

"I heard it once in college, San Francisco Opera."

"Are you a tourist?"

"Navy, at Pearl. And you, how did you get here?"

"How does anyone?" She started to move off. "I have to clear the tables."

"Would you give me your phone number?"

"You're very bold." I think she registered me then. "I'm sort of with someone." She nodded toward the piano at the front. "With Franz."

"Isn't he too old for you?"

She shrugged at the obvious – she was too old for me – and went into the kitchen. I paid the check and left, unsteady from talking to her. Or the schnapps. I'd parked on a side street, though I couldn't remember where and stopped, trying to recall. I heard someone call out "Wait!" Aisling caught up with me and handed over a slip of paper with tiny writing. Her hair had fallen out of the bun she wore and hung loose on one side. "If Franz answers, hang up," she said. She was out of breath, turned to look behind her, then closed my hand over her phone number and held it. "What's your name?"

"Andy Jackson. Everybody calls me Jack. Unless they call me Mr. President." She looked blank. "You know, Andrew Jackson?" She shook her head once, squeezed my fist and ran back quickly, her tight skirt hindering her stride. She slowed as she approached the pub, swaying slightly in medium heels, and I saw Franz standing outside the door, smoking a cigarette. We were both watching her hair bounce off her shoulders.

I let a week go by, then another, logging reports, eating at the Officers' Club, drinking too much. One night I was stopped by a cop while driving home in my uniform. He was a Haole who looked like Jack Lord from *Hawaii Five-0*, which had just started to appear on TV. He was sympathetic because he'd been in the Navy himself and let me off with a warning; if he'd been a Kanaka I'd probably have gone to jail. Another evening after work, again in my officer's whites, I paid a surprise call on Lynda, a girl I'd been seeing who also lived in Manoa Valley. She was about to teach a macramé class downtown so we chatted a few minutes and she introduced her new roommate, a Japanese woman named Michiko. It was obvious right away. I went out the door with Lynda but deliberately left my uniform hat on the top of the refrigerator. I sat in my car a few houses away until she drove off, then went back to the apartment for the hat and screwed the roommate. Drunk driving and sexual misconduct inside a week. Book 'em, Danno.

But Aisling's scent trailed me like an unfinished dream. Maybe I say that because her name – it's pronounced "Ashling," by the way – means vision or dream in the Irish language. She was a vision, and I couldn't understand why she would hook up with a gimpy kraut. I considered going back to the Bierstube as a check on my feelings, but in the end I rang her from my desk in Pearl one bored Monday afternoon. She answered and said right away she was anxious to meet, but not in Waikiki.

"Where, then?" I asked.

"Do you live alone?"

"A small apartment in Manoa."

"Give me the address. I'll be there at eight."

"Shall we go out to dinner?"

"No, no dinner," she said.

She arrived late, out of breath again. She wore a shapely green dress and her red hair was like fire against it. "We couldn't find it," she said; "I don't drive a car."

"That's difficult in Honolulu."

"Franz takes me wherever I want." She smiled. "Not tonight. I came by taxi."

We sat down; she looked at the snacks I'd set out, then around the room without taking it in. I offered her a drink. "Wine," she said, "I like white wine." She was nervous, her face was flushed. She got up once and sat down again, stared for a while at the geckoes on the outside of the window. I put on Miles's version of "Some Day My Prince Will Come," which calmed her a little. She played with her glass, turning the stem. At the end of the track she said, "Strange, isn't it, how something so beautiful can come from something so stupid?"

"What?"

"*SnowWhite* Disney1937 Music FrankChurchill Lyrics LarryMorey. You've seen it?"

"Maybe as a boy, I don't remember."

"You're still a boy, aren't you? How old?"

"Twenty-three. And you?"

"Ha." She drank her wine in one go, dropped the empty glass on the carpet and stood up. "I have to leave."

"You just got here, we've just – "

"Just started, haven't fucked?"

"That's not what I was going to say."

"No, no, I see the whole dreary thing already, you take me to bed, I fall in love, you get tired of me, I'm left with the same shite as now, only worse because I'll miss you. No, no." She picked up her bag, some kind of cotton Indian thing with mirror work, open at the top. A lipstick spilled out, and loose dimes. "Where's the telephone?"

"I'll drive you."

"No, no, don't trouble. It was my idea to come, it was stupid, I'm sorry, I'll just call a taxi – why do Americans call it a cab? Short for cabriolet, I doubt you ever heard of one." She looked at me, expecting an answer. "Light TwoWheeled Carriage FoldingTop SingleHorse?" She dialed a number from memory, ordered the cab, set down the handset without hanging it up, then

135

moved towards me and stretched out her bare arm, freckled white, vulnerable in the dim light, and touched my face with a red fingernail. Suddenly she grabbed my shoulders and pulled me to her, as the bag dropped to the floor. The phone was bleating; I could taste the wine in her mouth. We were in bed in a minute, and she showed me a few things; she was older, after all. I'd never seen such abandon. Her skin smelled of vanilla.

We were dozing after a second foray when I heard a car horn. "Your cabriolet is here, old lady," I said, and she laughed for the first time.

She scrambled into her dress. "I have to get home before Franz. I told the boss I was sick."

"Won't he guess anyway?"

She laughed again and went to the door, then saw the things that had dropped out of her bag and got down on her hands and knees to collect them, sweeping the carpet with her hand. "Don't come to the pub," she said, then went out, leaving the door open. As I closed it I saw her get in the front seat of the cab, gesticulating as it drove off. The next day I found a dime she'd missed. A Roosevelt.

The weather turned rainy in December and chilly. The trees in my neighborhood always seemed to be dropping moisture, even during sunny periods. I called her once but got Franz, so I hung up, feeling guilty. In the evenings they were both at the pub. Exactly a week later I got home about 8.30 and found her sitting on the outside stairs in front of my door in the rain, a folded Honolulu *Star* over her bare head. "Do we have a recurring appointment?" I asked.

We went in and without another word about it she was there the next three Monday evenings. She'd changed her night off to be free from Franz, and was no longer trying to keep our relationship secret, though she still wouldn't go out in public. "People already laugh at him," she said, "it wouldn't be fair to shame him as well."

"Why do you stay with him at all?"

"Should I move in with you?" As if there were no other option. For the first time I felt unsure of her – of her character, I suppose I mean – and let it drop. We had wonderful conversations, though, about jazz and art, Irish poetry, the strangeness of

Hawaiian culture. I hadn't met anyone in Honolulu so intelligent and well read. And the sex was wonderful too, better than anything, which turns a young man's head.

My parents came from California for two weeks at Christmas, so Aisling and I missed three Mondays. One of my new friends at work was transferred suddenly and I was offered his room in a house about halfway up Wilhelmina Rise, shared with Norm Steinhaus, another lieutenant j. g. at Pearl. I moved in right away, even though I lost rent on the Manoa place, and didn't get around to telling Aisling. She called me at work the next Tuesday.

"No phone, no flat, no word, we call that an Irishman's resignation."

"How did you get this number?"

"Your personnel office. There's a charming young man here who helped me, a – what did you say, Bill? – yeoman first class."

"You mean you're down the hall?"

"Can you get away?"

"No. Look, I'm sorry I didn't let you know, it came up suddenly. You're not easy to contact. I left a forwarding address with my landlady. She lives next door."

"She wouldn't give it me. Said I was too old for you, the bitch. I think I'm about to do something embarrassing."

"I think you have already. Just a second." I excused myself in the office and went downstairs. She was standing in the corridor dressed in white, with a long cream scarf flecked with green around her neck. I thought of Isadora Duncan and fateful beauty. A seaman, also in white, was swabbing the deck, his bell bottoms rolled up as if on shipboard, pretending not to look at her. I hustled her outside into the sunshine. "Why did you do that?"

"You could have left a note on your door or at the restaurant." I reminded her that she knew my parents were coming. She said I should have introduced her, I said she wouldn't go out with me, she said she'd make an exception for parents because it would prove I was serious.

"Serious?"

She looked at me with emerald eyes. Then she turned slightly and stared at the ships below us. From the steps of the Service Force HQ you could see right down to the harbor, the Pearl of the Pacific, the quays lined with warships, some at anchor, destroyers, frigates, amphibs, service ships, grey metal upon grey metal, huddled like Agamemnon's fleet bound for Troy. "Don't you want to see me?" She continued to look into the distance.

"Your ... your circumstances, they're complicated."

"They are, aren't they? I don't know what to do about that." She turned her foot outward like a dancer and looked at the white planks of the porch floor. She was wearing sandals with gold straps, bright red toenail polish, and had a thin line of dried blood on her ankle.

"What happened to your leg?"

She looked at it, surprised. "A stone, who knows? Listen, Jack, my grandfather, he was from the coast of Donegal in the west of Ireland, he used to say: If ya can't keep the boat afloat, let the bastard sink." We were in sight of the Arizona, sunk in the Japanese attack a quarter-century before. Its memorial is the ship itself, lying mostly submerged in the harbor.

"How did you get here?"

"What does it matter?"

"Are you deliberately mysterious? These sudden appearances – couldn't we have a normal date, you know, a guy and a girl, dinner, movie?"

"I don't like American movies. If it's food you want, I'll cook."

"I have a roommate now, a housemate. You won't like that."

"I'll cook for you both. See you at six."

"Tonight? What about your job?"

"They can bugger off."

Norm was out for the evening but she made an extraordinary meal anyway, a starter, as she called it; then roast lamb with vegetables, two kinds of potatoes in the Irish style, a salad, a baked tart, a final cheese course, though she complained she couldn't find decent cheddar on the island. She'd even brought the wine. The kitchen was a mess and we didn't eat until almost ten, delayed by testing out my new mattress. She stayed until midnight, later than ever, and I was still washing the pots when Norm came in at one. I was wearing the Bavarian apron Aisling had taken from the pub. "Hi, Norm," I said. "Hungry?"

138

So began gourmet Tuesdays on Wilhelmina Rise. Once he discovered the quality of the cooking, Norm joined us whenever he could. He'd volunteer to do the dishes; my contribution took place elsewhere. "Do you cook this way for Franz?" I asked one evening. We were already in February and the rains had stopped.

"He doesn't eat much," she said. She started to hum "Summertime" softly as I drifted off.

"Good tune," I said.

"MusicGershwin LyricsHeyward *PorgyAndBess* 1935.

She sang it softly. The phone rang in the kitchen and Norm knocked on the door.

"It's for you, Jack, Nazi accent." Norm had no tolerance for Germans. Aisling looked frightened, put her finger to her lips, and shook her head. I pulled on my pants and went out. "I told him you were asleep but he said to wake you up."

I picked up the phone. The accent was not so obvious as at the pub, no longer a joke. "I know Aisling is there."

"She's not."

"I know she is."

"How do you know that?"

"It doesn't matter how. To you I need to talk. Do you realize what you do to her?"

"She's doing it to me as well."

"Don't be stupid," Franz said, "she has no control."

"Nobody's forcing her. Except maybe you."

"You don't understand. She is very delicate, an artist of the soul. She needs protection from herself. And if you will excuse me saying so, from you also."

"Your opinion is noted. But I do understand her."

"How can you? She's almost thirty-seven. Fifteen years older than you, I figure. Old enough to be your mother. You're an educated boy, you must know Freud. Do you have an idea what you do?" Aisling had come out of the bedroom and was sitting in the nude on the sofa, hunched over with cold or pain. Norm went into his room. I put down the phone and covered her with an afghan. She didn't look up. Franz was still talking when I picked up the phone again, something about how he met her, wandering the streets in a daze near the pub late at night.

He was aggravating me and though she couldn't hear him, he was turning Aisling into a zombie. "Look, Franz," I said, "if she doesn't want to see me, she won't. If you can convince her she shouldn't, that's all right too. But in the meantime, let her make her own decisions."

"Of course she wants to be with you. I saw you in the restaurant, you're a handsome boy, intelligent and sensitive. I know you talk about music and books. And sex, she needs sex and you give her that. Did she tell you I'm impotent? Can't manage to–" he made a coarse humpf sound. "An accident years ago."

Aisling seemed to be in another place, hearing something else. She began to move her lips and though Franz was still talking I heard her singing very softly, repeating one line over and over. I can't be sure but years later I heard an Irish tune called "On Raglan Road" and it might have been that: "On a quiet street where old ghosts meet …." I wondered if Franz was simply jealous. I couldn't understand why he would tell me such intimate things, and that made me self-conscious and brittle and I interrupted his monologue. "Goodbye, Franz," I said, "don't call here again."

The next time I saw her she was physically altered. She had stopped coming on Tuesdays but about two weeks later appeared one Saturday late afternoon. I was going out the door when she arrived – I had a date with Lynda or her roommate, I can't remember – but Aisling wanted to talk. Her manner was disturbed, her eyes dull and unfocused. She'd been taking some kind of prescription narcotic, claiming she couldn't get rest otherwise. She'd given up her job and spent her days wandering through old Honolulu, trying to find, she said, the place where she lost herself. I said that's very melodramatic and didn't know what it meant. "Oh, you understand," she said, "you understand."

I asked if she wanted a drink. "I don't drink anymore," she said, "or eat much either." She did look thinner, not so lusciously rounded, wearing jeans that were too loose. "I've lost interest in everything." As an afterthought: "Except one thing." She smiled in a crooked, ironic way.

"What's that?"

"Ha," she said, and just stared with accusing green eyes, but I couldn't tell if she was inviting me to make love to her or daring me to try. I made no move and after a while she looked away. She was again sitting on that coffee-stained sofa we had in the living room, her elbows on her knees. She lowered her head as if she were feeling sick and spoke to the floor. I asked her to repeat it. "I'm seeing a psychiatrist, Franz is paying, somebody called Doctor Bleu if you can believe it, and he wants to give me ECT." Her head was still lowered. "Do you think I should?"

"What's that?"

"You're so young. Electro-shock, electroconvulsive therapy, zap zap zap! Tie me down, rubber bit in my teeth." She threw herself down on the sofa with her arms above her head and started to shake and convulse. "Hm-hmm, blapt-blapt-blapt, huggh!" She collapsed as if dead, then burst out laughing.

"It sounds like torture."

"It is torture, that's why it works." Then the heavy Dublin accent she joked with: "Shocks the feckin' be-Jesus out of ya, believe it, youse. Or it kilts ya, then ya're truly fecked."

"You're a beautiful and talented woman, Aisling. You'd be crazy to submit to that."

"Franz thinks I am crazy. Do you? Don't answer that." She stood up and brushed her jeans. "I know I do crazy things." She looked wide-eyed and tense, but may have been faking it. "So if we're not going to bed, I'll be off."

"I'll drive you, I'm going out anyway." For once she didn't object, and asked me to drop her at Waikiki. She was quiet on the ride down the hill. I had an open-topped Triumph TR3, which didn't encourage conversation. When we got to the Royal Hawaiian, the traffic slowed and she opened the door before I'd fully stopped. I thought she might fall or be hit. I slammed on the brakes and she walked away without a word. I watched her stride into the hotel.

I was, as she once said, naught but a callow youth, and I put her out of mind. I was tired of her inscrutabilities and boundaries, angry she could be taken only on her terms. It didn't occur to me that I might have been catalyst to her deterioration. She warned me at the beginning what would happen if she fell in love but I didn't think of that. I didn't love her, I knew that much, though I loved the sex and her company and her voice, singing or speaking, like bright water falling over rocks. But driving in the sunlight I had noticed some grey hairs among the red. She was no longer convenient.

She phoned early one morning at Pearl when I was still putting together the admiral's briefing. There had been an unusual number of CASREPS received from the ships overnight – that's Navy shorthand for casualty reports, the Navy loves aggressive-sounding acronyms – boiler troubles or winch jams or pump failures and a flooding in a hold. For once I was behind in my work and couldn't talk. She sounded strange, but she often did. The captain in charge of the operations division yelled across the room, "Jackson, goddamnit, get that board ready." I apologized curtly to Aisling and said I'd ring her back. But the day stayed busy and I didn't.

The phone went about two in the morning. I was deep in sleep and assumed it would be her, but it was Franz looking for her. The last time he was cynical and knowing but now was seriously worried. I convinced him I hadn't seen her for almost a month. She'd been undergoing a series of ECT sessions, he said, three times a week, and they were draining her of all energy. She'd become incoherent and dislocated, in a fog or wandering daze. "Too much, too much, so many shocks." I asked why he didn't stop her from going. "You know when she has an idea, you can't get it out. I wish I could stop her." As his stress grew his accent became stronger: I vish I coult schtop her. I began to feel sorry for him, a pitiable little man on the edge himself. He begged me to call if she appeared.

I went back to bed but couldn't sleep. I turned on the porch light in case she managed to get up the hill to me and sat on the ugly sofa in the dark. Our landlord, a big Kanaka who sang Don Ho songs as he mowed the lawn, had a large mango tree in the back overhanging a shed. He used a long bamboo pole with a blade and net at the end to pick the ripe fruit. At that time of year, though, the mangoes would fall of their own weight onto the corrugated tin roof of the shed, making a loud bang that echoed in the night. I listened to them drop, one by one, until after six in the morning, when the green light began to rise on the sea beyond Diamond Head, and counted eight falls, though one might have been a car backfiring. Aisling did not appear.

A few Saturdays later she phoned me in the afternoon. I was at the end of Joyce's *Ulysses*, a battered old Modern Library copy, trying to travel from the empty world I lived in, an absurd job supporting a hateful war, hedonistic pleasures, the Rainbow Isles with their ancient life destroyed by American missionaries who put muumuus on the girls. Aisling sounded reasonable. The ECT was over now, she felt much better, it was a bizarre few weeks but somehow the treatment worked, no one understood how or why. She remembered very little and had slept most of the time. She had no idea where she went the night Franz called me, or when she got home. I thought of Molly Bloom, her Dublin ancestor, but Aisling was more complex and, at that moment anyway, more coherent.

"What are you going to do now?" I asked.

"Recover. The doctor tells me to rest in bed at least two hours during the day."

"You're still seeing the psychiatrist?"

"Not him, another doctor over at Kapiolani, a woman, very sympathetic." I heard music in the background and asked what it was. "Only Bach these days, flow of notes, one after the other, order."

"Sounds like one of the cello suites."

"Well done, Jack. It's the first one." Then in her recitation voice: "G-major BWV1007 About1717Köthen." There was a pause; I could hear her breathing. "Jack," she said at last, "I want to see you."

It was my turn to hesitate. "I think," I finally stammered out, "I think it's really over, don't you? There's nowhere to go."

She sighed; I heard the music swell and fall. I could tell it was the Sarabande, slow, mournful, melancholy. "I suppose you're right," she said. "Can I see you one more time anyway? No sex, no craziness."

"I think that's not a good idea."

"Don't you want to?" I let the silence linger once more. "Oh, well," she said, "at least I'll have something of yours."

"What do you mean?"

"Goodbye, Jack, darlin' Jack. Thanks for the—" But she hung up before finishing the sentence.

When my marriage ended some years ago I had to clear out my clothes and in the back of the closet I came across an old brown suit, made in Hong Kong in my Navy days when the ship put in for R&R. I hadn't worn it for years – the color was ugly and it didn't fit any longer. In the right hip pocket of the jacket, in one of those

little inner pockets for coins, I found two ticket stubs from June
first 1968 for the Honolulu Opera Festival, row T, seats 30 and 32,
at the Hawaii National Centre outdoor arena, price $4.50 each, tax
exempt. I'm sure I wore the suit after that but somehow the tickets
remained in place, through many moves and visits to the cleaners. I
put the tickets in a little cedar box of treasures along with my
boyhood blue shooter marble, a hundred-yen note, my lieutenant's
silver insignia, and Aisling's Roosevelt dime.

I found the box a few days ago and I'm holding the tickets
in my hand. It was a blissful Hawaiian evening. I went with a nurse
from Pearl and though I can't remember her name or face, I
remember the production. It was *Don Giovanni*, the first time I'd
heard it, and I was amazed by the mixture of farce and seriousness,
music swerving from joke to tragedy, Mozart a few years from
death, not sure what to make of his material. Dona Ana was not up
to the challenge, but Zerlina was marvelous, a crystal soprano who
reminded me of Aisling when she sang Mozart the night I met her.
That's not nostalgic invention because at intermission, lining up for
drinks, I saw her standing off to the side, laughing at something
Franz had said. He had his arm around her in a protective way and
adjusted a purple shawl over her shoulders. She was obviously
pregnant, about six months along. Flourishing. Even from a
distance I could see the flush was back in her face. Her hair was like
the last rays of sunset over the water. She didn't look my way.

I was jealous, ridiculous as it sounds. We'd never discussed
birth control after the first night when she said she had it covered.
It had to be my baby and without knowing I'd given it to an
impotent stand-in. When she asked to see me one last time, did she
want my help? What would I have done? I tried phoning her many
times in the next days but the line was disconnected and no new
number available. At the Bierstube they told me she'd quit months
before and Franz was on extended leave. I never knew where they
lived and they wouldn't tell me. A few weeks later my Navy service
was up and I left Hawaii for good.

Il Dissoluto Punito Ossia DonGiovanni OperaBufa TwoActs
Libretto DaPonte Prague1787.

During the second act I unraveled the meaning hidden in
the music. When Don Juan sank into the pit of hell with a piercing
cry, condemned for his sins, Mozart actually wanted to pardon him,

and so did I. That self-satisfied sextet at the end, with the surviving characters singing in triumph over his death, still rankles me. I didn't know what I was doing, I say to Jack Lord, and he replies: ignorance of yourself is no excuse.

All that was half a lifetime ago and Jack Lord is long dead. I wonder if Aisling walks the earth, I wonder where the child is. Was it a boy? Did she name him after me?

JEANPAUL FERRO

The Dead River

Jack Linton had been floating down the Dead River for three long months now. Early in the morning, the sun would turn the crown of each wave a different hue of golden-brown, turning a flat black as each swell slouched down and became a rapid at Elephant Rock and Mine Field.

The river was ancient compared to a man, and each morning it seemed to get older; but at thirty-eight, Jack felt this enormous power come up within himself, something that he had never felt while he was working his nine-to-five job over the course of the past twenty years. Up in Maine, Jack could become the man he'd always wanted to be – fit and muscular with no one telling him what to do or how to do it.

Northern Maine was a beautiful sphere atop New England. White pines grew down in the valleys and up along the shoulders of the mountains and hills. Blue lakes dotted the landscape with horse-like moose and deer around every green corner.

It had been exactly three months – three months since he had left Groton and General Dynamics for the calm waters of Jackman, Maine. Three months of floating down the Dead River, the Kennebec, and the Penobscot. Three months of having to drive the old school bus through sylvan tracts of spruce to get down to the dam. Three months of trying to forget her when he could feel her in every second.

Being in Maine made Jack look at things differently now. Being a guide on a river instead of on some soft blue computer screen gave him hope again.

He first noticed it after working at the rafting companies for a couple of weeks. With the constant sun turning his hair the same color as a wheat field back where he grew up in a southern county in the black hills, he noticed that not only did he see himself differently, but everyone else saw him for someone he didn't know he was.

"You're a frontiersman!" one woman from Albany told him when they hit the big rapid on the Kennebec and the raft didn't turn over.

"A real Renaissance man!" a woman from Georgia told him when he cooked steak for forty people one night.

"I wish my husband were like you," a very sad twenty-something girl from Mississippi said as Jack hung up on a line all the wetsuits for the entire company one night after dinner.

Each time Jack soaked it in, parsed it, moved it around his veins and intestines, knowing he really wasn't any different than any other man. It felt good having other people, especially women, especially women he would have been interested in, thinking he was someone totally different than the person he really was. This was the feeling that motivated every man. A man wanted power and money and prestige and fame for the same reasons. Wanted to be thought of as someone different and perfect and not as he was in the secret recesses of his mind at night.

The girl had arrived in late September with her husband and another handsome couple who'd bowed out of the rafting trip after the first day on the Dead River. All summer long he had been watching wives like this one.

"I want to sit back by you!" she shouted to him as she climbed into his raft on the last day of the excursion.

Jack nervously looked back at her husband. He had these humored eyes and this bulging fat face and swollen red neck that didn't seem to match the subtle beauty of his wife. He was laughing with the man from Syracuse as they stood on the big rock beside the raft. The man from Syracuse had come here alone and the husband had adopted him for the weekend.

"He doesn't care," Jack heard the woman say half under her breath.

He looked at her. She stood in her blue and yellow wetsuit. She was blond and thin and flat-chested. There was something irresistible about her existence. He could see the pain she wore in her eyes. She was about twenty-six or twenty-seven, with an overconfident gaze, gray eyes, and a mouth always poised and ready to say something original. And she was a firstborn, like he was. He saw it the minute she walked up to him in the lodge and introduced herself. "Helene Thalhofer," she said as she slipped her hand into his. "My friends all call me Kat." When she said this he felt as though maybe they had known each other in another life – maybe somewhere on the Delta off in Tanis or on the northern Sinai coast in ancient Egypt.

He looked at her now as she sat in his raft. Her eyes kept surprising him. They were the same color as the Kennebec: blue like when the river flattens out around the corner and catches the last light of day on its surface. Her eyes unnerved him. All the eyes of the other women hadn't moved him until now.

He helped her husband and the man from Syracuse down into the raft, then the six happy college kids who were up from Northeastern.

It was dark and gray out that morning. It was cold when Jack put on his wetsuit in the tent. There was a mist in the air and some of the leaves on the sugar maple and the yellow birch planted around the camp had already started to turn into their autumn shades of orange and yellow.

Jack took a deep breath as he untied the raft from shore. He pushed off away from the rocks. He straightened out, to maneuver with his paddle. He saw the man from Syracuse paddling the wrong way. "No! No!" Jack shouted over to him. "You're not Dennis Conner. Do what I told you to do!"

The man looked back. "Sorry. Sorry."

Quickly, the raft moved out onto the rapids.

Jack shouted the commands he had taught his novice crew back at the lodge.

They moved through the granite canyon and out into the open blue river.

Some days the wind would come up from the north and Jack could smell the bitter decay of the paper mill from up in the hills. But that morning the mist and the clouds blunted the smell from coming down.

The blond woman kept looking back at him instead of paddling. The rapids grew larger and more powerful and everyone was smiling nervously like at a great play or on a roller coaster.

Jack shouted more commands as the water broke and crashed over them. He turned straight on, right for the big twelve-foot rapid they called Magic. He knew he had to hit it straight on or risk turning the raft over.

"Go! Go!" he shouted.

They hit the huge wall of water, sunk down into the blackish-gray gulch, then came up the other side.

Jack felt the wave in his stomach. It felt like the second after kissing a girl for the first time.

He smiled.

"Great! Great!" he was yelling at them. "This is what it's all about! This is what it's all about!"

They drifted downriver, passing some of the other raft companies near the waterfall where the Kennebec turns flat and gray.

Jack tried to ignore her now. He didn't want to embarrass her husband, but she kept trying to talk to him; but this was mean, defensive talk, and he didn't say anything back to her.

They went ahead downriver for an hour, and then he put them on shore and took the passengers for a walk through the woods to get their legs back. There were woodpeckers and blue jays up on branches in the trees, every branch waving and trembling in the wind, patches of black muddy ground everywhere one stepped. Jack began to pass out some trail mix he had put together the night before – Chex cereal, raisins, walnuts, M&M's, pecans, and popcorn.

The blonde woman, Kat, trailed behind everyone else. Jack saw her blonde hair matted down and wet and she had color in her cheeks now. The sense of her beauty began to rise up in him and he wanted to feel it.

"This job you have?" she said as everyone drifted ahead of them. "I'd die to have your job. I'm stuck in a room without any windows all day. Some days I don't even know if the sun's out."

"I know," he said. "Last year I was locked in a room teaching technical writers how to version their documents. A zero-point-a is not the same as a one-point-one." He saw her turn and look back at him. "It's not much of a life," he said. "I just couldn't do it anymore."

"I know," she said, nodding.

He watched her as she stopped in the middle of the trail.

The rest of the group, ahead of them, turned a corner. Jack bumped into the woman. He saw her turn and look up at him.

Her mouth was gentle. He noticed that she stared at him like they had always known each other just like he had thought.

He pretended this was a mistake. He tried to walk around her.

"Don't you believe in fate?" she said, her voice shaking.

Jack watched her reach out for his hand. He could feel her shivering from being in her wet suit for too long.

"You let water get into your lining," he told her. He looked into her eyes. "No. I don't believe in fate. Not anymore." He thought about it. "I was locked in a room for too many years to believe in fate."

"I know," she said. "But I've never, all my life …."

He pulled away from her. A wet linden branch brushed against his cheek as he moved back, slightly cutting his face.

He could feel the warmness of the blood as he wiped it away. He touched it and saw some of the blood on his hands. He tried not to look at her. He looked straight ahead for the group, but they were gone.

"What are we going to do?" she said.

"What can we do?"

Jack dropped the bag of trail mix and slumped to the ground like a baseball catcher. His face fell into his hands as the wind picked up and the mist and water dripped down from the canopy of the needles and leaves above them.

He began to think about his mistakes. Twenty years earlier he had loved this girl and he had let her get away. There were reasons. A million reasons and excuses and explanations. His parents wanted one thing for him. Her parents wanted one thing for her. Neither of them wound up with anything. He wanted never to feel like that again. There were all these rules in other peoples' lives. But what rules were there up in Maine?

Jack watched the woman kneel beside him. He felt her try to put her arms around him, but he pushed back. She leaned into him and forced her warm mouth against his neck, but it lasted only for a second.

And then they could hear the voices of the husband, and the man from Syracuse, and the six happy college kids from Northeastern coming back down the trail toward them.

Jack looked at her, because he knew what he wanted, but he had spent his entire life doing the exact opposite.

He jumped up and cleared his throat.

He saw her hold her hand over her mouth as she stood up. There were tears in her gray eyes.

"There they are!" the husband shouted to the man from Syracuse.

"Come on! We found another waterfall," one of the college kids shouted. "It's so beautiful."

"We'll be right there," Jack said. "We're coming."

He started to walk toward them and the woman followed behind.

Jack followed the trail that he knew much better now, and he watched the sky through the trees and saw some holes of blue begin to open up. He sensed the slight smell of the paper mill as it began to come up in the air.

He saw the waterfall ahead.

He stopped with the woman just before the end of the trail.

Jack felt her trembling right beside him.

"You'll find someone else," he said to her.

He kissed her gently on the forehead. Just as he did he began to feel the same way he always had, and it scared him to feel this, here, too.

He heard everyone shouting for them again, and he could smell the stench of the paper mill begin to grow strong.

Jack and the woman let go of one another. He ran his hand against her cheek. She was different from the others. He knew it. They were just like each other, but then there was all this other make-believe stuff too.

"I'm only a guide on a river," he said to her. He watched as she closed her eyes and let out a deep breath.

Jack took her hand and gave her a little push. He saw her looking at him, but slowly and deliberately pushed her to walk out in front of him. Together they went over to where the others waited for them, where they Ooh-ed and Aah-ed with everyone else in front of a waterfall that Jack had seen a thousand times before. And neither of them said anything, and they just stood there and pretended just like everyone else.

JAMES BABBS

It Was Nearly Summer We Sat On Your Roof

I remember your room
posters on the walls and
your bed covered with stuffed animals
I remember your long blonde hair
blowing in the wind and
how every time I touched you
I knew it wouldn't last
and it didn't matter
whether or not you loved me
I remember the way you tasted
when I kissed you on the mouth and
how we mixed peach schnapps with Sprite
lying on our backs
looking up at the stars
and you made wishes
but couldn't tell me what they were
because if you did
you said
they wouldn't come true
I remember your father
coming to the window
telling us it was late
and it was time for me to go
that was the year it stopped raining
and everybody's lawns turned brown
every day
announcements on the radio
warning people against burning outdoors
I remember you
standing in the driveway
the sunlight
teasing the ends of your hair
I remember
the way you put your hand up
when I slowly drove away

JAMES BABBS

Frank

she was in there warm and dry
when I came in
from out of the rain
she looked startled at first
then she pointed at me
You better get out of those wet things
she finally said
she brought me towels and a blanket
later
she gave me a cup of coffee
while I sat on the couch
wrapped in the blanket
she handed me the whiskey
Here
she said
This will help you get warm
I poured some into my coffee
watched the steam rising from the cup
Frank's dead
she said
What?
I asked her
How long?
I drank some of the coffee
felt the burning in my throat
8 or 9 months
she said
Maybe a year
I don't know
she started sobbing
holding her head in her hands
What happened?
I asked
the heat spreading
crawling over my face

They shot him
she told me
forcing the words through her tears
she fell against me
and I buried my face in her hair
I don't know
how long we stayed like that
before she stood up
and pulled her dress off
over her head
she was naked underneath
later
when I felt her body
shifting next to me in the bed
I rolled over
reaching for the whiskey bottle
I found it
and brought it to my lips
and I heard her
murmuring something in her sleep
I emptied the bottle
then let it drop from my hand
when it hit the carpet
it didn't make a sound
I didn't know what time it was
I listened to the rain
hitting against the house
I wondered
how long it would last
and I thought about Frank
I guess
I needed to find out
where he was buried
I thought
maybe tomorrow
we'd go visit his grave
she murmured again
and I wondered
if she was dreaming about him

I rolled over
and pushed myself against her
she moaned
before I felt her reaching out
and pulling me toward her
she opened her arms and legs
as she moved beneath me again
pressing me into her
our bodies churning together
slowly in the dark

PATTI ABBOTT

Bach Cello Suite No. 1

Cello students often begin serious study of the instrument with Bach's Cello Suite No 1.

Prelude

When he first saw Nanette de Fiore, she was seated in one of the practice rooms at Oberlin College. From his perspective, the instrument seemed to be playing itself, its shadow falling on the clean white walls with Nan's outline somehow submerged within its sharper profile.

She couldn't have weighed more than ninety pounds and her hair looked sculpted, drawing attention to her perfect skull. Her neck was long and delicate, her back perfectly straight – cello-like. A pair of unfashionable ochre cat-eye glasses teetered mid-nose. It was those glasses, in their descent, that sent the arrow straight through him.

Once recovered from the assault, Eli realized her bowing technique needed work; there was too much tension in her wrist, producing minute but discernible breaks in the music – the skittery sound he'd often heard discussed by musicians at his home in Northampton.

"Look, would you mind if I corrected your position?" He'd never summon up such masterfulness with her again.

"People more experienced than you haven't found my *position* wanting." She squinted up at him and suddenly seized the tottery glasses from her nose and stashed them in the music stand. An unspoken *so there* hung in the air.

Back away, a voice in his head warned him.

Ignoring both her comment and the voice in his head, he continued, "And, while we're at it, I really don't care for your thumb placement." He moved closer. "Make a ball of your hand – like this."

He demonstrated, and when she didn't move, he took her hand (and a cold hand it was) and closed it, placing the correct part of her thumb in the proper place between the frog and the grip.

Eli Hauser didn't play the cello. He wasn't studying music and, at nineteen, had no college major at all. But both of his parents were in a chamber group (violin and viola) and he recognized good technique. He'd been raised in the constant company of fine cellists.

Reluctantly, Nan drew the bow across the strings. She looked unconvinced for a split second, but then, liking what she heard – a smooth, continuous sound – she looked up and smiled. "How long have you been playing?" She drew the bow again and grinned.

He paused, wondering how to answer that without losing the slight edge his deception had won him. The door to freedom lay only twelve feet away, but he turned his back on it.

***

Allemande

Nan was so devoted to her practice of the cello that it was difficult for Eli to lure her away. Ignoring interested glances and even explicit overtures from other girls on campus, he hung around Nan's practice room as if it were a hive and he, a drone. He admired, resented, and misunderstood her commitment to her instrument, lacking such devotion himself. He was, in fact, reminded of his childhood, the years when he was dragged across the globe, only to stand in the wings or wait with non-English-speaking child-minders in hotel rooms while his parents performed in the great concert halls. Perhaps he'd been trained for this task – this standing and waiting – and nothing more.

"Is she very good?" he asked his mother when his parents came to campus to give a recital. He'd lost the capacity to assess Nan's ability long ago. They were standing outside a practice room eavesdropping while his father took his afternoon nap.

His mother frowned, patting his shoulder. "Ah, Eli. Well, she'll never be a soloist certainly. But she might find a position in a second – or perhaps third – tier orchestra. Or with a good regional chamber group." She listened a bit longer. "She has a certain feeling for the music. Bach's Suite No. 1, I see." She nodded approvingly.

Was her judgment too harsh? Her son knew about harsh verdicts.

At age twelve, Eli awoke one morning to find his violin missing. In its place was an expensive camera, one he'd been privately coveting for months. He never asked about the missing violin, and no one ever mentioned it again. In fact, when he saw his former teacher at a recital, both of them averted their eyes – as if deeply embarrassed by their joint failure. Neither of his parents suggested that he try piano or clarinet (something he expected but dreaded), which probably meant he lacked the proper feel for the music. This was a criticism his parents leveled at many of their private students just before dropping them.

His disappointment was eventually soothed by his proficiency with the new camera, and he turned its lens toward his parents and their associates. A lucrative business took shape before he'd finished high school. His musical knowledge, his eye for placement of musicians and their instruments, his intuition of what would please, guaranteed success. By his senior year, he was designing flyers and taking photos for professional programs.

"Hey, you," He'd crept into the practice room between movements. "I have tickets to a concert at Severance Hall." He waved them in front of Nan's eyes. "Tempted?"

"Yoyo Ma?" she asked. He nodded.

And later that Friday night, for the first time in the many months he'd pursued her, usually fruitlessly, she gripped him as enthusiastically as she did her cello. He pushed down the tiny knot of panic that swelled inside him.

***

Courante

Progress with their romance was measured. When Nan wasn't practicing the cello, taking required classes, or listening to her peers perform, she had important recordings playing on her CD player. Or she was studying video tapes of technique. He could sometimes lure her away for a concert or for a movie with an interesting musical score. (Bergman's *Cries and Whispers* was her absolute favorite.) But any suggestion of a football game, a Hollywood comedy, or dinner, met with little interest.

"I can't really spare the time," she said unapologetically. "I'm hoping to be invited to perform at a church in Chagrin Falls next week. Their regular cellist has mono."

Sometimes his patience was rewarded with a quick tryst. But those times were often more depressing than gratifying. He could feel a symbolic chucking of his chin, as if she were saying, "There now, that's done. Off to play."

He could also sense a certain rhythmic quality to her performance – as if she were mentally playing her instrument while permitting entry from his.

"Has she improved?" he asked his mother in his junior year.

"Oh, yes," his mother said. "Nanette's doing nicely."

"So she'll be invited to play with a good orchestra or chamber group after all?"

His mother shook her head. "She wouldn't be a candidate for a position at a major orchestra, I'm afraid. Times being what they are." She listened for a minute, droopy-eyed.

"Still working on Suite 1, is she? My goodness."

"Sometimes I imagine, or maybe even hallucinate, that her hand and the bow are one," he said, squinting. "Do you see it? Right now!"

He'd read hallucinations were not necessarily a sign of insanity, and he clung to this.

"See how they seem to merge on the forward movement?" He nudged his drowsy mother awake. The effect of him was seismic. He could actually feel a shift in the room.

"See what?" his mother said, not really listening to him – as was so often the case.

He wondered if Nan knew she wasn't first-rate. Had her new instructor, a Korean gentleman named Dr. Seung, warded off high expectations?

"So is this Seung a good instructor?" he asked Nan later. "Has he inspired you?"

"We are very simpatico," she said.

He wondered if that meant she was sleeping with him. It was unlikely she'd risk the purity of her relationship with Seung with a dalliance though.

If her hand and the bow were one, shouldn't she be first-rate? Shouldn't such a perfect unification with her cello mean something? It was only when she stepped away from her instrument, out of its orbit, in fact, that he saw her clearly – without the tremor of cracked spacings – a concept in art that explained the phenomenon. Cracked spacings occurred when a painting was split after completion, leaving impressions of the original state in both halves. Nan without her cello seemed incomplete – a loss of the centaur moment, in fact. Her hands looked bereft without a bow, a fingerboard. All of it.

***

Sarabande

They married soon after her Master's degree was complete.

"You understand?" she said on his proposal. "You understand how it is?"

He froze, expecting some distressing confession to pour from her mouth.

"You understand that the music will always come first." Her foot tapped rhythmically on the floor.

He nodded, relieved. This was how it'd always been; he wasn't sure he'd know what to do with a surfeit of devotion.

Eli was on the road a lot after that, following classical musical groups and occasionally a pop one with his camera. He placed a photo in *Rolling Stone* and another in *Spin*. He had a gallery show in Chelsea, another in Chicago. Overnight somehow, they became affluent – not that she was impressed or even seemed to notice.

"I'm home," he yelled from the foyer, dropping his overnight bag on the tiled floor. Her one demand in their search for a house had been a music room where she spent most of her hours.

He could hear music. The location of the music room insured any piece played there would swell throughout the paneled walls of the brownstone. Like her body's relationship with her cello, her music occupied every crevice of their home. She was playing Britten today. Sometimes it only seemed like she played Bach continuously. Despite his weariness of Bach, he was wary of a change in atmosphere and the possibilities it might signal.

"Nan," he yelled again. The music stopped and he heard her sigh. The acoustics were good enough to pick up even a frisson of displeasure.

"I was nearly finished …. Now I'll have to begin again."

For a second, he wondered if she'd forgotten his name. Why did she always have to begin again? If she erred, even on a final note, she started afresh.

"Wait. I've brought you a present, Nanny." Silence. He bounded up the steps and found her fiddling with her pegs. "Did you hear me? I brought you something special."

He'd been in Munich for ten days and had missed her every minute. He searched her face for a familiar expression, a sign. Had she even noticed his absence? He held out the bright blue bag. When he wasn't home, did anyone stop her from playing night and day? Sometimes he cursed the thickness of their walls, which hid her obsession from their neighbors. Only an open window gave her away.

Nan looked up and smiled, finally seeming to know him. Pulling out the wrapped gift, she opened it excitedly. Usually he brought home rare CDs or autographed sheet music. Gifts she loved. But this was something special, he hoped. In seconds, she was holding up the music box. Hesitantly, she opened its lid. He knew she was worried that the music would be a violin piece, an instrument she barely tolerated.

"Can you really abide that screeching sound? I know your mother plays violin, but …." She had said such things on many occasions. Brought up on the violin, he didn't hear what she did. The instruments – when played well – were similarly melodic to him.

"It's Dvorak," she said a second later, the gift wrap lying at her feet. She sounded puzzled. Puzzled and a bit annoyed.

"There's a shop outside Munich, which has quite a selection. Even Philip Glass."

She giggled nervously. "Surely, not Glass!" She listened a second or two longer then shut the lid.

"Thank you, Eli. Very artfully done."

He knew she was referring to the case and not the music inside. The case, decorated with a Bavarian woodlands scene on a lovely cherry wood, was nothing special. The music itself was a recording by Jacqueline du Pres.

She saw the look on his face. "Well, I can't help but wonder, Eli – why not Bach?"

Why not Bach indeed?

***

Minuet

Five times in six – no, perhaps, nine times in ten – Nan practiced the Bach suite. Eli seldom entered the house without hearing it cascading down the stairs, spilling into the dining room, tumbling into the kitchen. If she wasn't playing it herself, she was listening to her many recordings.

"Cellists spend their whole life deciding on the correct reading of this piece," his mother explained to him in a hushed phone call. "Attaining a correct balance between the romantic and the scholarly interpretation – and what exactly that interpretation is – is the constant debate. Some say Bach wrote his suites much like you'd publish mathematical theorems." She paused. "Is she playing it now?" He held the phone up. "I think she's leaning toward the more aesthetic approach. Interesting but predictable. No one can say she suffers from a lack of restraint."

"We've been married for three years," he said. "In all that time, she has never once played outside this house, Mother. If she only plays for herself, is it anything more than masturbation?"

He could feel his mother freeze. "I don't think we can consider Nan's music in those terms," she finally said. "You don't understand, Eli. Not being a musician yourself. And although you're a talented photographer, I don't think you share our obsession." This was clearly meant as a slight, but he was long inured to such observations from his mother. "Maybe Nanette is your obsession."

He shrugged this off. "I do understand what complete self-absorption is. When I picture her, it's always with that instrument in front of her." He thought again Nan as a centaur – of an illustration of cracked spacings. If he found a way to separate Nan from her cello, would she lose the mania that defined her? Would she be irreparably incomplete, broken?

162

"Maybe it's you who has the problem," his mother repeated. "Be glad she cares about something more than shopping trips, decorating, or making obscene amounts of money." She sighed. "And I think you need to examine this: how is Nan different now from the girl you were attracted to eight years ago? Didn't you in a sense create her? Is she the end product of submerging your own ambition for someone else"'s?"

She babbled on about how they shouldn't have taken away his violin, shouldn't have sent him to Oberlin, should have introduced him to a nice fourth-grade teacher at the right age.

***

"I think you should look for a job," Eli told Nan later. "You could teach, work for a non-profit even. You need to get out of the house. Live more in the real world." Having children though was beyond her capacity for – well, he wasn't sure what – nurturing?

"I didn't realize we needed a second salary," she said, putting down her cup of Oolong. "I thought we had an understanding ...."

"That understanding was based on the idea you'd perform. I had no idea ...."

"And I will perform," she snapped at him. "As soon as I'm ready. Madame Giroux thinks next spring. I have the brochure for the local spring music season at the arts center. They're inviting guest performances." She opened a drawer and withdrew it, slapping it down on the table.

He took the brochure and looked at the section she'd circled in red. A quick scan made it clear it was meant for high school, or, at best, college-aged musicians. Not a cellist who'd now studied her instrument for more than 15 years.

"You underestimate yourself," he said tiredly.

That night when he passed her music room, he was sure he saw her face intersected by the strings. At the far end near the peg box, they seemed to bite into her. Cruelly even. Should a string snap, she could be seriously injured. Her cello, one he himself had purchased from an excellent luthier, was taking on the size of a bass fiddle in his head.

163

***

Gigue

The Bach Suite was playing again when Eli came back from Chicago. He could hear it on the street now that the windows were open. Several neighbors seemed to be listening from their stoops. He wished he could show Nan the pleasure they took in her music, the look of joy on their faces as they listened. Maybe then she'd find the courage to play on stage.

But strangely when he came inside, he found her in bed, the CD player turned off. She looked dead. "Men only kill the thing they love," went through his head. That poem Wilde had written in jail.

"Nan," he said softly. And then he said it a bit louder. "NAN."

She sat up suddenly – like a puppet whose strings had been yanked. And it was all right then. He lay down beside her and together they absorbed the silence, entwined their fingers, tangled the sheets, slept. She seemed to intuit they needed a rest from it – from whatever was lurking in the music room. For a week or two, she left the house with him for various events. A concert, a play, a dinner with some business associates. She seemed normal if tired; their life was ordinary for once. But normal for most people wasn't normal for Nan when you thought about it.

And however he defined her normalcy, it was short-lived. He came home to silence again but knew his wife was in the house because her coat was on the coat rack, her keys on the hall table. At first, he thought the music room was empty. It took several seconds before he saw her face, looking plaintively out at him from behind the bridge of the cello. Her skin seemed to be part of the wood, layered onto it in some ineffable way. Marquetry perhaps. The cracked spacings had merged.

"How did you get in there?" he asked, alarmed.

The strings, which had before seemed to cut across her face before, now seemed to imprison her. Her cries for help seem to spring out of the blasted f-holes, cello-like in sound. The entire instrument was a prison. Why hadn't he seen it before? When had the cello taken control? When had she submitted to it? Why had he allowed it?

"Don't worry, my darling. It won't take me more than a minute to free you."

He looked around wildly for a suitable implement to destroy that thing that jailed her, thinking suddenly how difficult, how painful, such a separation might be.

ZDRAVKA EVTIMOVA

Thursday Again

It was Thursday again and that meant at 9 pm Becky's husband would visit her. He had emailed her, had called on her mobile, and had sent a fax message warning her to be in her bedroom exactly at that hour, but Becky hoped that at least today she would break the established routine. Theo had some important/official meeting in Bonn and odds were that she would be in luck; he was already ten minutes late.

She dreamt of going to Bonn herself; she loved the cold, humid air, the intimate fog hovering above squares and statues, the sluggish dark river, but above all she enjoyed the closed faces of people. Their cool, unobtrusive presence put her at her ease. She was wind or dust on the sidewalk, and the feeling of solitude was sweet. She adored the loneliness of the houses; although they were arranged in strict straight lines, each one had an ancient facade and a little fountain which spoke of the owner's frivolity. The marble arches cast their quaint shadows on the squares full of legends and history. She felt the stares of men on her skin; their parasite eyes delved deep into her flesh and sucked delicious juice from it.

Her husband's business partners were civilized enough, but Becky guessed that at the end of the day they had one of the expensive girls in their hotels. She imagined the services the men wanted and felt appalled. Thinking about men was an appalling occupation, for it made her remember Theo, her husband, and the Thursday nights he spent with her.

Becky hated Thursdays.

Bakaloff, one of the business partners of Becky's husband, had so far behaved in a very friendly manner. He sent her discreet flower gift baskets on the mornings after each official dinner. At the last working lunch, the seventeenth in a long, tedious series, Becky mentioned something about the film "Titanic" just for the sake of participating in the conversation. Theo had warned her not to be silent like a statue even though she looked as beautiful as one. Out of pure politeness, Becky took part in the discussions. She dropped a question in the sphere of culture she had prepared beforehand — finance and politics were perilous zones and Theo had cautioned her not to poke her nose in it, pointing out how narrow-minded her way of looking at things was. In general, he did his best to stress her overall inability to cope with anything outside cosmetics; because of that Becky asked Bakaloff her well-prepared question, "Have you seen the film *Titanic?*"

Perhaps the question was downright stupid, but pronounced by her beautiful lips it acquired weight, and the businessmen, feeling the ennobling female presence, commented on "Titanic." Unlike all the rest of them who kissed her hand and bowed silently, the bolder ones discreetly directing their eyes down the neckline of her dress, Bakaloff on the following day sent Becky a disc with the film.

Becky had made up her mind to indulge in a small adventure with Mr. Bakaloff. She needed neither sex nor the sugary porridge of love; Bakaloff attracted her with the fact that he had not lowered his eyes to the neckline of her dress nor had he attempted to swim in the stream of the topic of how beautiful Becky was. He simply established a dear little tradition to send her modest bouquets of snowdrops on Mondays, Wednesdays, and Fridays. Becky appreciated them all the more because on these very days Di, the strange girl, came to her house and massaged her body with such intense concentration as if that was her favorite occupation in the world.

When Bakaloff brought Becky to his villa in the country, and she saw him naked, whitish, and flat like the undulating shapes of tapeworms she had seen as a schoolgirl in her biology classes, the iceberg of repugnance hit her throat. Becky did not want Bakaloff. She imagined his hands, scraggy, overgrown with transparent hairs, touching her; then she saw his thin colorless lips closing down on her mouth, and she thought she would throw up. Bakaloff caressed her and Becky was scared by his dry palms moving rapidly all over her, his unnaturally quick fingers planting warts in her skin as they touched her. The experience was all the more unpleasant because of the question that Bakaloff constantly kept asking her, "Does it feel good?"

Finally Becky answered that it felt good, hoping that he would calm down, but he sank into her all the more intensively leaving dry pain in his wake. There were thin grooves of saliva running from the corners of his mouth on which Becky concentrated. Yet she could gain considerable advantage from this situation; Bakaloff's blue, almost transparent eyes swam in fog, his eyelids slid downwards, his mouth kissed her persistently as his body swayed on her like a buoy tied at the bottom of the sea. She could examine him closely and had the chance to experiment with him; she scratched his back, ready to avenge herself on his body for the humiliation and the splitting ache he gave her. Then she hit him.

Last Thursday night, while her husband Theo was making love to her, she scratched him as well; and he hit her. That was the only time he had ever done that to Becky and after, when he had gone, the money left on the bed for the week was three times more than usual. From that time on, Becky suspected he nurtured a vein of sneering and sadistic malice; he tried to humiliate her in public, and since she was not a woman given to procrastination and suspicions, she told him plainly, "Next time you hit me you're asking me for a divorce."

"You won't divorce me," Theo answered, his gray eyes hungry for her. "You need my money."

Becky did not object and did not explain anything.

"Try me," she said.

Becky scratched Bakaloff's back again, but instead of leaving her alone he blurted out, "You are great, you are great." He sounded credible, as if he really believed what he said. His saliva dripped on her breasts and she hated that, but the exhilarating feeling that she was a researcher experimenting with a species unknown to science never left her. She could push and scratch and beat and bite him. She could do anything to him, and for a moment Becky was sorry her imagination was so poor she could not invent anything twisted and deviant.

"Stop!" Becky ordered him. He ceased moving and sat up, whitish and undulating in his glass jar of acid where the tapeworms were preserved in her biology lab at school.

"I love you," Bakalov said, but Becky saw his shiny saliva and the whitish hairs piercing his colorless skin. "I love you. Marry me! Abandon your husband!'

She hit him once again, this time on the mouth, and instead of yelling, he tried to kiss her. At that moment, Becky saw in her mind the dark hands of the girl who massaged her, and was unable to catch her breath.

Becky drove on the way back home and Bakaloff slept, the streams of his saliva dripping onto the seat of his expensive car. She suddenly wanted to make him feel pain; her desire was so irresistible that she drove her fingernails deep into his wrist. Bakaloff woke up and looked around expecting that somebody wanted to break his neck. Becky stopped the car. It was so cold and wet that for a moment she wanted to throw Bakaloff out in the street and go on without him. She kissed him instead, and bit his lip, bit it savagely, feeling the taste of his blood in her mouth. He shouted with pain and as Becky let him go he whispered, "I love you."

Becky thought about the hands of the girl who massaged her and remembered that it was Thursday again. That meant that Theo would be home at nine pm. His gray eyes — if the lewd gloss between his eyelids could be called eyes — would pick a spot on the floor, then he would order, "There!"

Sometimes he did not speak at all but it made no difference to Becky. She accepted his visits on Thursdays with the same reserve as her appointments with the dentist: the sooner they were over, the better. Theo did not allow her to be a researcher intent on scratching, hitting, and dissecting him closely. Very rarely, perhaps one Thursday a year, her husband would snort "You are pretty, damn it."

"I am cold," Bakaloff muttered from the seat of his expensive car. "I am cold and I love you."

She had totally forgotten about him.

"I will not leave Theo," Becky said, and thoughts of the girl who massaged her every Thursday blissfully flooded her. What a pity her husband had chosen Thursdays to make love to her. She wished the girl stayed after he went out to work in the city. She wished Theo never came back to her life.

STEPHANIE SMITH

Graveyard

You and I wade through weeks
of erratic weather
without a single word
spoken to each other
Just your arm in mine,
holding on to the impossible
Syllables are sins
sung from dirty mouths
I'd rather clutch your throat
to bring another day to its death
to end the ennui
like a record skipping endlessly
like my beating heart
being ripped to shreds

STEPHANIE SMITH

Between

Can you hear the space between the sounds?
The silence that comes with a final heartbeat
A last gasp
The gap between the living and the dead
The path between Heaven and Hell
and the journey from night to day
The din of death on drunken highways
with the screams of the innocent
stinking up the backseat of a car,
traveling far away from here
Only to end up
right back where it started from

D. H. SCHLEICHER

Down Gallow's Way

The name Galloway Downs seemed appropriate for my new digs off the pike as it was here deep in the heart of Atlantic County where the down-and-out went all the way down. It was the spring of 2010. I was just finishing my first semester as an adjunct sociology professor at Richard Stockton College over in Pomona. In '08 I had left my position at Temple in disgrace after an indiscretion with a female student. I didn't regret the indiscretion, only that I had chosen such a dramatic girl. I had been out of work for over a year and ran through all of my savings at the casinos in Chester and Bensalem before eyeing Atlantic City and landing the "temp" gig at Stockton. I was forty-three years-old and I was moving into the shanty house of a woman named Clementine.

Clementine wasn't her real name. I think it was Cynthia. She had adopted the story of being a fine southern belle from Atlanta-way, and she drenched her speech in sweet molasses as if she did voice-over work for a series of audio recordings of William Faulkner novels. The truth was her momma had originally been from Alabama, down Montgomery-way, and she had moved up here a piece to be with a man (not Clem's daddy but some long haul truck driver) back in the '70's when Clem was just a girl. You see, she was really from Clementon, not faraway up the pike. It didn't take much imagination to see how she conjured her fake moniker.

We had met one night outside a strip joint. My darling Clementine was a "talent manager" there. ELO's "*Do Ya?*" was playing on the radio of her red convertible when I first caught a glimpse of her Amazonian body. "My momma died of the sugar cancer 'round Christmastime. She left me her house," she said four days later. "It sure is lonely there. Why don't you move in with me?"

It was through Clementine that I learned of Bibbs and Saundra, the most infamous residents of Galloway Downs. Bibbs was some sort of truck driver—local delivery, not long-haul. Saundra was a domestic engineer, meaning she stayed at home watching Lil' Bibbs and gossiping with the other unfortunate victims of circumstance in the Downs, many of whom seemed to have reserved their spots at the foot of the gallows of life. Whether they were waiting to see someone else break their neck or were awaiting their own execution was never clear.

Saundra was attractive, comparatively speaking. She worked out with Clementine at the gym, so her body was fit for her age, or what I had determined to be her age … mid-thirties perhaps. She also had a little side business selling cosmetics and skin care products, like Avon I guess, but something cheaper and fly-by-night. When she wasn't in the company of Bibbs or Lil' Bibbs and she was advertising her products at the local Target or Shop-Rite, you might say she was a looker. As soon as you knew she was with a man like Bibbs, you began to wonder, "What the hell for?" She tricked you into thinking she could do better. But then you found out about her tramp stamp (some ridiculous Chinese tribal thing) and the "dedication" decal on the back window of her pick-up truck. When her baby brother passed away in an accident where he was the drunk driver back in '06, the family couldn't afford a proper headstone. *In loving memory, Christopher "Jer-Jer" Moore, 1984-2006* was on her window for all riding Saundra's tail to see. Oh, yeah, and there's also that grotesque image of her smiling baby's face tattooed above her left breast.

Bibbs was as Clem would say, "scandalous." This was funny, because I had always suspected Clem and Bibbs had something going on, not just because I actually caught him at her place one morning (before I had moved in and he was supposedly fixing a broken rail on the back porch) but because he frequented the strip joint and was known for favoring the management over the talent. Bibbs was tall, tightly wound by bulging muscles, bald and tattooed, the type of guy you wouldn't want to run into alone in a dark alley, but when you got to talking with him he was always quite amiable. He was a scumbag for sure, but also a bit of a dumb lug who couldn't help himself. His name allegedly came from his penchant for grilling up some of the sloppiest, dripping barbecue ribs come summertime – stuff so dirty you needed a bib when you ate it. I suspected the name came from even further back to when he was an over-slobbering toddler who always needed a bib well past the age bibs were socially acceptable. No one seemed to know his real name. Hell, maybe Bibbs *was* on his birth certificate as Saundra once claimed.

Then there was Lil' Bibbs (I think his real name was Joey — the baby on the breast tattoo) who was nearly three and still not potty-trained. Saundra still referred to his age in months as if that would cover up that he was behind a little bit developmentally. I never could understand how a kid could talk about taking a dump yet still do it right there in his pants. Seems to me he was being willfully defiant. But otherwise, he was an okay kid I guess, quiet, a bit clumsy, and he smelled. But at that age you can only blame the parents.

So when I moved into Clementine's house just off the pike, the little blue rancher with the overgrown lawn and rusted metal fence that stood in the center of a clusterfuck of lesser homes and doublewides nestled at a fork in the road, we were in the middle of that blasted April heat wave. After the wretched winter of the snowpocalypse where we were hit with record snowfall amounts and left to trudge through mountains of the stuff that seemed like it wouldn't melt until May (it was gone by March), it seemed a welcome slap in the face to be hit with record heat just after Easter. Clem's AC didn't work, and I was no handyman. So we spent those nights in Saundra's chilled-to-the-bone doublewide drinking beers and watching the Phillies' games, passing Lil' Bibbs from knee to knee, bouncing all the way until he was as Clem liked to say, "right tuckered out." Bibbs was, of course, always out on the road working. He was probably doing more lying of pipe than driving, I imagined, but Saundra seemed blissfully oblivious.

"So you teach like anthropology and stuff?" Saundra would inquire.

"Sociology, anthropology, yes," I would answer cautiously.

"That like the study of people in Africa and such?"

"And such, yes." I was pretty good at hiding a smirk even when drunk, but I guess holding that back made me look constipated or shifty, as I could tell Saundra thought of me as a bit of an uppity know-it-all, being a professor from the college and all.

"I could've gone to college, but then I met Bibbs. He don't like people to be smarter than him. I could still go to cosmetology school, ya know. Don't know 'bout all them other fancy 'ologies though. But you ga'head with your teachin', mister professor."

"Wow, hun, you and Bibbs have really been together that long?" Clementine remarked.

Saundra looked insulted. "How old do you think I am?" She was cradling a sleeping child in her arms. Maybe referring to Lil' Bibbs' age in months made her feel younger. She stood up to take him to bed, a beer bottle balanced between her bosom and the child's stomach.

"Wanna take a ride to the city?" Clementine whispered, referring of course to the city that was … *always turned on* … and just a hop, skip, and a jump down the pike.

"You bet," I said.

Even though the heat wave was short-lived, this became routine for three or four nights out of the week that month. It would always end at five or six am back at Clem's place, booze sweating out of my pores, a hole in my pocket, and my body collapsed and stripped down to my boxers, with Clem, always somehow sober, sitting at the end of the bed in her bra and panties slathering that awful smelling moisturizer from Saundra all over her arms and legs. I would admire her while on my back. Sometimes her body would spin and sometimes the clicking of the ceiling fan whirling above me sounded like gunfire. Her revolver and holster stared back at me from atop her bureau. It made me feel secure knowing that she might be the dangerous type.

"This ain't such a bad life, is it?" I would ask, half smiling in the darkness. Hell, it was surely better than staying at the efficiency apartments along the pike.

"Naw, I've known worse." Clementine would assure me with a touch of her hand on my leg. That made me wonder just how old she really was and how long she had been carrying that gun. It seemed to me then, down Gallow's way, people were ageless.

The next day, before heading off to my afternoon classes, would be filled with aspirin-taking, French toast-eating, coffee-fueled diner trips and a requisite call from Saundra crying about the "disturbance" she and Bibbs had gotten into when he got home sometime 'round three or four in the morning. This was, of course, after she had Tweeted about it at five or six a.m. for all her followers to read. I think even the local cops followed her Tweets. Why she felt the need to regale to me personally all the minutia surrounding the fight was beyond my comprehension. I suppose she would've done so to Clementine had she not already left for work. I guess I was just the lucky one who happened to be there. As for the Tweets, it didn't puzzle me as much, as it was clear through her nervous body language face-to-face that she was so desperate to connect with another human being even if that was limited to 140 characters over a ridiculous social-networking site.

One night in May, Bibbs never came home. The Tweets were instantly hysterical. The next day, Clementine left for work but never arrived at the club. She, too, never came home. I ignored Saundra's texts and voice mails. I put up as my Facebook status, "Stuck *at Stockton with extended office hours during finals week*." Saundra left a comment, "*Call me PUHLEASE!!!!!!!!*" Three days passed before I finally went to her house. I didn't have the heart to tell her what I really thought, you know, that Clementine and Bibbs ran off together or something, but I couldn't avoid her forever.

I stood at the screen door peering into the dark musty house. I could hear the television on ... cartoons. I knocked gently. Lil' Bibbs came toddling towards the door sleepily and rubbing his eyes with the dusty sunlight streaming into the darkness through the torn screen.

"Daddy?" he asked pathetically while looking up at me and trying to adjust to the light.

I was surprised to find him wearing a Phillies' t-shirt and Superman underwear. Could it have been that overnight he had trained himself? Maybe he thought if he started acting like a "big boy" Bibbs would come home, though I often wondered about a child's sense of time and expectations. Maybe Saundra finally laid down the hammer. If Bibbs was gone, Lil' Bibbs was going to be the man of the house now.

"No, it's not Daddy," I told him softly as I carefully opened the door and stepped into the house. "Where's Mommy?"

"In the baffroom," he said.

The place smelled like sour milk. As I surveyed the mess in the living room and kitchen, the child stayed by me, close to my leg, his one hand touching my pants by my knee. Surely his hand was sticky.

"Where's Daddy?" he asked me.

"I dunno, Bubb," I said to him, which was odd. It was as if right then and there I had decided his new nickname would be Bubb, and he accepted it as if that had been his real name all along.

176

The era of Bibbs had already closed, and the two of us together, in psychic complicity, had decided he wouldn't be coming back. Not now. Not ever.

When Saundra came tumbling out onto the scene with her usual histrionics, Bubb retreated from my side and collapsed on the floor in front of the television amongst a field of battle-worn trucks and slain stuffed animals.

"Didn't you see my Tweet?" she asked me as she came up and gave me an inappropriately tight and long embrace.

"I'm sorry, I've been so busy. These damn kids and their finals, you know."

She whispered, "Somebody from the DEA was here this morning asking about Bibbs."

"Damn, you don't think he was—"

She swirled me into the kitchen with her waving arms and hands. She poured herself a cup of coffee. "Want some?"

"I'm fine."

"Suit yourself. Look, I logged onto that SOB's Facebook and started talkin' with all his good time friends, ya know? Askin' what's up, how's it hangin' and these bitches were all messagin' back askin' where I've been and what's goin' on. All worried about 'im and shit."

"So nobody knows where he is?"

"Well ain't nobody tellin'. But I got the feelin' this DEA prick knew somethin'. I think they're about to bust up the club. I'm surprised they haven't moved in on that crystal meth house downaways, but maybe they got bigger fish to fry at the club, ya know?"

"I don't know."

"And where the hell is Clem? Gawd, you don't think she's involved in this, do ya?"

And suddenly that horrible ELO song was playing in my head. *"Do ya do ya want my love?"* All over again it was that first moment I saw Clementine standing by her red convertible in the parking lot of the club talking on her cell phone. I remember she had this strange look in her eyes, a serious look. I had never thought about who she might've been talking to at the time. Maybe the song was blasting so nobody would hear what she was saying, and it was too dimly lit in the lot at night to read anybody's lips.

"Naw," I said. "Hell no, I mean ...." But did I? Clementine was on her cell phone an awful lot, all secretive-like. Were she and Bibbs running something out of the club? Drugs? Girls? What kind of *talent* was she *managing*?

When I got to the office that day, I was told a man had been by to see me.

"Looked like somebody from the FBI," the young female student who answered the phones said, her eyes wide and giddy at the thought that I could be wanted by the FBI ... or by anybody. She was looking at me the same way that girl at Temple did, you know, all intrigued by the fact that maybe this mild-mannered professor was bad news.

It was then that it dawned on me that if I were to be questioned, I wasn't even sure I knew Bibbs' and Clementine's real names. Hell, Clem never received any mail at the house. I always assumed she kept a P.O. Box. I had always thought her name was Cynthia (had Saundra told me that?) but who really knew?

"Did he leave a message?" I asked the girl.

"No, said he would try you at home later." She looked at me trying not to smile as if she wanted me to reveal something, tell her more. I must've sneered at her. Her desire quickly retreated into a dumbfounded look of defeat in a slouched position. She flipped a switch and was perky again, shoulders up and breasts out. "The other profs are ordering out for lunch. You want in?"

"No, I'm not hungry."

That night Saundra convinced me to drive down the pike towards Atlantic City.

"What if he passed out driving and his truck is in a ditch on the side of the road somewhere?" she said to me.

"Don't you think somebody would've seen it by now?" I asked. But then I realized maybe she was formulating some story in her head where Bibbs and Clem did run off together to Atlantic City, and then maybe last night or this morning he finally decided to come home but then ... dun dun dun ... he fell asleep behind the wheel! I still found it too fantastic a notion to think nobody driving along the pike would've noticed or stopped or called the police. And if that was her new story ... why the hell would she want that POS to come back to her?

"C'mon, ya know there's always cars parked on the shoulder

of the road, abandoned ... people see that shit every day and don't think nuthin' of it," she reminded me.

Part of me thought she just wanted to get out of the house. So 'round midnight, we packed up Bubb into the back of the cab of her truck where he happily slept in his car-seat and we headed down the pike, me behind the wheel and Saundra navigating. Along the way we passed the club, which appeared abnormally black, boarded up, and with no cars in the lot.

"Would you look at that?" Saundra whispered hotly. Maybe the gossip about the club getting busted and shut down was true.

She took me down back-roads, off the pike, and through the marshlands. We drove down a road towards a small regional airport where a private jet was taking off. It passed over us and was so close I thought the noise would wake Bubb, but in the rearview mirror he slept soundly. In a flash, I imagined myself commandeering a jet and flying off the coast out over the Atlantic Ocean until the plane ran out of gas and it fell and crashed into the water.

We drove all over, up and down the pike and on detours out into the Pine Barrens, the only place I knew of in the world where you could be driving down a dirt road into the woods and then get stuck in the sand. If Clem or Bibbs were out there, surely we would never find them. I thought what if that was an FBI agent looking for me at Stockton today? Maybe it was someone with news. News of finding a body. It was scary how quickly macabre thoughts would enter your mind even when you knew it was just the hysteria of the woman in the truck with you slowly infecting your mind. I had no real fears about Clem's whereabouts. She was the type who could handle her shit. Bibbs, on the other hand, I could see him getting into a bad spot ... but where? And were we already too late? And should we even care? Bubb had already moved on. Maybe so should we? Were the ribs Bibbs cooked really that good? I hadn't a chance to sample them yet. Summer was creeping in already.

In the hazy coming of dawn we were pulled over to the side of the road so Saundra could get out and smoke a cigarette underneath the giant windmills on the outskirts of Atlantic City. It seemed so calm and quiet then, the windmills nearly silent, their breezes calm. There was some cooing of birds out in the marshes and insects buzzed calmly not wishing to disturb the peace of the sun rising in the east out over the casinos. I leaned against the grill of the truck and thought of how badly I wanted a drink right then. All that driving up and down, out and over … for nothing. My arms and neck and back ached. My right foot was falling asleep. Inside the truck I faintly heard the sounds of Bubb waking. I walked around to the open driver's door and peered in at him. He looked lost and confused, and I felt a sudden camaraderie.

"Time to get you home, Bubb," I reassured him. "C'mon, momma, time to head in," I called out to Saundra.

Back at the house, Saundra poured me a drink in the kitchen after putting Bubb down in his bedroom. There was nothing quite like a good stiff drink at six in the morning. Saundra appeared exhausted but willful. She wrapped her arms around me while the bourbon slipped down the back of my throat and burned. "I want you to teach me about all them tribes in Africa and such, mister professor," she whispered into my ear, as if such things were a turn-on for academics. "Ga'head, do with me whatever you want." She began to suck on my right earlobe. Maybe Saundra had taken a cue from Bubb and was ready to move on. We began to kiss and she led me into her bedroom. What was the name of that girl who answered the phones for the Sociology department? Had she been in one of my classes? I knew this would not end well.

I went onto campus the next day un-showered, unshaved, and reeking of booze and Saundra. The girl answering the phones was not the same one from yesterday. Were they volunteers? This one seemed stern and uninterested in my shenanigans. Instinctually I went home to Saundra's house after my extended office hours. We ate pizza on TV-trays and watched *American Idol.* We shared a bottle of cheap red wine, showered together, and retired to bed early. We didn't have sex. We just lay there together.

"I filed a missing person's report today," she whispered to me before we both drifted off to sleep.

Around three in the morning she woke up screaming in my ear. My head was pounding as we sat up in bed, and her nails dug into my shoulders as she cried into my chest. I could find no words to comfort her. I wondered if she had awakened poor Bubb in the next room.

"I'm sorry," she cried. She tore herself from me and gazed

off into the darkness on her side of the bed. "I had the most horrible dream."

I lay back down on the misshapen pillows. My neck was killing me. "Ga'head," I said not realizing I was mocking her South Jersey accent. "Tell me about it."

"I dreamt they found Bibb's truck out in the Pines," she began. "I could see the flashlights, ya know, and his truck half sunk in quicksand or something. The windshield was all dirty and smeared with bug guts, and then there it was ... just his head ... sitting there, smiling on the driver's seat. And I could just feel it in my gut ... his body would never be found."

I could see his head, too, and he was singing to Saundra that Nirvana cover of the old Lead Belly song, *"My girl, my girl, don't lie to me; tell me where did you sleep last night? In the pines, in the pines, where the sun don't ever shine, I will shiver the whole night through."*

Saundra rambled on for a little more, but I didn't hear her. Though part of me felt special because she chose to share this with me before any of her Facebook friends or in a 140 character Tweet. Some things needed to be spoken, even if only partially heard.

A few more days would pass and finals came to an end. I had signed on to teach a summer course, Sociology through Popular Music. I was actually looking forward to it, though I wondered if they would have me back to Stockton in the fall. At some point during the week I picked up most of my things from Clementine's house and took them over to Saundra's. On Friday night I went over to just "check up" on the place, only to find the locks had been changed. Peering in through the big window by the front door, the place appeared empty.

"There was a big movin' truck here while you was out down campus," one of the neighbors said. "Damn Clementine locked, you out, huh? Ain't she the funny one? You think Bibbs gonna have one of his famous barbecues soon?"

"I couldn't say," I said, and I strolled back downaways to Saundra's place.

Early Saturday morning there was a knock at Saundra's door. I had been tossing and turning all night, still drunk and wide awake. I stumbled quietly out into the living room to see who it was. As I opened the door, it was still relatively dark outside, and crisp night air billowed in through the screen. I flicked on the porch light and there stood a youngish-looking serious man in a golf shirt and khakis.

"I saw your office was closed for the summer," he said quietly. "I apologize for the early hour call on a weekend."

"Do I know you?" I asked.

"I'm a colleague of, um-hum," he coughed mechanically. "Agent McThune."

"I'm sorry, do you have the right place? Who are you looking for?"

"Umm, you. I was told I could find you here now. I have something for you that she wanted me to pass along." He held up a white, letter-sized envelope. "May I?"

I cracked open the screen door just enough for him to slip it to me.

"Thank you," I said. I was puzzled by the idea of a letter. I could see the handwritten ink on folded-lined paper through the front of the envelope. "Couldn't she have just called or emailed?" I still wasn't sure who she was, though something in my gut told me it was Clementine … or Cynthia … or my wife even. Though the truth was I hadn't heard anything about or from my wife since April when she was trapped in Copenhagen under the Eyjafjallajokul ash cloud, and I had only learned about that from her Facebook status. Even I couldn't help but look, though there had been no updates in nearly a month. Who this Agent McThune was I hadn't a clue.

The young man smiled. "Well, professor, in this day and age, a personally hand-delivered, hand-written letter is about the only thing we can't track." He stepped down from the porch and disappeared into the morning darkness still enshrouding the Downs.

I turned off the porch light but left the door open for the cool air. I sat down on the couch and flipped on the lamp on the side table. I read it quickly, didn't digest it all, half-read like I half-heard Saundra's description of her dream. Maybe I was afraid if I heard or read the whole thing the person I thought I was would disappear.

She wrote … *I couldn't just leave you like that. I know the signs too well. I know some people tied to AA back in Philadelphia. Here are their email addresses. I think your wife deserves a call too. I really started to care about you. I should've never allowed myself to get so close and compromise the operation, but I knew for sure you weren't involved in any of it. And sometimes life does funny things and you can't control who you meet and who you like. I hope you don't hate me for lying to you, and I'm sorry about the house, it never was mine, just a front. I hope you can understand, and part of me thinks you can because I always felt like you were playing a role, too, hiding away out there under cover. I know you won't let anyone, not even poor Saundra, see this letter. I trust you. I wish I could tell you everything but I can't. I wish you well. I wish we could've met under different circumstances in better days. And please, you have to start taking better care of yourself. —Your darling Clementine.*

Before I knew it, sunlight was streaming in the through the windows and the screen door. An hour or so must've passed and I must've dozed off. Little Bubb had awoke and got into some kind of mess in the kitchen. He was sitting next to me fully dressed in a t-shirt and shorts with just his left shoe on and chocolate (perhaps from some cookies) smeared on his left cheek. His hands were unidentifiably sticky, too, and he was pretending to drive a car, his little hands gripping an imaginary steering wheel as some car commercial played on the TV. "Vroom, vrooooom!" he imitated the sounds form the television.

It was then I realized how long it had been since I went for a spin in the old Bella Vista neighborhood where so many fond memories had gone to die after the incident with the female student at Temple. Suddenly I felt compelled. With his momma asleep we could steal away and make a great escape.

I took his dirty hand and said, "C'mon let's get you cleaned up."

"Why?" he asked.

"Do ya wanna go for a ride?"

"Where?"

"Into Philadelphia."

"Roy Halla-halla-halladay!" he sang. He really did pay attention to those Phillies' games.

"Sure," I told him. "Maybe we'll see Roy Halladay. But I can't promise that."

"That's okay," he said patting my leg. "Let's go for a ride!"

Ga'head, take a ride, his momma would probably say if she were awake. For a moment I thought we might never head back down Gallow's way, but part of me wanted to be there with Saundra when she found out the truth about Bibbs. Yet another part of me could see my wife standing in front of our house in Bella Vista and asking, not in a scolding way, but sincerely and with a twinge of exhaustion, "And just when is this little sociological experiment of yours going to end?"

BZ NIDITCH

Adrienne Rich's gone

One short year ago
on a cold March day
trailing dust
snow and ashes
you passed us by
in the early dawn
you were never late
for a woman's expression
to astonish us
with words, glances, pain
even at your readings,
you rightly disturbed us
we watching your wise face
with lively silver threads
from your pocket poems
now opened up
to feminine freedoms
from hidden woolen scarves
and a daughter's handkerchief
of controlled tears
you, Adrienne knitted out
those kept oppressed
by some man's power trip
in bondage and shelters
from home wreckers
and violent quarrels,
you offer a way
through a poetry
of confessional talk
to look at our nature
differently.

DAVID SYNDER

NPC

It was immediately hailed as a masterpiece. A work of interactive art. A revolution in gaming. A gift to the world.

For Karina, it was a gift to herself, and to Darren. An engagement present she could be proud of. One that Darren could not otherwise provide. In the year of their relationship, he had bought them so many things: in this room alone, there was the couch, the loveseat, and the easy chair, all brown leather, each almost unnervingly yielding to weight. And then there were the cars, matching convertibles with "HIS" and "HERS" license plates. The trip to Disneyworld, where Darren had pranced around like a marionette, posing with every anthropomorphic animal he came across as Karina giggled, aimed and shot. And, of course, there was the house itself, Darren's engagement gift, which they had moved into just a week ago. An oversized colonial in Westchester, it was four stories of tasteful luxury, all selected and purchased by Darren. His company had developed the property years ago, but he'd only now bought it himself. He said he'd been waiting for his proper princess.

Karina, unable to match Darren's spending power, had also failed to equal his whimsy or general competence. She'd bought video games he already owned, knitted ill-fitting socks, and blackened cinnamon rolls, the icing congealing atop each one like a burn cream. Only one of her gifts could be labeled a success, and that one had left a smattering of resentment on her end. She'd made a few calls and arranged for a celebrated centerfold photographer to compile an album of lingerie shots, the first and only time she had posed that way for a professional. It deeply rankled her that she was paying for the arrangement rather than being paid, but Darren's reaction justified the act. When he became truly excited about something, like photos of Karina on a bed of velvet, nearly nude, staring out with her sultriest gaze, then his body would tense and his eyes expand, and the overall effect was that he reminded her of the first boy she'd slept with: the awed look on his face, mind blown over by the sudden reality of a living, naked woman in his presence.

Darren had that look now. "There you are!" he squealed once the console was running and he'd entered the game's realm. He held the controller in his lap, firmly but carefully, like a breakable thing, and the way he rubbed the joysticks reminded Karina of the massages he was so fond of supplying. As he pushed and pulled, the landscape on the screen – a meadow, a wispy blue sky, waves of grass so well rendered that you could see the reflection of the sun striking and stroking each blade – slid along, reflecting the main character's (Darren had named his Maxwell) changing perspective as he moved forward. And as the character moved, so, too, did his companion. "She even walks like you!" said Darren.

She did. The character, Anya Odelay, moved like Karina, stood like Karina, stared like Karina. Her voice was Karina's, recorded over the course of hundreds of sessions, thousands of hours of Karina reciting an infinite-feeling variety of words and phrases and noises, each with multiple inflections. "Where should we go?" she'd said, and "Where should I go?" and "Where should I go?" and on and on. She had worn a special black bodysuit bedecked with microchips and sensors and cameras, giving her the appearance of a hi-tech, uncommonly svelte bondage slave. On a wide blue square mat surrounded on three sides by lime green walls so much brighter than the rest of the studio space that they seemed to summon and swallow all other light, Karina had walked, she had run, jumped, climbed, swam, sat, danced, slept, wept, smiled tenderly into a series of impassive cameras. There were other model-actors, too, but only occasionally. For the most part, there were only engineers and programmers in the studio, in the dark outside the mat, and Karina alone in the green.

Karina considered herself a model by trade, but it was a difficult classification to defend. Several years past prime modeling age, she had booked no shows and had graced no covers; a few department store catalogs and a single magazine advertisement were the total of her accomplishments. Consequently, she'd had to support herself with a series of clerical positions. Even this recent job was not particularly lucrative. But the lack of compensation didn't bother Karina. It wasn't about money. It was about establishing herself. This was her star-making performance – modeling and acting. An achievement to be proud of. She may not have developed the game's software or written the dialogue or digitally created the world, but it still felt like a pure product of herself.

Darren had stopped Maxwell's forward progress and was now manipulating the controller to examine Anya in greater detail. She stood passively, shifting her weight from one foot to the other as Darren panned up her long legs, over her compact torso and dangling, somehow silky arms, ending on her pale face, smooth yet defined, as if whittled from soap. Her short brown hair lilted in the game realm's wind.

"You look beautiful," Darren said, his voice rising with that childlike wonder of his. Karina, watching him, felt all the unavoidable worries that accompany an engagement dissipate. She could see a future with this man. One of comfort and delight.

Darren put down the controller. He faced Karina. His smiled flattened into a familiar smirk, his eyes into a familiar leer. "Don't you want to keep playing?" asked Karina, slipping off her left sock with her right foot.

"Yes, I do," said Darren.

She laughed and, under his steady weight, sank into the couch. As he nibbled on her earlobe, he whispered, "I used to have a crush on Princess Peach. I suppose this is as close as I'll get."

Karina licked his neck and gripped his thigh. "I have a tiara," she said.

She felt Darren stiffen.

Twenty minutes later, they were rollicking in bed, he on top of her, the tiara atop her head, digging into her scalp with each push. Karina didn't mind, though, for Darren was performing even more admirably than normal. And he always performed admirably. The new mattress was still novel to her and, like all the furniture Darren chose, too soft. They found their balance, though, and were cavorting along when, abruptly, Darren's rhythm altered, became irregular for fifteen or so seconds. Under his breath, he hummed a complementary tune, a calypso rhythm. Unless Karina was very mistaken, Darren had taken a moment to thrust to a rough approximation of the Super Mario Bros. theme song. For the rest of the session, Karina debated whether she should appreciate this as yet another example of the silly inventiveness and unselfconsciousness which she loved, or if she should resent that he'd indulged his own whimsy while he was with her. In her, in fact.

Afterwards, they lay together, her sweaty shoulder on his sweaty chest, the tiara resting awkwardly akimbo on her head, tangled with her hair. After an exaggerated exhale, Darren said, "I shouldn't have been a developer. I was made to be a plumber."

"Sure," said Karina, "and I should have been a princess."

Darren chuckled. "Well, you're a model," he said. "That's pretty close, right?"

Karina edged herself off of Darren. "I don't think so."

"You're my princess, anyway," he said. He kissed her cheek, rolled over, and was soon asleep. She spent a few minutes attempting to extract the tiara from her hair, but it was like a bird's nest, held together by sweat and mousse, and ultimately she surrendered, falling asleep still affixed to the crown.

* * *

The game broke every sales record there was. Within a month, it was the best selling game of the year. Soon thereafter, the best of all time. It was estimated that thefts of this game outnumbered total sales for all others. Video game retailers joined software titans and energy giants at the top of the stock market. Government revenue derived from the sales tax on copies sold accounted for a fifth of all U.S. revenue.

Karina's fame spread, in a sense. She spent most of her time in New York, taking a train in from Westchester in the late morning and meeting Darren for dinner near his firm's office downtown. In the interim, she loved strolling through the city without a menial job or bills to worry over, with no real responsibilities or tasks to complete other than occasional check-ins with her agent, Marie. Most of all, she could now indulge herself, thanks to the recent melding of hers and Darren's bank accounts. If a dress or a hat or a pair of shoes caught her eye, she did not feel any guilt or even doubt about buying. She wouldn't admit it, but it was one of the best things about her and Darren's recent engagement.

And as she wandered New York, shopping and strolling, she was finally recognized. A British tourist asked if she'd mind posing for a picture, and a few days later she saw a Japanese teenager in Times Square wearing a promotional t-shirt with Anya's image printed on the front. For the first time, her signature was sought for non-bureaucratic reasons, although the recipients oftentimes seemed disappointed when they saw what she had written. Everywhere she went, she noticed passersby stopping to gaze at her, ribbing their companions and pointing, brightening when she smiled and waved. Karina brightened with them. She had long desired fame, and now she had it. And even though it wasn't exactly Karina who was being recognized, it still satisfied. Prior to this, she had only been recognized by a stranger once, and that had been Darren.

It was just over a year ago, in line at a coffee shop during her lunch break. The pastries pleaded with her to accept them into the nirvana of her digestive system; particularly insistent were the bite-sized cinnamon-vanilla muffins, looking forlorn and endangered, surrounded as they were by the more mountainous treats. Karina was famished, but she had not resisted the hot dog vendor and the pretzel cart just to lose her willpower now. She ordered a low-fat cappuccino. The barista stepped away to build the drink and Karina focused on ignoring the nearly audible pleas of the delicacies. Then the man behind her said, "They look good, don't they?"

Karina, doubly annoyed that she was being accosted at her lunch hour and that he was also further torturing her empty stomach, had intended to tell the man off. When she turned, however, she was immediately disarmed by his debonair beauty, sterling silver hair, his fine suit, and the delight which seemed to illuminate his face, as if he knew that this, right now, would be the best moment of his day.

She did not demand that he leave her alone. She said, "Very tempting."

"I've never been one to resist a temptation," said Darren. To his barista he said, "I'll take a mocha latte and the little muffins there."

"How many?"

"You know, I think I'll just take all of them." To Karina, he added, "I have a feeling I'll really like them."

Karina smiled. She felt that she should be put off by the showmanship, but overriding that was the pleasure she took in having a handsome, confident, clearly well-off man play with her.

He reminded her of a few of her more successful model friends' husbands.

Then he said, "You look different dry."

A cold alarm materialized in her chest. "Excuse me?"

"Before today, I'd only ever seen you shampooing under a waterfall. That was you, wasn't it?"

The panic evaporated, replaced by a form of affection that Karina had never known. He was referencing her lone magazine advertisement. While a number of her friends had reached the upper echelons of the modeling world, fashion shows and music videos, Karina had trailed behind in complete anonymity. Now, no longer complete.

"I had to step out for a minute," she said. "It's bad for your skin to soak too long. It loses its luster."

"Oh, I don't think you need to worry about that. You're looking plenty lusterful to me. Positively radiant."

Darren's barista handed him the bag of muffins. He pulled one out and held it before her, to feed her. Normally, Karina would feel hugely embarrassed by such a gesture, and would react indignantly at the forwardness. Now, though, she slipped out her tongue, and Darren, like a doting parent, fed her the treat. As she chewed, luxuriating in the comforting sweetness and the knowledge that her hunger pangs would soon soften, her own barista returned and gave her her cappuccino. The heated porcelain warmed her hands. Karina swallowed. "Thank you," she'd said.

* * *

It was labeled an RPG, but only for lack of a better term. The game was not like any other. It did not have a single, easily-conquered primary campaign, nor was it open and endless. There were many storylines, many plots to pursue, many mysteries. Play progressed in different directions for different players, to the degree that no two gameplay experiences were alike. Players moved through, not levels, but rather eras in their characters' lives. The circumstances would change drastically between these eras: the character could start as a detective investigating a homicide, then become a traveling bard loved by man, a boxer hated by all, the lone survivor of a tragedy. No matter the scenario, the character was

191

always consistent, defined by the player's choices throughout, and players felt that as their characters grew, so, too, did they.

The media, unable to get anywhere near the finale prior to its release, had based their reviews on thirty to fifty hours of gameplay. Had they had more time, and had they not been so utterly overwhelmed by its scope, its story, and the sheer brilliance of its control system, then their reviews may have warned readers that the game required an investment of more than money, that players could and should expect to devote hours and hours and hours to exploring its myriad possibilities, and much emotional energy in its outcomes.

Across the globe, plants and pets were neglected as the game consumed huge swaths of each player's day. The world economy dipped and sputtered as productivity decreased across the board, while sick and vacation days proliferated with abandon. Video games joined narcotics and alcohol in the American Psychiatric Society's definition of substance dependence.

Websites and forums dedicated to gaming were overrun by posts from players requesting assistance and sharing their own experiences in concerted efforts to vanquish the game. But the game's storylines were so sprawling and so delicately predicated on what occurred previously that these efforts were futile – each player's progress was too singular for another's to be of use. Weeks after the game was released, no reports had surfaced of the end being reached, and like pressure systems, a heavy sense of frustration began to amass and swirl inside each and every gamer.

* * *

As Karina entered the house, she heard Darren cry, "Bullshit!" The TV was on, and she could hear a controller being clicked and swiveled.

"Darren?" she called.

He didn't respond, but his mutterings fluttered from the den to the foyer, disconcerting her. Darren was not the sort to display aggravation. Despite the pressures of his career as CEO of a billion-dollar land development group, she could only recall a single occasion when he'd betrayed any real sense of inward disturbance. Three months ago, her friend Therese had obtained a last-second invite to a posh lawn party in Long Island and Karina, eager to see another titan's particular form of lavishness, had canceled dinner reservations with Darren without much notice. When she saw him next, Darren was short with her, conspicuously unfrivolous, and, for the few hours his mood lasted, Karina had become hyperaware of his true age – he had seemed, for the first time, like an older man, weighted and worn by life. Barring that lone exception, though, he had always appeared totally in control and capable of handling anything. Especially a video game.

He was hunched forward on the sofa, curved like a shrimp's shell, and just as rigid. His loafers and corduroy pants blended in with the dark brown leather of the couch, cocoa-colored rug and mahogany paneling, as if it was all of a single entity. His left cheek indented as he chewed at it. As she crept in, Karina felt like a servant invading her master's privacy out of concern for his health. "Everything okay?" she asked.

Darren startled, and it looked to Karina like he momentarily considered stashing the controller between the cushions. His reaction reminded her of the time she'd caught him masturbating. On that occasion, after the first surprised second, he'd abandoned pretense and asked if she could lend him a hand with something, and she had laughed and done so. Now, he recovered, but his stiffness didn't leave him completely. He said, "I didn't hear you come in."

"Um, okay," said Karina. She sat down beside him as his attention returned to the game. The landscape was dark, with low, shadowy buildings hovering above a cobbled road. Somber-faced laborers marched on both sides, some carrying bags or baskets, all of their clothes drab and ragged but for the computer screens embedded in their sleeves. This was one of the characteristics of the game: it blended aspects of the past and future into all of its environs. The effect was destabilizing, imbuing a sense of dreaminess into an otherwise meticulously realistic world.

"I spoke to Marie today," Karina said. "I'm doing a fashion show in Budapest in December."

"Wow, that's great," said Darren. "That's awesome. Because of the game?"

"Might have something to do with it."

"See? I told you. All you needed was a chance to show these

designers how great you are at walking. Your walking in this game is superb, by the way. Really graceful."

After a moment, he noticed her silence and turned to her. Seeing her expression, he said, "Hey, you know I'm just kidding. Haven't I always told you that your break was coming? Didn't I keep saying that?"

Karina had to admit that he had. In times past, she had at times become desolate, and she had lamented to Darren that she wasn't good enough, that she'd peaked with a shampoo advertisement. She'd needed Darren's reassurance and comfort, and he had provided. "You've always been supportive," she said.

"And I always will be." He grinned, then returned to the game.

Karina watched him play. Maxwell ran along the streets, turning at times, ignoring any characters that seemed inclined to talk, following some directive which Karina couldn't discern. On the edge of the screen, Anya's left leg and arm occasionally appeared, never quite reaching Darren's character.

"We need to set a date," said Karina. "For the wedding."

"No we don't," said Darren, his face faintly lit by the television's glare. "It's all taken care of."

Karina waited for Darren to elaborate, and when he didn't she said, "What do you mean?"

"I already booked everything. The first weekend in March. Six months should be plenty of time to figure out the rest."

"You booked 'everything?' What's everything?"

"Hotel, caterer. I guess that's it. I'll get to the rest soon enough."

Generally, Karina liked Darren's initiative, that he freed her from worrying about logistics and other practical matters. But this was much too much. She said, "Cancel them."

His eyes flicked toward her.

"You need to consult me before you make these kinds of decisions," she said. "We need to discuss them."

Karina saw his grip on the controller tighten, the bones of his fingers like spider legs, the same fine hairs. A long moment passed, and then he eased back and said, "Sure thing, babe. No problem." His thumbs started to roam over the controls once more.

Karina leaned further into the couch. She thought about the

furniture here in the den: all smooth leather, all too large, too spongy. What they needed were some solid, wooden chairs. Maybe with creeping vines carved into their straight backs. But now there was no room, and she regretted not taking an active role in the furnishing process.

She watched Darren, not comprehending. Every character he passed looked up, as if willing to engage in conversation with Maxwell, but Darren kept him moving forward. "I still don't even know what this game's about," said Karina. She'd said so many lines of such variety, she had not been able to detect a narrative.

"It's not really about anything." Darren glanced at her, then dipped the controller deeper into the hollow of his lap. "Want to play?"

She knew what he meant, but pretended as though she did not. "I told you, it'd be too weird. Seeing myself like that."

"You get used to it," he said.

Maxwell was now crossing a small courtyard filled with merchants selling newspapers, fruit, watches and plane tickets. In the center of the square was a crowd, moping without apparent purpose. Maxwell maneuvered around this assemblage, skidded down an alley, then hopped through a dark doorway. Darren unfurled his back, waited. Nothing happened. After a moment he had Maxwell spin around. Anya was noticeably absent.

Darren groaned. Then he had Maxwell head back towards the courtyard.

"Problem?" asked Karina.

"No, no," said Darren, working his way through the crowd, looking at each face now. "Not a problem. The game can get frustrating at times. You get sidetracked." As he said this, Anya filled the screen and Maxwell stopped moving. Karina recognized her own lips and remembered speaking the words as Anya said, "What now?"

"But it's totally worth it," said Darren, and flashed that winning smile.

* * *

Desperation set in.

Unlike other challenging games, this one's difficulty did not stem from hordes of weapon-wielding zombies or gap-filled race tracks or well-hidden keys. The trouble was that players had to regularly make choices whose consequences would only become apparent much later in the game – performing a rescue mission now meant that a more significant quest was no longer performable, or a player might retrieve an item for an important character only to discover that that same item was needed by an even more important character, and the player's course was therefore elongated by a dozen more hours of gameplay. Weeks passed, and still not a single player managed to provide proof of completion.

Betting sites began to offer odds, accepting enormous wagers on the date when this feat would finally be achieved. The headline "Game Remains Unbeaten" became a standard facet of every news site's homepage, the story unchanged each day save for an update on the duration. TV shows covering addicted players' interventions rose in the ratings. For the first year ever, deaths from heart-failure caused by excessive video game playing reached the double digits, and then the triple.

Internet message boards swelled with invective. Threats were crafted, targeted at the most obvious source of gamer frustration: Anya. It was soon considered a matter of fact that this character's tendency to get lost, need saving, or require the completion of otherwise unnecessary quests was the only real flaw in an otherwise perfect game. There were more than a few death threats impotently aimed at this fictional character.

Karina read them all. She couldn't stop. She would retreat to the bedroom early, leaving Darren playing in the den, and she would sit cross-legged in the middle of their massive mattress, reading on her laptop. Hours later, she'd notice the house creaking and whistling with the night wind, and Karina would feel like the two floors above her were full of phantoms. She'd momentarily consider going upstairs to dispel her inane fright, but this urge would soon pass. She'd cover her head with a pillow and try to sleep.

One morning, she told Darren about the death threats. He was sitting at the table, watching the news, eating a glazed doughnut. "Maybe you should stop reading them," he said.

Karina looked through the pantry for something tasty and healthy. She only saw the former: sugar-soaked cereals, another box of doughnuts. Karina was realizing it would be difficult to maintain a respectable weight in this household. Although Darren somehow managed. "That won't make them go away," she said.

Darren chewed, then said, "The threats aren't really about you, though. They're about the character. No one wants to kill you."

She closed the pantry. She'd thought that this was what she wanted him to say, but hearing his dismissal annoyed her. Leaning against the pantry door, feeling the metal handles as though they were girded to her back, she said, "You don't know that. Maybe they'd want to stop me from making a sequel. There are plenty of reasons why someone would want to kill me."

For a moment, it seemed to Karina that Darren didn't know how to respond to this. But then he chuckled, walked beside her, patted her butt, kissed her temple and said, "Whatever helps you sleep at night, babe." Then he left for work, leaving Karina in the kitchen with nothing she needed to do.

* * *

There were protests.

Everywhere, all at once. An internet-originated mass uprising against Anya. They congregated in all major cities with nearly revolutionary furor. There was no real objective to these demonstrations other than the collective release of pent-up disgust.

On that day, Karina was once again in New York. She had come into the city to meet with her agent, and it had gone poorly. Marie informed her that the Budapest show wasn't happening. Or, rather, it was happening, but not with Karina. When Karina had demanded an explanation, Marie had assumed a patronizing expression and said, "You have a bit of an image problem, dear."

Afterwards, Karina decided to distract herself with shopping. But while she told herself that it was the professional setback and death threats which she needed to be distracted from, really, she knew it was Darren. Despite his assurances, they still had not discussed a new wedding date. Whenever she brought it up, he became exhausted and stressed from work, and if she complained that he had seemed perfectly energetic beforehand, he'd point out that that was easy for her to say – she wasn't working. She couldn't argue with that. She strongly suspected that he had not actually canceled the original bookings.

And then there was his underwhelming response to her death threat situation. It wasn't that he hadn't made any effort to protect her; it was that he was so sure that she didn't need protecting. That she was unworthy of purposeful violence.

Hours later, Karina emerged onto Columbus Circle and saw the crowd. They hovered around the statue of the space's namesake, ringed by a thin strip of manicured brush, white and pink flowers and leaping streams from hidden sprinklers. They jostled and shouted, chants of "An-ya must go!" and "Fu-uck An-ya!" Their outcry surmounted the rumbles and roars of the surrounding cars, and the hostility smashed into Karina like a solid wall of humidity after the cool of air conditioning. It was stunning to see such anger and revulsion. She realized that she'd never before seen anyone react so strongly towards her.

There was no leader initially, but as she watched a young man climbed onto the base of the statue, holding something limp and white in his hand. He spread it out, revealing that it was a t-shirt with Anya's image on it, one of the game's byproducts which had sold well initially and then not at all. It was the same t-shirt she'd seen on the Japanese teenager in Times Square, when she was first encountering her fame. She watched as the man pulled a lighter from his pant pocket and, to the crowd's roaring approval, set the shirt on fire. And as she watched her doppelganger's image burn, she noticed that the arsonist was that very same Japanese teen.

For a moment, Karina wished that Darren was there, just so she could prove that he was wrong and she was right. Then she fled, dashing down avenues and occasional side streets, hopping through traffic, wondering whether the mean glares she noticed were due to her behavior or creation. She quickly tired and stopped to rest against the plyboard covering a nearby building. As she leaned against the weak wood, catching her breath, she noticed that right underneath the black stenciled "POST NO BILLS" someone had spray-painted a crude caricature of Anya. They'd covered it with a red no-smoking sign, and added the caption, "Just Say No To Anya."

* * *

Karina awoke in the night. Darren was not beside her. Earlier, she had once again brought up the wedding arrangements, and once again Darren had deflected her concerns, telling her not to worry about it. She told him she should worry about it, and Darren shook his head but offered no rebuttal. Later they'd had rougher-than-usual sex, Darren splaying his elbows so that his full weight bore down upon her. There had been none of the usual playfulness, and afterwards they'd not spoken, just rolled to their own sides and slept.

Now he was gone, and Karina heard the echoes of repeating gunshots. She knew that there were guns in the game, having held a dozen or so surprisingly heavy models. But overall, it had not seemed particularly violent.

She nimbled down the stairs, through the hall, and peered around the wooden support beam. Darren was on the couch. His character moved through a metallic hallway, like an oversized heating duct, and he had a pistol drawn. Maxwell turned one corner, then another, and came face to face with Anya. Anya had her own gun and raised it towards Maxwell, but before she could fire, Darren clicked. There was a splash of red particles where Anya's head had been. Her body collapsed, then dissolved.

"What the fuck?" said Karina.

"Did I wake you?" asked Darren, eyes not leaving the screen. "I'll turn it down."

"Why did you shoot her?"

"Oh, that wasn't Anya. That was some guy from France. They added a deathmatch mode; you can play as whatever character you want."

The moment he finished explaining, another Anya appeared, and once again, Darren delivered a fatality. Karina wondered if there were any areas where Darren was unsuccessful.

"I'm going back to bed," she said. "Good night."

"Love you," said Darren. His tongue slipped through his sealed lips as Maxwell danced and exchanged fire with a distant enemy.

As she hiked back up the stairs, Karina heard the sound of Darren's gun reloading.

199

* * *

That night she had a dream. She was walking through the house and seeing it as though she was playing the game: all things faintly luminescent, flattened out, nothing quite random enough. She reached the den, and yet it did not look like the den. All the furniture was gone and the dark wood walls had been replaced with metal siding, glinting with light from an unseen source. Darren was there. He looked like himself, the only facet of this world which had not been rendered into the game's visuals. But he moved like a character in the game, just shy of human, and his face was utterly expressionless as he raised his pistol.

He didn't fire, though. He just kept it aimed at Karina, and Karina, even after she realized that he was never going to shoot, remained in its path, unwilling or unable to move. She couldn't tell which.

* * *

There was rejoicing.

Celebrations in the streets, booze rolling through sewer grates like runoff. Fireworks over rivers and lakes, spontaneous parades. It was like the Fourth of July, Mardi Gras, and Cinco de Mayo combined into one worldwide day of revelry. Border disputes were paused as they had been for the ancient Olympics, allowing enemies to lock hands and sing. Fewer murders were committed in this 24 hour period than in any previously recorded.

The game's creators had released a downloadable patch which allowed players to delete Anya from the game entirely. Nothing else was affected. You could play through the game as though she'd never been there.

Karina was devastated. Despite the scorn, despite the unanticipated blow to her career, she still felt a brutal loss. Her only creation of any note or value, and it was being washed away from the world by popular demand. She wondered if a single player would opt to save her from oblivion.

When Darren found her, she was in the couch in the den, curled into herself like a cat. He gently lowered himself next to her and stroked her hair, the slight pull soothing her scalp. "Hey, I'm sorry," he said.

"Not your fault everyone hates me," she said, not letting go of her coil or gloom.

"No one hates you. I don't hate you. And besides, that's not what I meant. I mean, I am sorry about that, but I'm also sorry about me. How I've been treating you recently. I know I haven't been giving you the support you need." He moved his hand from her hair to her body, her back, side, stomach. Karina flinched when he reached there, the softness which had once been firm as dry ground. But Darren didn't balk. He kept on caressing, until finally he had coaxed Karina out of her loop. She tucked herself into the crook of his arm, nestled until comfortable.

And yet she wasn't wholly comfortable, because she didn't want to be. She wanted the grief. She just couldn't resist letting Darren draw it from her, and knowing this made the comfort distasteful. She felt like she was living in medieval times and he was the physician, blood-letting his default solution, and Karina sensing that it wouldn't work.

"I promise to do better," he said.

Karina did not know what he meant by that, and she doubted he did, either. It seemed impossible to her that Darren would or could be anything other than what he was. Hearing his words, his vague promise of improvement, Karina was once more reminded of her first boyfriend, in the days after her lost virginity as he misspoke and misstepped, still learning how to navigate a serious relationship. But Darren was not a young boyfriend. Darren was her fiancée, and nearly twice her age.

Wiggling to create enough distance for her to see his face, Karina said, "I don't think I can handle the wedding prep for a while. Do you think you can take care of all that?"

Darren smiled, that same boyish smile. Too many teeth, Karina thought. Too happy. He said, "No worries, babe. Consider it done." He pulled her in tight again. "You don't need to worry about anything."

"I'm glad," said Karina.

* * *

The next day, Darren left for the weekend, a conference in Detroit. For the first time since moving in, Karina would be alone in the house for more than a day. She visited the kitchen, the bathrooms, the exercise room, the library, the spare bedrooms. Room to room, examining the furniture, the rugs, the paintings, the paint, looking for anything that she'd chosen, that she'd supplied. She found only one item of consequence: a framed blowup of one of her lingerie shots that Darren had insisted on hanging in the corner of his walk-in closet, hidden except when parting his winter coats. She removed it from the wall, finding the silver frame heavier than expected, and brought it down into the den. There was a painting of a hibernating bear there, rolled into a ball, one ear sticking straight up from its cocked head like a dorsal fin. This was Darren's playful nod to the room as man-cave. Karina removed the print and replaced it with her lingerie photo. The pale gleam of her curving skin shone out from the darkened, earthy wall.

Then she turned on the game. She intended to open up Darren's campaign, to see if Anya was still there. But once she reached the main menu screen, Karina decided not to play as Maxwell. Instead, she began a new game. She named her character K and started playing.

And kept playing. Hours and hours. She couldn't stop. After an initial period of struggle, she became accustomed to the controls and began to see what made the game so popular, its players so passionate. It had everything you could want: compelling storylines, mysteries to solve, worlds to explore, romance. The romantic tension between K and Anya was tantalizing. Anya was charming, seductive in her gazes and movements. Karina remembered it all, and she didn't see how anyone could possibly hate her. She kept playing.

The sun set, the sun rose. Karina stopped briefly to use the bathroom and to drink a huge glass of water, but that was it. The old hunger pangs from her diet days returned, the ones which she had so despised in the past. Now, she welcomed the growling and gnawing. It was revitalizing. She kept playing.

Finally, after a whole day of nonstop play, she started to hate Anya, too. She needed help too often, distracting Karina from more urgent objectives. She would get lost, would ask for supplies, would lag behind. After realizing that Anya's helplessness had caused K to miss an important delivery, Karina, starving and exhausted and feeling very twitchy, drew K's gun and aimed it at Anya. Anya reacted like Karina knew she would: a shriveled, pouty face, the epitome of pathetic. She remembered making the face, and the idea that she was capable of such an expression depressed her.

Then there was a flicker. Maybe it was the lack of sleep, or maybe the lack of nourishment, or maybe she really lost her mind for a moment, but the screen seemed to calm itself, to cease its electronic buzzing. Anya became calm, too. Her expression was peaceful. Karina watched, her controller inactive, as Anya, her face a crooked grin, reached forward and took hold of K's gun-wielding hand. Anya brought the gun to her own temple and, staring straight at the screen, at Karina, nodded and closed her eyes.

Karina shut down the game.

* * *

She imagined him returning. Announcing, "Babe, I'm home!" Dropping his bag as he swung shut the front door. Climbing up the stairs, peeking into the bedroom, calling, "Babe?" He'd go back down, check the backyard, the pool, the kitchen. He'd be irritated that she did not let him know where she was going, when she would be back. He'd stow his annoyance, decide to play the game for a while.

She imagined him falling to the couch, a puff of cushion displaced. He'd turn on the television and the console, pick up the controller, wait. Nothing would happen; the screen would stay black. He'd heave himself off the couch with a groan, crawl down to the lower shelf of the entertainment center, hit eject on the console. It would be empty. Confused, he'd pull open the drawer, flip through the cases, the games he used to play but had ignored utterly since the arrival of this one. She imagined him finding the proper case, unclicking the plastic clasps, and ripping it open, only to discover that the game was not there. Discovering, instead, the note she left. Reading: The princess is in another castle.

SIMON FRIEL

The Retreat

The retreat sat at the top of a high valley. It faced an old town, a couple of kilometres away, which rested beside and grew up impressively from the narrow river that ran through the valley's centre.

Our room was on the lower level of the retreat's complex; the part that had been excavated directly from the rock face. The name plate on our door read *Lorca*. Our neighbours were *Dalí* and *Buñuel*.

Natural smoothed down stone made up the back wall of our room. It swelled out at its centre like the belly of a pregnant woman, creating a natural border between the two single beds. The crying episode during the previous night's sex made me feel like that wasn't going to be a problem.

Inma, or Carne, sat out on the sun filled terrace that cut a semicircular swathe before the line of the rooms. I walked carefully towards its edge and glanced down at the steep incline of jagged rock, parched sandy ground dotted with sporadic green bush, and the still turquoise water of the river.

The two hour drive inland from Valencia had been awkward. It got worse when I asked why she told me her name was Inma but her emails said they were from Carne. The answer she gave was garbled and inconclusive and the discomfort that the question heaped into the already strained mood within the car meant that I had to let it go.

The last hour of the journey had then passed in silence as we drove into a landscape that was increasingly brutal and beautiful. Our final destination was an extension on this theme and seemed to be located somewhere close to the very centre of isolation.

I looked out across the valley towards the town and wondered how many words it had taken to bring us here. Excluding a few emails, I estimated that it could not be any more than a thousand.

The night we met in Arambol was our most verbose. She was struggling to speak in a heavily accented English with a tall Russian that looked like Jesus as I entered the quiet cafe looking for a sign of life. I was not an expert on India and I had failed to understand that Goa only came alive two months later, when the monsoon stopped and the regulars migrated down from the Himalayas, or returned from the season in Ibiza.

Russian Jesus was fucked on ketamine. When he stood up, he swayed round in tight circles that sent his purple sarong flapping open and closed to reveal his cock.

I said something to the girl in Spanish to distract her from the show, either out of pity or out of arrogance, and when she turned, surprised and expectant at hearing her native tongue, I knew instantly that something significant had started.

Jesus disappeared with a dubious looking older English man, whose bad intentions were clearly excited rather than tempered by the Russian's mental state.

Inma and I sat on cushions on the floor of the cafe, drinking warm *Kingfisher* and smoking charras from Parvati valley. An excitable Ukrainian played excessively loud hard-trance and told too fast stories that he hoped she would understand. We shot each other knowing glances and exchanged intimate foreign banalities for the rest of the night.

The evening ended in a drunken, smoky haze: the good natured and infinitely sad Ukrainian in tears as he presented me with a bandana from the 1984 Sarajevo Winter Olympics. He had found it beside him in the middle of a field after being thrown there from a car crash that had left his best friend dead.

Nothing happened that night between Inma and I. We said our goodbyes and left each other as though it were forever. An only partly-fortuitous encounter in the same bar the following afternoon led to the discovery that our separate flights to Delhi got in at almost exactly the same time. We found each other easily enough in the lowly-lit, dusty chaos of baggage reclaim at Indira Gandhi airport, shared a taxi from the airport into Paharganj, and did nothing to correct the man on the desk of the hotel when he assumed we were a couple in search of only one room.

Inma touched my elbow gently. I snapped out of my wanderings into the lost past of little more than one month ago and looked down to where this stranger now sat beside me.

She smiled and rested her head naturally against my side.

"We go to the town?" She asked in the dreamy, hesitant tone that characterised her English.

"Si, vamos al pueblo," I agreed, hooking my arm softly around her neck and kissing her on the top of her head.

We walked down a narrow trail through the valley. The newness of this place and the warm pleasantness of the late afternoon unshackled and released us from the tension of our previous unease. The sun, falling behind us, cast our long, skinny shadows over the lifeless, blanched sand of this steep and narrow decline. Spindly grey branches of vicious flowerless tress snagged maliciously at our clothing and lashed small cuts across the bare skin of our legs, feet and arms as we passed.

In the town we ate a poor meal of dry, bony fish and drank cheap white wine in a noisy restaurant filled with drunk, chain smoking Spaniards clad mostly in Lycra.

The noise level made our quickly restored silence seem more natural, but beneath the toxic smoke cloud and the aggressive conviviality, I accepted that this needlessly extended relationship would not live beyond my 9 o'clock train back to Barcelona the following night. The adventure was over.

Delhi, Agra, Varanasi, Kolkata, Mamallapurum, Pondicherry, Varkala, Arambol. I knew nothing of India other than the names of the places I had stayed. My abiding memories of the trip were of cows, a news report of Usain Bolt winning Olympic gold, cow shit, a plane crash in Madrid, and the way the golden foil crackled and peeled away to reveal skin, hair and bone as another fresh corpse dissipated to dust on the main burning ghat in Benares.

I had put up walls and insulated myself away from the country and the possibilities that I might have hoped existed there. I had run, eyes closed, in fast forward from all of the experiences and challenges that I was not brave enough to face.

Inma assuaged my fear and postponed failure. She was a simple and familiar salvation.

A few correctly spoken words and extended glances. A couple of touches that lingered a part of a second too long. Then sex; an act that absolved me of all blame and allowed us both to feel as though we had in fact had a good time.

Now that we were here, isolated and far away from the fruitless promise of the exotic, everything seemed tawdry and sorrowful. I knew that soon I would wallow hungrily in the melancholy of this situation, and that she probably deserved better than to be thought of as simply another victim of my romanticised masochism.

We took a walk up through cobbled streets in the direction of the old fort that loomed overhead and dominated the town with all of the history and fantasy implicit in its nine centuries of longevity.

Las Cuevas del Diablo was written in black gothic letters on a red sandwich board resting in the middle of the pavement. Inma arched her right eyebrow at me in an upside down V of suggestion. I shrugged my shoulders and twitched my face back at her in acquiescence.

The *Devil's Caves* burrowed through the upper part of the hill on which the town had been built. Its corridors were dark and cluttered with clunky iron bicycles, pedal sewing machines, large empty casks, and oversized wooden wheels.

The antechambers that ran off from the corridors smelt of cat piss. More junk filled these rooms and the walls were adorned with photos of the moustachioed devil posing with Spanish B and C list celebrities.

We fled in the direction of the light, offered through an open door, away from the stank of damp decay and the cloy of prescribed mediocrity, and found refuge on a deep, open terrace. The devil was here pouring lemonade to two children from behind a bar. The sapphire sky of the fading day was fast dwindling from dusk to night. Lights flickered on in the retreat up on the opposite side of the valley. And the slither of what must at times have been a gushing river smeared a dead black trail through the centre of the valley's darkened floor.

Across the road from the caves, an old cinema had been converted into a museum. Long, unsteady tables with thin foldable legs were covered in postcards, copies of the local newspaper from the days of the Civil War, and Franco era stamps and coins. In the centre of the far wall there hung the stuffed head of a huge black bull.

We climbed some rickety ladders to reach the area that housed the cinema's cobweb-covered projector. Ancient farming tools were incongruously spread about the floor here.

A rusty, long bladed scythe. A hand drawn plough. Pitchforks. Spades.

I wondered on the life more honest and real that had once relied upon such simple instruments for survival. In that longing for something more authentic, I realised how I had shared nothing beyond the flimsiest level of superficiality with Inma. It was an easy default to dismiss and destroy rather than make even the slightest of efforts, but something had brought us together in this place where neither of us belonged.

I took up the pitchfork from the floor and spoke to her of how it seemed to me that the world's most basic values had been lost and left behind somewhere in the past. How more and more it felt like each step forward was just another virtual leap into a world I had no faith in. And the way progress seemed to be defined as little more than a succession of unjust wars and a blind march into a mass annihilation of the self.

I wanted her to soothe me, even though I understood that the words I used were not really my own or ones I especially believed in. I wanted her to recognise and protect something deep inside of me that I was too afraid to comprehend and confront alone.

I became conscious of my poor Spanish. The sounds stupid and wrong; each one rightly sabotaged and belittled the falsity of the words and sentiments they struggled to express. My mystification of the past and the desire for a forced connection was only serving to further sour the paucity of our present and increase the distance I felt between us.

I shut up.

Inma looked at me with tenderness.

"Why do you think you have to be special?" She asked.

Her response caught me off guard. There was only honest enquiry and interest in her words but I couldn't help but feel hurt and embarrassed by them.

"I just want to be better," I lied, looking down and pretending to study the weighty handle of the scythe.

A goat was slaughtered for dinner.

There were not many other guests staying at the retreat so the long fully prepared dining table felt wasteful and overly extravagant. A Swedish couple smiled a lot but could speak no

Spanish and excused themselves quickly after eating. One other couple sat directly across from Inma and I. The girl was dark haired and very petite. Her hair fell forward and hid most of her face. Her partner was a tall, dark and handsome latino cliche with broad shoulders and his hair pulled back tightly into a short ponytail. He was loud and made unfunny jokes that the Argentinians who ran the place pretended to laugh along with. On a couple of occasions I caught his bright green eyes looking at me a little longer than was necessary, encouraging me to join him in his fun. I flicked him a half-smile and took some bread and another tomato from the plate in the middle of the table.

We headed straight back to our room after dinner. Inma was tired. I stayed out on the patio in the darkness. I sat on a reclining chair and stared up into that impregnable ocean of infinite cold and celestial light. Shooting stars flit from within it occasionally like the dying embers of silent fireworks. Lower in the sky, beyond the dim outline of the castle walls, whispers of cloud unfurled into nothingness to reveal the faded lustre of a red crescent moon.

I had never known the night sky. Its portentous shadow show of ploughs, big dippers, and bears was not an education I had been afforded. I had silently feared the violence of its enormity but its implications were something that my innocence, ignorance, and hubris had conquered. I eschewed and extinguished its significance with speed and an insistence on those simple earthly pleasures that would always be awaiting me around the next corner.

In the darkest part of this night I recalled a dream. A man appeared there. He crept out from the corners of my consciousness and rested there in silence. He was important but I could not remember why. The realisation of who he was and why he came was always just beyond the reach of my comprehension. The letters and the words of the answer formed in my mind but they were impossible for me to ever fully grasp.

There was no malice in the man, but he moved slowly and forever away when I went towards him. His face was a horrific mask of compassion and fear. He wanted to help me but he was aware that it was his very presence that brought about my consternation.

He left as quietly as he had come. In his absence I felt the most profound emptiness and fear. My bones chilled and I would awake paralysed by the terror of the not knowing. In stages, the feeling would fade and a new idea began to take hold; a worse one – the possibility that he was in fact not important at all.

I stood up from my chair and opened the door to our room. A shallow strafe of light from the red moon trickled across the floor. Inma had pulled the two single beds away from the wall and together.

I undressed silently, got into the empty bed, and ran my fingers gently through the softness of her cold hair.

The next morning was beautiful. The sky was a soft, cloudless blue that shimmered with an intensity that verged to white above the town where the sun slowly rose into view.

Inma was sitting out on the terrace, talking quietly with the couple that had sat across from us at dinner. I squeezed her shoulder gently as I joined them. The girl looked down as I tried to acknowledge her. The guy stood up to offer me his hand.

She was Maria. He was Iván. His handshake was surprisingly weak and clammy.

Iván said that he knew a walk that we could take together down to the town. I wanted to spend the time alone with Inma but I could see she was keen not to disappoint her new friends.

We set off up the road that led away from the retreat and soon came to a small village that was set around a simple square, empty except for a stone cross in its centre.

A few children, playing with a ball, stopped their game and waved as we approached.

An old lady continued beating dust from a rug hanging across a line.

The murmur of invisible TVs reached us through the increasing heat of the day.

At the edge of the village we came to an unmarked fork in the road. Iván motioned for us to continue to the left, then hung back as he stopped to light a joint.

He was an attractive man and he looked good with the joint resting between his fingers, the sun reflecting in the clean sheen of his black hair. He played his part well but I was not surprised to notice that he failed to inhale the smoke he brought so casually to his mouth. There was something too smooth and too rehearsed about this man. It was clear to me that he was not a person who could be trusted.

He acknowledged the fact that I had been watching him by pointing the joint in my direction.

"Quieres?" He asked with a smile and a flash of his straight, not quite white teeth.

"Gracias," I replied, and took it from him.

The strip of asphalt road that we had been following came to an abrupt end. We stood at the edge of a dusty path that stretched out into a vast golden plain. In the far distance the horizon was an undulating blur of heat that split the endless blue of the sheltering sky from the baking earth of the world. We all exchanged glances and then turned to retrace the route we had followed.

Back at the fork in the road we took the other path. The floor here was uneven and dotted with rocks and stones of various sizes. The tall trees guarding it on both sides offered us a brief respite from the now overpowering sun.

The valley came back into view and the narrow path opened out into a wide plateau. To the right there was a drop to another lower space that continued for around fifty metres until it fell away at the valley's edge.

In this alcove, an old car stood perfectly upright on its nose. The paint had faded from red to sun-bleached ochre and the windows were all missing, but the wheels were intact and the bodywork was undamaged save for an indentation in the centre of the bonnet. It looked like an accident but it could just as easily have been another artefact from the museum we had visited the day before.

The unrelenting sun was at its apex. There were no clouds. The path had become steep and difficult to navigate. To the left was the rock face and a sharp rise to the valley's peak. To the right a sheer fall to the now familiar vicious nature and the guarantee of broken bones.

My mouth was dry and my footwear inappropriate. I concentrated intensely on each step but I was unable to prevent myself from slipping along the wet surface of my flip-flops. A raw, red line of skin showed where the rubber thongs chaffed and brushed away the misty dust that covered the rest of my feet. Sweat ran into my eyes and down my back.

Something was wrong. I was moving forward but only out of habit and automation. My thoughts slipped in and out of a dozy consciousness. Disconnected images of places and people flashed and bit at my brain.

A dull repetitive thud throbbed throughout my head, building up into a deafening crescendo of an unintelligible word that gradually began to sear itself clearly into the back of my mind in bold black letters. I tried to reject it and chase it away with other, less threatening thoughts but it only began to run louder and louder, like a skipped record, in violent circuits through my head.

SPIKED

No. That doesn't make sense, I reasoned. If nothing makes any sense, then everything is possible, the same internal voice shot back at me like a whip across my face

I recalled Inma's two names. A profound sense of dread and acceptance immediately washed over me. My knees buckled as I moved forward into some trouble that I knew I had undeniably asked for.

I laughed out loud stupidly in an attempt to deny the sudden, clawing notion of this impending danger.

"A sip of water," I said, without having wanted to. The surprise articulation of the words jolted me back into reality, disappearing the new and perfect image of a single blue drop of water that had instantaneously settled in my mind as the only conceivable and wholly logical route back to normality.

I glanced behind me to see if Iván was carrying anything. There was something in his hand, but it wasn't a bottle of water.

"Are you ok, amigo?" He asked.

I pretended I hadn't heard and looked back quickly to find Maria, who was carrying a back-pack, but the path had turned up ahead and she and Inma were out of view.

"Keep going, Sam."

We had reached the highest point of the valley. A broad strip of land tapered out into a peninsula whose edge was a step into the void. A soft breeze blew. To the left and right the world slalomed off into the distance in thick brushstrokes of green. Directly across from us, on the other side of the valley, a small white church glimmered beneath the sun.

Iván's words had lost the fake flare of friendliness and sounded brusque and like an order. I turned to look at him. His eyes narrowed and a smirk distorted his face. He still carried the large object in his hand.

I rubbed hard at my eyes and moved out closer to the edge. My foot stubbed against the floor and my left flip-flop fell off. Blood trickled down my dirty foot from the broken skin of my toe, congealing in an ugly ruby pool as it ran into and mixed with the dusty ground.

"What are we doing here?" I mumbled.

"Do you still not know?" replied Maria.

I opened out my arms to Inma in supplication.

She shook her head and looked away.

Iván paced backwards and forwards in long strides across the open ground.

I understood what was going to happen. I understood and then the realisation of it vanished immediately.

"All I need is water," I laughed stupidly to myself.

Confused, I moved further forward to where the ground began to narrow and recede to the nothingness that was the colourless deadly air. I slapped my face hard with both hands. Opened my eyes wide. And found a second of solace in the lapis coloured ribbon that the river cut through the valley floor a long way below.

I took a deep breath and leant slowly down to take up some weapon from the floor. My fingers brushed over an object's surface. It was hot to the touch and as soft as skin. I had no strength to lift it.

I closed my eyes and fell forward onto my knees.

There was not a single sound. I looked up and savoured the wonder of the emptiness around me. The light from the sun was incandescent and merciless. Everything was equally and perfectly illuminated. Beyond the white building, the vacant sky was an infinite orb of the purest blue.

One of the girls let out a strangled squeal of excitement.

Iván charged at me. His right arm tore towards my head. The scream had dragged me up from my holy reverie. I ducked to avoid his blow. A part of the stone clipped me sharply above the left eye.

I hurled myself up and at him before he had a chance to turn and come at me again. My body was too slow and too weak. He stepped back from my pathetic lunge and struck me hard in the face as I collapsed down to the spot where he had been standing.

He punched wildly at my body, grunting and snorting like an animal, as I struggled vainly to rise to my hand and knees to face him. He kicked me hard in the side and rolled me over onto my back.

My vision was drowned and blinded in the onrushing light of the sky.

Iván stalked my prone, defenceless body.

There was an almost imperceptible scratch on the earth as it was broken close by and I understood that he had picked up the tool that would be my end.

He stood over me. I felt grateful for the shadow that covered me in soothing shade.

"It's time, amigo."

There was a snap of light. And in the new darkness he brought the rock down hard onto my face.

The world thundered and blitzed in a shrieking burst of opal light. My face lay flat to the ground. I gazed out across the void to the white building and the perfect border that framed it.

Iván's shadow retreated once more, and I was kissed for the last time by the brutal horror of the sun.

MEG JOHNSON

My Father Throws a Party Because
I Broke up with a Boyfriend

Even though I am states away
I can hear the crackle of the fire.
I can smell the assorted meats
on the grill and the sticky light
beer. He has never before been
so happy to see one of my
relationships end. The neighbors
won't know the cause for celebration.
He'll simply say *my kids are doing*
well and offer more food, almost
holding back a wily smile.

MEG JOHNSON

The Old Couple Remake

I'm an Oscar, not a Felix.
You can find where I am in
the apartment by the trail of
empty pop cans. My boyfriend
suggests we host his co-worker's
baby shower and I raise my eyebrows
like Walter Matthau, scrunching my
forehead into disapproving lined
sections. I have a laundry pile knee
high, mostly of deceptively girly
lace thongs. My boyfriend's
t-shirts hang on white hangers,
color coded. Who knows… If he
wasn't putting out regularly, I
might throw his frittata against
a kitchen wall.

MARC PIETRZYKOWSKI

Mobius

The mountain in the rear view mirror
purses its lips and throws me a kiss
and all the cars behind me shimmer
like a breeze-blown curtain
on a late Saturday afternoon, sunlight
stretching its paws up the wallpaper.

And on the mountain, a door, bright red
and brass handled, and behind the door
her skinny toes curling crooked
over the couch arm, a chipped
and dormant teapot, a dusty mirror
reflecting a dirt road that leads away,
a rattling sedan crawling it like a roach.

The face around her mouth (an O
like an eclipse, like a moray's discreet
door, a mineshaft on an asteroid)
is settled as a cairn, and points the way
home. Home was fingertips reading
the story of a spine, and now?
A cardboard motel in a glass desert.

I toss cards at a hat, as I learned to do
from movies full of sharp-faced men
who wait. I toss them to make myself
believe I am waiting, and I am, for a day
unlike any other to come. A day like the one
before the mountain rose, before it was
a dark valley, before molten stone and scattered
bits of star finding each other in the crevices
between past and not-past. The day
it finally goes still, perfectly smooth,
all the jokes told and crevices filled in.

MARC PIETRZYKOWSKI

And I am not Afraid

I have tasted the flesh of the zombies who live
    behind the gates of work/play communities,
tried to understand them virally, on the scale
    of the scourge. I have supped
with vampire monkeys on rooftop gardens, watching
    helicopters plummet in the sunset like cherry blossoms.
I have raised my tiny fists in triumph with the over-diagnosed,
    the over-determined half-time celebrants, all
to no avail: my mind's right as rain, Pancho, it's this world,
    this mad, bad, stupid world
that turns my very love for it to maggotry.

KRISTEN FALSO-CAPALDI

Of Man and Mouse

Henry, to say the least, was quite ordinary. He'd wake up in the morning, put one aching foot to the floor, followed by the other. The creak that he heard as he pushed himself off the mattress may have been the floorboards. He wasn't sure. He needed to be at his post outside his classroom door at exactly 7:30 am, and it was Monday. Again. Outside his second floor window, the traffic on the main road across the parking lot sat still. It was cold; in deepest January, without the Christmas lights twinkling in the gas station window across the street, winter was a wasteland. It was 5:00 a.m. and Henry was bleary-eyed and twitchy from not enough sleep.

Henry lived alone, a timid, pudgy man with the years like scattered trash behind him and a couple of decades – more creaking floorboards on bleary-eyed Mondays – ahead of him.

"I want ... I want ...." Henry would mutter to himself, his chin propped on his fist, as he looked out the window on these mornings, but he'd never complete the thought.

He'd watched too much TV last night. Again. Nightly, from 6 pm until he fell asleep on the couch at near midnight, Henry drifted into the nighttime programs. It didn't really matter much what the show was, but he had a few favorites. In one of them, a biker gang ruled a small California town, in another several people battled zombies in an apocalyptic nightmare. How he dreamed each night in bed! Sometimes he was the handsome bad boy biker, the young one with the pretty wife and the ability to both kill and love. In others, he was the brave policeman-turned-zombie-chaser with the sharp-shooting skills. Henry woke from these dreams with a pounding heart and the inexplicable feeling of something that felt like hope. Then he was fully awake. And the morning ritual would begin. Feet to the floor, the movement toward the window, and the involuntary declaration escaping his lips, nearly inaudible, "I want ... I want ...."

Sometimes before his eyes had caught up with the rest of his body, he'd stumble into the bathroom and flick on the light. In the second it took his eyes to adjust, he'd look into the mirror and he'd see the most remarkable .... No, it couldn't be. For just a second he'd see the blond biker or the brave cop. They'd blink at each other in the mirror, and then he'd be Henry again. He'd grip the cold porcelain sink with his chubby fists, leaning into the mirror, his eyes darting over his reflection, nose nearly touching the glass. But of course it had to be his imagination.

One evening, while watching a new program about a rogue hunter of supernatural forces, he saw a man he'd recently seen on the cover of several magazines in the checkout line at the supermarket. In some photos, the handsome young man was alone, staring intently into the camera with a look that said, "I dare you." Dare you to do what? Henry wasn't sure. But there was a challenge there. In other photos, he was accompanied by others, the cast of the show, Henry assumed. In these photos, the man looked at him (well, not at him, exactly, but at the camera) with that same look, "I dare you."

Henry left the store and felt that perhaps he wore that expression himself. He wasn't sure if he really wore that expression or if he'd imagined it, but one woman walking past him into the store seemed to make a bee-line around him. "I dare you," he thought, as she scurried away.

In the program, this man, whose name Henry did not know, was involved with a woman who seemed to need him completely. It was probably unrealistic, Henry thought, but then he couldn't be sure. He watched as the plot unfolded in that episode. When it finished, he watched a second episode. Then, a third. A glance at the clock told him it was past two. 5:00 was looming. It didn't matter. Yet another episode later, he watched the character get shot and saw his beautiful lover stand over him, weeping. He thought he could feel the wound, hear the beep of the hospital monitors. He could feel the warmth of tears spilling against his face.

He woke up to the ringing of his telephone sometime around 8:00. In a daze, he scurried to the dark corner of his bedroom for the previous day's clothes. They were wrinkled and soiled with the chalk dust and dirt of the classroom, as well as the spilled contents from his lunch. Nevertheless, he pulled them on and headed to the bathroom to straighten up his appearance for another day. He fumbled through the familiar routine. Then, as always, it happened. The flicker of light, the image in the mirror not quite right. He blinked. Once. A second time. A shock went through him and he sprang back several steps, cowering from what he saw. The rogue hunter stared back at him.

He shook his head from left to right. He blinked again. Surely, he'd change back to Henry. He didn't have time for this on today of all days. In the previous encounters with the men in the mirror, he'd morphed so quickly, he barely noticed the change. As when one sees ghosts, he'd convince himself that the thing he saw wasn't really the thing he saw. Ghosts, he'd found for most people, could smash a glass against a wall and the witness could dismiss this action with, "hmm, it must have been the vibration from the furnace below," or "the wind from the open window could have blown it off the counter." Such was the case on the other occasions with Henry. But this time, it was undeniable. He tried everything. He scampered back and forth, then rolled his neck and shoulders, hoping to reverse the transformation, but the rogue hunter did the same in the mirror.

"I'm not sure where to go from here," thought Henry. "I can't show up for work this way."

He pictured the faces of the graying secretaries in the office, how their eyes would grow wide with wonder as he walked into the office. It occurred to him that maybe he should have been happy, but the idea of the rogue hunter strutting among those women, who munched on hard candy and donuts all morning, their breath stinking of vending machine coffee, their hands covered in liver spots, made him tremble. He'd been privy to the manner of conversations these women had about men; celebrities or young male teachers, men they'd never have. They would shamelessly drool over him! He turned 180 degrees and closed the bathroom door where a full length mirror greeted him. Just as he'd feared, the rogue hunter stood, his stance imposing and angry. Again, the look, "I dare you." Henry still wore his own wrinkled, soiled clothing, but on the rogue hunter, his black slacks and button down shirt fell loosely, stylishly. A shudder ran through him, visible even in the mirror. He thought of Maggie, who spoke to him with a polite detachment as she hurried past him to her classroom. Maggie might notice him, speak to him. "I can't," he whispered to no one in particular. As he froze with this new fear on that morning, Henry noticed something more remarkable than his transformation. While inside, Henry felt terror, in the mirror, the rogue hunter's face held disgust as he stared back at him.

Henry thought he might go back to bed and see if he could possibly sleep it off like a drunken binge. But the phone rang again and he grabbed it. It was Betty, one of the secretaries. He told her he had developed a sudden cough; indeed, he felt he had taken on the voice of the rogue hunter, which sounded like the low rumble of an old car engine. This whole ordeal is straight out of one of the scripts from the show, he thought. In the show, the rogue hunter and he would switch places, but of course the story would be told from the hunter's perspective. What a turn of bad luck, to turn from the handsome sure-of-himself towering powerhouse into Henry, meek teacher of middle-schoolers. The hunter would spend the entire episode searching for an antidote, for sure. In the end, he'd switch back, and Henry would perish.

As for Henry, being the rogue hunter was not convincing his boss, who had just taken the phone from Betty and was begging Henry, in his usual unctuous way, could he please, please try to come to work today? It would be difficult at best to find a substitute, he said. Many of his teachers already were out with the flu, and anyway, to phone at the last minute without a substitute in place was an anomaly. His students would lose valuable instructional time. The principal was an old man, at least two or three years past the age of retirement, who wandered the halls making small talk with faculty and students, but doing little in the way of discipline or order. On more than one occasion, Henry had smelled liquor on the old man's breath. Henry knew he wasn't worried so much about the students as who would have to look after them in Henry's absence. Henry's students were the repeaters, the ones who worked little and unleashed their own brand of jovial havoc on their best days. On their worst days, vitriol and fistfights erupted. Henry did not take many days off, but on the days he had to do so, substitutes left him angry handwritten diatribes with the familiar subtext: the blame for their behavior belonged exclusively to him. They were poorly behaved, had no self-control, they said. They had no respect for rules. Over the last several years, Henry had, every spring, written a memorandum to his principal as well as the head of the English department, requesting a different course load. Surely, he thought, they can give me just one honors level or even a college preparatory class? Surely, he wasn't destined to teach only the discipline cases for the rest of his career? But each year, both parties responded similarly. "While I will take your request into consideration," his department chair wrote last spring, "there may be no "wiggle" room again next year. If that is the case, you will have to make the best of the situation." On the phone, the old man continued to admonish Henry; he should put his students first, bite the bullet and so forth, but it was unnecessary. As it was not in Henry's nature to make trouble for anyone, he began to acquiesce. Then the rogue hunter spoke.

"Listen, asshole," the rogue hunter replied. "I'm telling you that I can't make it in. If you have a problem with that – "

"What?" The old principal replied.

"Um," Henry began. "No, I didn't ..."

"We must have a bad connection, Henry," said the man. "I'll see you in a half hour then? Doris from Mathematics can cover you till then." Then he hung up.

"Ok," Henry said to the empty line. "I'll get there as soon as I can."

The rogue hunter slammed the phone down, growling at Henry and calling him a weasel, and crossed the room to the hook where Henry kept his car keys.

"So, it's a possession, then," mused Henry. "Remarkable! It's just like in the show."

In Henry's car, the hunter's hands firmly gripped the wheel, his eyes alert on the road, as if he could see every possibility. He had little tolerance for weaker drivers, swerving left, then right, then left again to move beyond them. He checked his rear-view mirror often, as if there were someone there, chasing him; yet Henry noted that he drove like a predator. In the mirror, Henry was gone. But yet he existed, now buried deep inside. He wondered how to reverse the spell, how to escape. As soon as the thought formed, of course the rogue hunter knew. In the rear-view mirror, he took in a deep breath and stared Henry straight in the face. They locked eyes for too long; the rogue hunter nearly slammed Henry's car into the stopped volvo at the light in front of him. At the last minute, he swerved over, making an obscene gesture to a group of teenagers in the beat up Jetta he'd nearly hit. Henry watched in horror, as he recognized some of the kids as former students, now in high school and cutting class. None of them saw Henry.

In the parking lot, the rogue hunter slammed the car door and stared ahead, his legs propelling him across the pavement, his arms swinging at his sides. From inside, Henry shuddered as the hunter strode up the front stairs to the double doors and jerked one open. He was heading for Maggie's room when he nearly bumped into the old principal and Gloria, another secretary, who both greeted him with affected smiles. He stepped past them without even a nod and shot up the stairs. Henry, though he was terrified, was curious; whom would Maggie see when she looked at him? He surveyed his body; there was no longer the protruding belly, no longer the belt fighting to suck everything in. His shirt fell easily over his pants front, and the fabric across his thighs no longer bunched up.

As the hunter headed toward her classroom, Henry thought about what he wished for. What did he want to see in Maggie's eyes today? What could he say about Maggie on a typical day? She wasn't cruel. She tolerated him. She was friendly, in fact, though never familiar. Is that what he wanted from Maggie, the familiar? The thought made him quiver. When the rogue hunter reached Maggie's classroom, he could hear the chatter of thirty thirteen-year-olds vying for attention. Maggie was just shy of forty, but still young and full of life. The students cheerily entered her classroom even on the rainiest of days. Henry, whose classroom was just a few doors down, liked to stand in the hall and sneak peeks at her through her open doorway while she taught, sitting effortlessly with one leg tucked under the other on the desk in front, or, if she was wearing a skirt, sitting demurely with legs crossed. He cringed as the rogue hunter crossed her threshold, causing her to stop what she was saying in mid-sentence. Henry felt trapped and he silently pleaded with the hunter to end the pursuit. Maggie followed him into the hallway.

"Hello," she said; there was a question mark there. Did she see the flash from the mirror? Something was happening for sure; Maggie looked at him differently.

"I needed to see you," the hunter said. Then, to Henry's horror, he reached his hand up towards her face, meaning to tuck a loose strand of hair behind her ear. It seemed, even to Henry, a cliché, but it was standard for the hunter.

"Oh, come on!" Henry exclaimed, as he fought the hunter for control, pulling his arm back before he made contact and tucking it tightly by his side. Maggie just blinked at him.

"Is there something you need, Henry?" The spell broken, she nodded toward the open classroom behind her. "I can't leave them alone for too long." One of her students, one of Henry's former tormentors, made a gesture at Henry behind her back, his friends snickering. The rogue hunter leveled his gaze at the boy, who looked downward, fear darting through his features.

"No," Henry said. "I was late today and wanted to say good morning." Henry babbled a hasty goodbye and scurried off, not wanting to see her puzzled expression. Henry felt his chest might explode. Inside, the rogue hunter peppered him with questions. Why, the hunter wanted to know, when you were given the chance to get what you want, did you shut me out? You silenced me in favor of *you*? It's foolish, Henry.

Henry continued to his classroom. There, Doris, the ancient mathematics teacher, stared his pupils down with a glare that she turned upon Henry as he entered. "They were hideous," she said to him as she grabbed her belongings and walked out, closing the door behind her. After she left, Henry tried to proceed with the previous day's writing lesson, a refresher for the upcoming standardized tests. As he turned to write a sentence on the chalkboard, the boys in the back began to mock him, the girls laughed at the boys, and so it was like every other day. Henry looked down, and he could see the rogue hunter's physique was still there, though it seemed to hold no magic for the pupils.

Henry spoke to the board about verbs. "Verbs are action words," he said. "And just like some actions are more powerful than others, some verbs are more powerful than others." Henry droned on, pretending not to notice the smattering of chatter behind him, the taunts and subsequent laughter, until a full water bottle whizzed past his face and smashed into the chalkboard right where he had finished writing the sentence, "The man wants to be a mouse."

"What the hell does that sentence mean?" Jimmy, one of the boys in the back, said. "What man would want to be a mouse?"

Henry wasn't sure. He'd written that sentence only seconds ago, underlining the word "wants" three times, yet he didn't know why.

He cleared his throat. "What are some more powerful verbs to use instead of "wants"?

Nobody answered him; instead someone shouted something he couldn't quite make out followed by the familiar laughter.

"What do you think?" He tried again. "Other words for 'wants'?"

A voice in the back shouted an obscene word. More laughter. Inside, the rogue hunter was fuming. He turned from the board and stared the class down. For the first time since Henry had known him, the smirk left Jimmy's face and he was still. The rest of the class seemed to stop breathing.

"Desire?" a girl, Fiona mumbled.

"Wish?" a boy, Jonas, said.

"How about 'need'?" asked Naomi.

Henry didn't respond, and again the spell passed too quickly. Soon, the class erupted into adolescent jokes and the accompanying cackles. But the rogue hunter reached to a shelf above the chalkboard and slammed a heavy book to the floor. For a moment all was quiet. Then the bell sounded and the malcontents were replaced by a nearly identical group, who shoved their way into the room on a wave of crude comments and hilarity.

And so, Henry's day progressed in much the same way. Henry had many conversations with students, colleagues and even another with Maggie, in which the rogue hunter with his gestures and good looks and "I dare you" stare moved Henry a few paces off his familiar road. He talked sports with the old principal, flirted with the graying secretaries and even argued with his department chair over a lesson plan. Yet, in every circumstance, Henry fought him. True, Henry liked the rush it gave him whenever someone suddenly would blink and see him in a new way, much the same way he saw himself in those first few seconds in the mirror. It was a terrific surge; however, there would always be the moment when he felt fear and back-peddled to undo what the hunter had done.

On the way home, the hunter let Henry take the wheel and provide them both safe passage home. When they locked eyes in the rearview mirror, the hunter sighed, shook his head, then looked away.

Before getting into bed that night, Henry and the hunter stood before the mirror. The hunter glared and just shrugged. "The man wants to be a mouse," he said.

"That was *you*?" Henry asked.

"That was you." said the hunter. "Want, desire, wish, need ... it really doesn't matter, does it?"

"What do you want from me?" Henry asked. "What do you want me to say?"

The Rogue Hunter didn't speak again.

The next morning when the alarm clock went off at 5:00, Henry awoke to find himself quite ordinary. Everything, even the quick flash in the mirror, was gone. "I've blown it," he said to his reflection. He knew it was not a dream, the way he knew that as soon as he hoisted himself off the mattress, the traffic on the main road across the parking lot would be sitting still under the dark, cold January sky.

At the window, he paused, resting his chin on his fist. "I want ... I want ..." he muttered, then he turned from the window and began the preparations for another day.

MICHAEL C. KEITH

The Rules of Gravity

Jump up as far as you can. See how far you get.
— Joseph Paul

When his divorce proceedings began, Sid Barrington had been advised by his attorney to avoid dating for at least a year to get his head back in a healthy place. He did as his lawyer suggested, but one year turned into two and then three. It wasn't that he was deliberately avoiding the dating scene. He just couldn't find anyone he wanted to go out with. Not that he tried very hard to make it happen. Then things changed when a young woman joined his company. She caught his eye instantly, and for weeks he watched as she settled into her job as the billing clerk for the flooring outlet where he worked as a buyer. He gradually developed a casual friendship with the woman and finally gathered the courage to ask her out. She accepted and he was happier than he had been since the collapse of his marriage.

Sarah Pendleton. I even love the sound of her name, he thought excitedly, as he readied himself for his date. *God, I hope it goes well.* His nerves were raw at the prospect of his first hookup with the woman who had grown more attractive to him with each passing day. *Don't blow it, Sid. Don't blow it. Oh, shit, I probably will. Look, my palms are sweaty. Maybe a drink?* Sid rarely consumed alcohol, but on this occasion he figured it might settle him down some. He poured himself a substantial shot of Wild Turkey, a gift given him by his brother a dozen years earlier, and downed it in one gulp. For a few moments he thought he would suffocate because he was unable to catch his breath as the liquor coursed through his system. When he finally was able to inhale, he nearly vomited. *Oh, God, that's awful stuff!*

It took Sid a few more moments to get past the jarring experience, and when he had he could feel the effects of the powerful beverage. *Whoa! That's strong booze!* he reflected, heading out of his condo. As he drove from his driveway, he struck the garbage can awaiting pickup by the curb. *Easy, buddy. Don't get a DUI.* Halfway down his block, he felt something hit his bumper.

What the ...! Peering through his rear view mirror, all he could see was the blackness of night. *Another garbage can*, he thought, continuing on his way.

The remainder of his drive to meet Sarah at the cinema went without incident. By the time he arrived he figured most of the whiskey's effect was gone, but it had done its job by relaxing him. When he caught a glimpse of Sarah standing near the ticket window, all he felt was excitement. *God, she's pretty!* Unfortunately, over the course of the evening he discovered that she was more physically attractive than intellectually interesting. Throughout their dinner following the movie, she mostly talked about her two Siamese cats. When Sid tried to redirect the conversation, she would steer it back to her beloved felines.

"Would you like to meet Mimi and Pierre?" asked Sarah. "You can come to my place for coffee, if you want."

Sid demurred, saying he had an early rise to drive up to his brother's in Hartford, a few hours drive north of Baltimore. This was a pure fabrication, because by the end of the evening, he had lost interest in pursuing the striking brunette. While appearance was important to Sid, the substance of an individual's personality was of equal or even greater consequence to him. In that area, he found her totally lacking. He was surprised and disappointed, because she had seemed so much more engaging at work. Although they never went out again, they continued to be cordial to one another in the workplace. Two years after their only date, Sarah would leave the floor-covering company to be married.

*   *   *

The next morning a TV report caught Sid's attention. His neighbor had been the victim of a hit and run right on his street. It took him only a second to connect the dots. *Was that what I hit last night? Oh, my God!!* The person he now was convinced he had struck was well known to him, because he had been regarded as the scourge of the neighborhood since he and his wife arrived from Australia two years ago. Trevor Collins was a brute, and his wife was a lout as well. Both had alienated the residents of Furlong Drive with their callous behavior and blatant disregard for the appearance of their raised ranch and its surroundings. When neighbors had petitioned the couple to rid their yard of an assortment of debris—mostly rusting and decaying objects and plastic containers and soda bottles—they had been greeted with threats.

At least he's not dead, thought Sid, his panic rising. *And no one apparently saw me hit him.* Upon inspecting his car's bumper, he was relieved to find it undamaged. *Maybe it wasn't me.* But on closer inspection, a piece of red flannel hanging from beneath the fender convinced him otherwise. *His shirt … he was wearing a red flannel shirt the last time I saw him. Shit! What am I going to do? Go to the police? I'll go to jail! Hell, no! That can't happen. Nobody saw the driver. What about Trevor? The news says he has a concussion and broken bones but no recollection of the incident. Don't do anything.*

And so it was that Sid tried to put the mishap behind him, though he was not successful. His guilt weighed on him and forced him to confront his victim. A week after Trevor returned home from the hospital, Sid decided to pay him what he hoped would be a friendly visit. He had to know if Trevor had any inkling that he was the one who ran him down. If he did, he would try to make amends. Just how he wasn't sure. Since neither Trevor nor his wife had made an attempt to contact him, he felt he was likely in the clear, but he had to be certain.

"Yeah, what you need?" mumbled Sybil Collins, answering his knock—the doorbell was apparently not working.

"Hello, Mrs. Collins. I'm Sid. I just thought I'd check to see how your husband is doing," replied Sid, tentatively.

"Really? Trevor, you got company!"

The disheveled-looking woman waved for Sid to enter. The inside of the house was in no better shape than the outside. The furniture looked as if had been purchased at a flea market and old newspapers and magazines were stacked everywhere.

"Who is it?" called Trevor from another room.

"It's Sam from down the street."

"Sid … It's *Sid*."

"Get your butt out here, hon!"

Trevor entered the room on crutches. A soiled bandage covered a section of his head, which had been partially shaved.

"Yeah, what can I do for you, mate? I'm in a bit of pain here."

"Just want to see if you need anything?"

"We need *something* all right," blurted Mrs. Collins. "We need to find the bugger who done this to him."

"They don't know who did it?" inquired Sid.

"Naw, they'll never find the ratbag who hit him."

"You never know, Sibby. These jackals usually are found out," said Trevor, flopping into a chair. "Can you get me and … what's your tag?"

"Sid."

"Yeah, Sid, a beer. Would you like one?" asked Trevor, pointing to Sid with his cane.

"I'm fine. Not much on the booze."

"One of them tight-ass tea teetotalers eh? Well, just don't stand there, Sibby, get me a Fosters."

"Hold your horses," replied Sybil, trailing off to the kitchen.

"Some chips, too, while you're at it."

As soon as she was out of the room, Trevor began to snicker while staring at Sid.

"Guess we both know, don't we?" asked Trevor, arching his eyebrow.

"Know what?" replied Sid, baffled.

"That you were the one runned over me."

"Me?"

"Yeah, you. Got a look at your car before going under. A Jeep Cherokee, right?"

Sid was at a total loss for words. He felt like his heart would pound its way through his chest.

"That's what I thought. Guess I should call the cops. Unless we can work this out between us."

"I didn't mean to … It was an accident."

"Nearly killed me. Bad blow to the head and my ankle is all broken up. That should be worth some major compensation. Wouldn't you think … *mate?*"

"What do you have in mind?" asked Sid, feeling his world collapse around him.

"A monthly payment would help ease the pain. I may not be able to walk right again. How am I supposed to work construction if I'm disabled?"

"How much?"

"Let's say five hundred dollars a month for life. That seems reasonable, considering. Don't it, Sid? I mean I could sue your Yank ass for a hell of a lot more."

"That's a lot. Okay … fine."

"And don't say nothing to the missus," said Trevor, his forefinger over his lips as his wife reentered the room. "Where you been? Thought I'd never see you again."

"Oh, shut your yap, you old bludger. Here's your bloody beer and chips."

"Well, I guess I'll be going now, Mrs. Collins," said Sid, turning to leave.

"Keep in touch," responded Trevor, with a complicit wink.

"I will. Definitely. Thank you."

On his return home, Sid reached the conclusion that it might have been better for him if he had killed Trevor rather than merely maiming him.

*   *   *

Two days later, Sid received a phone call from Trevor advising him how to get him the agreed upon monthly payment.

"Cash only. No checks. Just put it under the front door mat on the first of each month. Best to do it after it gets dark so the missus don't see you. Got that, mate?"

As the years went by, the monthly compensation Sid was obliged to provide Trevor increased twofold. Eventually it became a financial burden to him, especially after the business he had been employed by for nearly twenties years went bankrupt and had to lay off its entire staff. Sid had managed to save a decent sum, since he had few expenses, but he could foresee a time when he might not be able to pay off his hit and run victim. *What the hell would happen then?* Sid wondered. *He's been extorting me for five years. If he says anything, he'll be in deep trouble, too,* he reasoned. *I should just stop paying the prick. Call his bluff.*

But Sid did not have to confront his blackmailer because he had fallen to his death from the scaffolding of a high rise under construction. *That's it. I'm out from under. No more monthly payments,* thought Sid, dialing the number of the funeral home where Trevor Collins was to be waked. At seven that evening he would bid his worst nightmare adieu and take back his life. For the first time in months, Sid felt optimistic about his future prospects. An interview the previous week had resulted in a callback for a second one, and Sid felt confident that he would soon end his period of economic strife, if not the continuing drought that made up his so-called love life.

*   *   *

It did not surprise Sid that the parking lot of the funeral home was mostly empty. There was no more than a half dozen attendees inside and none appeared to be in a state of mourning. As Sid approached Mrs. Collins, he caught part of her conversation.

"It was that crushed ankle of his from that hit and run. Couldn't keep weight on it for very long. Probably why he fell. Never too sure-footed after being run over."

The couple she had been addressing nodded and moved away leaving the new widow alone.

"Hello, Mrs. Collins. I'm very sorry for your loss," said Sid, extending his hand.

"Thank you. You're Sam from down the street."

"Sid, *Sid* Barrington, from number seventy-two."

"Oh yeah, you came to our house after Trevor's accident. I remember."

"Did he ever find out who ran over him?" inquired Sid, wiping his moist palms against his pants

"Oh yeah, he knew who hit him."

"He did?" asked Sid, sensing he was nearing the edge of a cliff.

"It was his stupid cousin, Quinn. Confessed not long after you visited us, as a matter of fact. Trevor wouldn't tell the cops. Kept it a secret. Didn't want his kin to get into trouble. Don't know why. His cousin sure wasn't any treasure. Now it don't matter anymore, does it?"

"No ... No, I guess it doesn't," answered Sid, catching his deflated image in the polished side of Trevor's coffin.

233

JENEAN MCBREARTY

The Truth about Thurman

Captain Thurmond drummed his fingers on the wooden bench, imagining a world with ashtrays and cigarette machines. He'd have smoked Chesterfield's because he had British relatives. But he wouldn't have won the Expeditionary Unit Triathlon if he'd mucked up his lungs. Health or cool. He'd made the right choice. The medal displayed in a Plexiglas cube on the mantle testified to that. But none of the women he'd tried to seduce over the years ever noticed it.

"It belongs in a black velvet-lined jewelry case," his mother told him. "You need to make a bigger splash, Gordon. What's special about a coin preserved in plastic?"

What indeed. He'd asked the jeweler if the medal could be extracted from its transparent casket, and could he buy a jewelry case? When he saw the rings, he decided it was time to settle down.

"Commander Benton will see you now." Thurman looked up at Benton's Admin—assist and wondered why the old man didn't promote a pretty young thing from the ranks. "Would you like some coffee?"

"No." He showed her a steady hand. "No jitters." Avoiding caffeine was another good choice, under the circumstances.

She ushered him through her part of the office. She was a plant aficionado and said, "Go right in," before opening Benton's office door.

He was staring at the TV, watching a curvaceous blonde report on the latest attack on an American embassy followed by film clips of Iraqi streets filled with shouting crowds burning an effigy of President Sandoval. "What do you think, Thurman?"

"After fifty years, I think they'd get another hobby."

"I like that. Gentle sarcasm. Sit down and fill me in on operation fuck up."

Thurman eased onto the sofa. "There's not much to tell. The chopper caught an RPG round and went down. Lt. Chandler and SSgt. Whitcomb were captured."

"How'd the jihadists find out Whitcomb is gay?"

"Whitcomb carried a photo of his wife. Husband. I don't know who's who, but what's important is that the photo had a loving dedication written on the back. There was one jihadist who understood English. Rachman Ali Alibi, a.k.a. Leland McKinney."

"Tell me about Chandler." Benton went to the bar and brought back two glasses and a bottle of Johnny Walker Red.

"A Jew from New York."

"Damn it! I told the DOD we should take religion off the dog tags." Benton's eyes bored through him. "You thinking what I'm thinking?" Even if he didn't come clean, he had the feeling Benton could read his mind.

"Sometimes death is sadder, but simpler," he said.

"This is one of those times, Thurman." Benton led out an audible humph. "All the god-damned jihadists in the world, and our soldiers get popped by an American whack job. Where's he from?"

"Atlanta."

Benton swallowed a healthy swig of bourbon. "What does he want?"

"To force our hand. Says he'll release one. Our choice." Explaining the ultimatum was more difficult than Thurman had anticipated. "The other one will be ... executed."

"Christ. Can it get any worse?"

Thurman looked at his shoes. Where had the dust come from? He pulled a Kleenex from his pocket and gave them a quick pass. His Uncle Mike became convinced that if he kept his hair parted in a straight line, nothing bad would happen to him. He could function outside the asylum as long as he took his meds and kept a good supply of hair gel, a comb, and checked his part every fifteen minutes. Was he becoming as obsessive about his shoes as Mike was about his hair?

"It is worse, Sir. Lt. Chandler's a woman."

He found a trashcan and tossed in the tissue. He felt Benton's eyes on him again.

"So that's it. Either way we offend somebody. How long do we have?"

"Forty-eight hours. Well, forty-six now." He was wrong. Benton wasn't watching him. He was still in his recliner, staring at a wall covered with Civil War art. A portrait of Abraham Lincoln, battle scenes of Manassas and Antietam. "Sir, shouldn't we notify the Joint Chiefs? Or the President?"

"So they can play political football? Not a chance. No publicity. That's exactly what Alibi wants. And we're not going to give it to him."

"But ... But ... a woman, Sir."

"Have you ever seen the movie Sophie's Choice?"

"No."

"A Nazi's dog forces Sophie to choose between her son and her daughter – and she chooses the boy. But the Nazi winds up killing both children anyway. Chandler and Whitcomb are soldiers – equally brave as far as I'm concerned. They'll comfort each other."

Who, Thurman wanted to ask Benton, will comfort their families? Who will comfort the nation? Somewhere Whitcomb's spouse was feeling grief grip his guts like labor pains as imaginings of torture crawled in and out of his mind and sucked at his heart. Was he screaming prayers or curses at God? No, he was on his knees pleading for a miracle, whipping himself for sending a picture of their last happy day together so Chad would have something lovely to hold onto when the desert nights froze his balls off and the days baked his California blonde hair.

God damn the cell phones that sent pictures of the two naked soldiers, blindfolded and shackled, to their speed-dialed loved ones back home.

*

Forty-four hours seemed like a long time before Benton made his decision to let Chandler and Whitcomb die together if the rescue mission failed, or if time ran out as it surely would. All the field officers reported is that what was left of the Cobra was somewhere near the Afghan—Pakistani border. The jihadists must have blown it up because Chandler's last transmission said she'd made a hard but safe landing.

Thurman went by the Wal-Mart on his way home. He bought a copy of Sophie's Choice. He'd decided not to split the cube. He'd put it on a piece of black velvet instead. He bought six yards. Enough to cover the mantle, and the mirrors in the bathroom, bedroom, and hall because covering mirrors is what Jews do when people die. He bought a set of black bedding including a queen-sized comforter, and black accessories for the bathroom.

When he got home, he took off his uniform and put on his old jeans and a T-shirt, and began painting the apartment with ten gallons of black paint he'd bought. Satin finish for the walls, semi gloss enamel for the doors, baseboards, and cabinets.

He tried not to think about Paige Chandler and Chad Whitcomb being raped and tortured and having their heads hacked off as a camera recorded their last futile pleadings for their lives, their last gasps of disbelief, their screams of pain. He concentrated on other things—like not getting paint on the carpet or the miniblinds, or the windowpanes—while Sophie's Choice played out on the TV screen. He paused it at the part when Sophie is holding her daughter in her arms. He made their bed, pulling the sheets tight enough to bounce a quarter. He replaced the Kentucky Wildcats bathroom accessories with the new stuff, scrubbed the toilet and put down the seat. He watched a frantic Sophie hand over the child to a Nazi. The child shrieked with terror. How could the woman she loved abandon her to this stranger? Benton was right. To be thought the insignificant one would be another torture.

Forty-three hours and forty-five minutes later, exhausted, he sat in front of the fireplace dressed in the black suit he wore to his father's funeral and his black well-polished shoes, staring up at Paige's engagement ring he'd had the jeweler seal in a Plexiglas cube. He'd placed it next to his medal, and placed his black-barreled pistol next to him on the end table. He turned on the news and waited as the clock threw away the minutes of life. If only … if only they'd told Benton that Paige was a little pregnant and they were going to be married as soon as she rotated out in three days. Three fucking lousy days after he'd left.

"Shocking video of the executions of two captured Marine pilots appeared today on you-tube …"

Just before the night swallowed the light, Thurman went to the hall mirror and lifted the soft black cloth just enough to see if the part in his hair was absolutely straight before he swallowed his pistol.

CONOR POWERS-SMITH

Word of mouth

[Monday]

"We offer a variety of services, Mr. Clark."

"For example?"

"Oh, anything from the simple anonymity of a long-range rifle to the personal touch of a ball-peen hammer. Knives, explosives, fire, piano wire. Let your imagination roam."

"I'd want ..."

"You may speak freely. We are known and respected in this establishment."

"I'd want him to ..."

"Suffer, if I understand you? That can certainly be arranged. Man is born to suffer, Mr. Clark. Perhaps you're ready for another?"

"No. Well, OK."

"Why not, hmm? It is an extraordinary day. Two more whiskey sours, Emanuel. And I believe my associate is ready for another lemonade."

"Does he ever ... talk?"

"Emanuel? He is loquacious enough, under the proper circumstances."

"No, your ... associate."

"Mr. Barrow. He does not. But I assure you, he more than makes up for his lack of interpersonal skills by his dedication to his calling. And that brings us back to the question at hand."

"Yeah. How would you ... go about it?"

"Entirely up to you, Mr. Clark. We place at your disposal all the thousand natural shocks that flesh is heir to, plus a good many about which the Bard knew nothing. I will—thank you, Emanuel—I will venture a suggestion: we begin by skinning the subject alive ..."

"Jesus!"

"I take it that option does not appeal? Another personal favorite, then: beginning with the fingers and toes, each joint is forcibly hyper-extended to the point of breakage. As you can see, Mr. Barrow is a powerful man. Next we ..."

"Christ."

"If I may ask, is your interest in the Son of Man solely maledictory? Because we have performed several crucifixions."

"That's hideous. No crucifixion. No torture."

"We appear to be working with rather different definitions of the word suffering."

"Look, just ... the hammer. That'll be fine."

"Fine as dandelion wine, Mr. Clark. Fine as soft rain in July."

"Yeah."

"Now, a special offer: our research has revealed that Mr. Reynolds has a wife and two young children. Normally, we charge by the head, as it were, but these are tough times, and we have recently introduced a package plan. Your payment, already gratefully received, would cover the entire family unit, if you wished to ..."

"Jesus, are you out of your mind?"

"Mr. Clark, I sincerely hope I am imagining the note of moral condemnation which seems to have crept into your voice. Such tones upset Mr. Barrow. See how avidly he regards you? One can only imagine the thoughts slouching torpidly to and fro behind that gaze."

"I'm sorry. I'm just not used to this. You're ..."

"Professionals."

"Yes. Professionals."

"That we are, Mr. Clark. We are nothing if not professional. Therefore you need not fear for Mrs. Reynolds and her rosy-cheeked cherubim."

"Good."

"One last consideration: would you like us to deliver a message?"

"No message. He knows what he did."

"Then you wish to remain anonymous in the matter?"

"No. I'd want him to ..."

"To know at whose whim he is being dispatched."

"Yeah."

"I suspected as much."

"Yeah."

"Yeah, Mr. Clark. Yeah."

#

[Tuesday]
The mutilated body of Stuart Reynolds, 36, was discovered this morning in the living room of his Olive Street home. Police say the father of two was beaten with a blunt, metal object, likely a hammer, and that Mr. Reynolds' wife and children may have been drugged to prevent them from waking while the murder was committed. However, police would not confirm the leaked report that each of Mr. Reynolds' bones was broken exactly once ...

#

[Wednesday]
        "Knock knock, Mr. Clark. Knock, as it were, knock."

        "Jesus. It's three o'clock in the morning. What are you doing coming to my home?"

        "Business, Mr. Clark. May we come in?"

        "I ... don't think that's a good idea."

        "You did hear the news? About Mr. Reynolds' untimely passing?"

        "Yeah. Thank you. But you've been paid."

        "You indicated you were satisfied with the services rendered?"

        "If this is blackmail—"

        "Mr. Clark. How can one help but be offended by such a suggestion? I thought we'd established our professionalism."

        "Yeah."

        "So professional are we, in fact, that, barely twenty-four hours having passed since the completion of our last assignment, here we are, in execution of our next."

        "Your ... next?"

        "Our next assignment, yes. I do wish you'd open the door, Mr. Clark."

        "No."

        "Mr. Barrow, perhaps you'd like to help Mr. Clark overcome his unfortunate lapse of hospitality?"

        "Jesus! Stay out! You'll wake up my wife—"

        "She needs must awaken, Mr. Clark. Your lovely children, as

240

well. You have a lovely home, by the way. We will endeavor to keep the mess to a minimum."

"What are you doing here? Get out!"

"I told you, Mr. Clark, business. Our client, the late Mr. Reynolds, was much more receptive to our professional guidance than certain other clients I could mention. Actively encouraging, even."

"What'd he ..."

"Oh, it's so much more rewarding when we reveal the specifics as we go. I will say this: Mr. Reynolds, a man who knows a bargain when he sees one, opted for our package plan."

"I'll pay! Anything you—"

"We have been paid, Mr. Clark. And we have never yet reneged on an assignment. I find I must again remind you: we are professionals."

"Oh Jesus!"

"Restrain him please, Mr. Barrow. One more observation concerning Mr. Reynolds, and then we may proceed."

"Mmphhhmphh!"

"As I was saying: Mr. Reynolds had a truly delightful imagination. We may be here for some time. I hope it's no imposition?"

"Mmmmphh!"

"Glad to hear it. We are looking forward to our stay. Mr. Barrow. The wife. The children."

TIMOTHY BEARLY

Quantum Eternity

It was a theoretical physicist – not a Spanish conquistador – who would eventually discover the proverbial fountain of youth.

The year was 2070. It was almost a century after Heisenberg's death. A century after leading scientists, Bohr and Einstein, argued over whether or not God liked to play Yahtzee – with both men assuming an unlikely premise that the man upstairs actually existed. Albeit, that was way back when ... back when the motto of the United States was still: "In God We Trust." An unsophisticated chapter. A crude and shameful blemish in the fibrotic tissue of our evolutionary history. But it is now the age of human cloning and sex robots – God no longer has a pulse. And the uncertainty principle – the idea that a particles location and velocity could not be simultaneously quantified – was now regarded as a patently erroneous conjecture; which, along fairy tales of talking snakes and three headed dragons, was only to be found in antediluvian encyclopedias.

Niklaus was just 16 years old when Danish scientists began successfully teleporting amoebas. It wasn't so much that they were being teleported per se, it was more of an elaborate cut-copy-and-paste process, an atomic deconstruction and reconstruction. In essence, hi-tech Xerox machines would scan, locate, identify, and break down the components of an organism, down to the tiniest vibrating strand of energy. The information was then sent to the "assembly chamber," where the subjects' constituents would subsequently be "rematerialized."

The young Niklaus – who's logical mind was offset by his morbid fear of death – attentively watched the press conference, as a PhD, in a white coat, stood behind an anachronistic lectern and over-enunciated his speech.

"Teleportation ... some say that it is a misnomer. Some say that it violates the laws of physics. Well ... naysayers be damned! Because we have successfully transported single-celled organisms from our facility to another facility 3000 miles away, without traversing the physical space between them. This has been a revolutionary scientific breakthrough."

Unbeknownst to Niklaus, twenty five years later he would be the one – with a PhD in physics – using this same technology to pioneer a revolutionary breakthrough of his own.

*

"Everybody dies Niklaus, it's a part of life," he recalls the soft voice of his beloved grandmother. A futile attempt, by an ailing old woman, to console a trepidatious child.

"Everybody dies."

"Death is a part of life."

"You get to a point when you're just ready to go."

"I am ready Niklaus."

Did she really mean it? Was she really ready to die? Or was she privately shitting her bedpan when she uttered those words? Niklaus was unsure. Nevertheless, he was certain of one thing – he would never be ready to die. Nothing was more frightening to him than the thought of facing his own mortality. Indeed, he was petrified of dying. But maybe … just maybe … he wouldn't have to.

*

Decades later, Niklaus, now 41 years old, stands before a crowd of inquisitive reporters.

"Behold the Rejuvenator!" Niklaus' baritone voice reverberates throughout the auditorium.

He draws the curtain, revealing a monolithic contraption, then begins his keynote.

"What if, when we got sick, the remedy could be as easy as throwing a switch?" Niklaus bellows, sounding something like a 17th century charlatan.

"What if, instead of performing an invasive surgery to remove a malignant tumor, we could simply dematerialize the neoplasm?"

"What if, in the wake of God's death, we could grant ourselves everlasting life with instruments of science?"

"Lo, this is our endeavor!"

The Rejuvenator looked like something straight out of a 1950s sci-fi film. With it's vintage aesthetic – complete with antiquated levers and knobs – it almost appeared as though it had been engineered by H. G. Wells himself.

"With the process of teleportation – along with our newly patented Foreign Body Modulation (FBM) technology – this machine, the Rejuvenator, is capable of identifying and extracting cancers, viruses, infections, toxins, and virtually any other unwanted biological constituent," Niklaus boisterously proclaims.

Oohh's and Ahh's ring out from the crowd.

"And yes, ladies and gentleman, give it a yarmulke and a copy of the Torah, and this machine can even dematerialize one's foreskin."

Oohh's and Ahh's hastily turn into eww's and uh's.

"Has it been tested on humans?" shouts an incredulous member of the press.

"I will be the first," Niklaus responds.

"And how ... exactly ... will it be tested on you?"

"I shall now publicly demonstrate this machine's remarkable capabilities, by teleporting my appendix out of my body."

A large metallic cocoon lights up and begins to split open. More Oohh's and Ahh's resound. Niklaus steps inside.

"Are we ready?" Niklaus asks his bug-eyed assistant.

"Ready sir!"

The cocoon closes, enveloping Niklaus. Bug-eyes gives the thumbs up.

"Beginning quantification sequence now," announces the voice simulator, apparently switched to the Stephen Hawking setting.

Niklaus is trembling as the Rejuvenator prepares to dematerialize his superfluous vestigial organ. He's thinking: All it takes is a few particles, a few misplaced electrons and, BOOM!, your intestines explode. He imagines his guts, a crimson colored mac and cheese, splattering all over an amused audience – with Heisenberg's ghost in the front row, laughing his ass off.

A large red button is flashing. Bug-eyes presses it.

"Initiating extraction ... Initiating extraction ... Initiating extraction."

The process is over as soon as it begins. The cocoon then slowly opens.

Extraction complete ... Extraction complete ... Extraction complete."

Success!

*

"Sir?"

Niklaus remains motionless, with his eyes still closed.

"Sir?"

He enjoys keeping em' waiting. Maintaining the suspense – like it is an escape act, and he is Houdini. But this is no magic trick, this is no sleight-of-hand deception, this is science.

His ocularly gifted assistant retrieves a glass tube from the assembly chamber, which encases Niklaus' appendix.

Niklaus opens his eyes, steps out of the cocoon, and extends his arms.

"Voila!" he shouts.

The crowd responds with a thunderous applause. Niklaus responds with a self-satisfied smirk.

"Painless ... affordable ... risk free. Yes, ladies and gentlemen, if you're a surgeon, you might want to start updating your resume. Your job will soon be rendered obsolete."

So smug. Typical PhD.

"Have you discovered the fountain of youth?" asks a reporter.

"No ... I have invented it."

Yeah, Typical PhD.

*

There was one hang up unfortunately. The Department of Medical Research was still not convinced that teleportation was safe; consequently the government was not yet ready to subsidize a mass scale production. Thus, needing private sector investors, it became necessary to take the show on the road and perform more demonstrations. And so, like a ringmaster in a traveling circus, Niklaus continued to mesmerize the crowds – extracting his tonsils, wisdom teeth, and any other bodily organ he didn't need.

"I envision a future ... a future where everything, every disease known to man, is curable with this apparatus," he tells his audience, which now fills lecture halls.

But following each demonstration his assistant noticed that the middle-aged physicist would emerge from the cocoon a bit stranger, with a peculiar look in his eyes, and that said a lot coming from a guy who looked like he had his eyelids perpetually clamped open.

It wasn't until a few months later that Niklaus became aware of what appeared to be side effects, which he noted in his journal.

"Persistent sadness, trouble focusing, lack of patience. Originally I thought I just needed to change my diet ... but now I fear the worst. I fear that I will suffer the same fate as Marie Curie and Carl Scheele, and that my love of science – my research – will ultimately destroy me." He decided to leave out the part about him not being able to get his cock hard anymore. Yeah, that part was inconsequential. No need to document that.

A lifelong teetotaler, he soon began drinking – heavily. "It's never too late to pick up a new hobby," he reasoned. Plus, now he could always teleport the cirrhosis out of his liver if he had to.

What was happening to him? Was this cutting-edge medical procedure diminishing his will and sapping his vitality? There were many speculations. Some suggested that – because the process of teleportation involved the deconstruction of atoms and molecules – it probably had something to do with radioactive decay. But in the end, no one quite knew what it was. Researchers in other countries were reporting similar findings.

A news headline from Germany grabbed Niklaus' attention:

"Guinea pigs show signs of depression in aftermath of teleportation experiments."

Sadly, the human Guinea pig in Denmark was suffering from the same side effects; and things were only getting worse for Niklaus. Fainting, hallucinations, a loss of touch with reality; and then came the voices – in particular, the voice of his dead grandmother.

"Everybody dies."

A few months later Niklaus was admitted into a psychiatric hospital. Well, it was more of a self-admission really ... with him bursting into the front lobby and demanding that they "Make it stop!" Nurses didn't ask too many questions. Admission granted! You've been accepted!

Not that they could really do much for him. Put him in an observation room, dope him up – the usual.

He's is lying in bed now. All of the drugs are ineffective. He continues to hear his grandmother's voice becoming more shrill.

"Death is a part of life!"

Her words don't seem as disconcerting as they once did.

"You get to a point when you're just ready to go."

He's wondering: Am I ready?

"Yes ... you are ready Niklaus."

He's wondering: What if our souls really did last for all eternity?

Now he's really delusional, he's starting to believe in fantastical illusions of immortality.

"Niklaus!"

He's wondering: Why am I not as afraid as I used to be?

"Do it!"

He's wondering: Why didn't they restrain me?

Everything, even a roll of the dice, can be forecast from it's initial conditions and the laws of physics. But no one could have predicted that it would end this way for Niklaus.

A bit of pressure on the carotid artery was all it took. They really should have restrained him.

NOEL SLOBODA

Middle-aged Pinocchio

Hauled in by the Office of Honesty
the puppet endures another chiding:
he has done his paperwork
wrong once again.

Receipts must be submitted
for each of his lies—
from the toll his shoplifting took on Gepeto
to how his last girlfriend paid

when he didn't reveal
that neon fungus bloomed
beneath his tattered lederhosen;
and he needs to account

for a recent refusal to face himself
naked in the mirror; admit
his life has half passed; accept
he has become brittle.

Handwritten documentation
won't do: everything must be
typed up, Times twelve-point.
The wooden man-boy makes soft noises

of assent, nearly convincing himself,
all the while thinking he needs to sneeze
and release the great pressure
built up inside his head.

EVAN W. STONER

Jesus can't swim

In 2013, Jesus returned to Earth. He opened a Twitter account with the handle @SonOfGodForReal. He tweeted, "People of Earth, there's no Wi-Fi in Heaven, so I've returned to answer your questions. Please tweet me any and all inquiries." The good people at Twitter quickly verified the account was genuine, and @SonOfGodForReal received a white checkmark in a blue circle. In 140 characters or less, the people of Earth started tweeting questions.

"@SonOfGodForReal, who got it right, the Protestants or the Catholics?"

"@SonOfGodForReal, does this mean all other religions are a sham?"

"@SonOfGodForReal, what about Mary Magdalene? Did you ever hit that?

"@SonOfGodForReal, if there's no Wi-Fi in Heaven, is there cell reception? I'd like to be buried with my smart phone."

"@SonOfGodForReal, are there taxes in Heaven? Who's responsible for maintaining the gold-paved roads? Should we tip these people?"

"@SonOfGodForReal, are you a socialist? You are, aren't you? I knew it!"

"@SonOfGodForReal, has your dad mellowed at all since the Old Testament? He certainly did some crazy shit back in the day."

"@SonOfGodForReal, are you single?"

After a few days, Jesus tweeted, "Enough. From now on, I will only take questions from children."

Children across the globe began tweeting Jesus questions.

"@SonOfGodForReal, what's your favorite color?"

"@SonOfGodForReal, can you really walk on water?"

"@SonOfGodForReal, do aliens exist?"

"@SonOfGodForReal, what about my dog, Ginger? Is she in Heaven like my mom says?"

"@SonOfGodForReal, what's it like in Hell?"

Jesus responded, "My favorite color is blue. I can walk on water, but only because I never learned how to swim." The next tweet read, "I'll get back to you on the aliens." This was followed by, "Hell is just like standing in a long line at the post office, and when it's finally your turn they're out of stamps." In the last tweet, Jesus wrote, "As for Ginger, she and Shadow don't get along, but other than that she is in Heaven and doing just fine."

Soon an unruly adult tweeted Jesus asking, "@SonOfGodForReal, so should we read these tweets as parables or what?" In a move that is still hotly debated in theological circles, Jesus retweeted the question without any explanation.

The media blew up in response to what CNN dubbed "The Jesus Tweets." The newspaper and blog headlines read:

"JESUS SPEAKS! IN PARABLE?"

"JESUS ADMITS: I CAN'T SWIM."

"MICHAEL PHELPS TO JESUS: I CAN TEACH YOU."

"ALIENS!!!"

"HELL IS REAL AND JUST LIKE THE POST OFFICE."

"POSTAL WORKERS STRIKE, DEMAND HOLY APOLOGY."

"POST MASTER GENERAL COMMITS SUICIDE, PRESUMABLY TO GO TO HELL AND STRAIGHTEN THINGS OUT."

"WHO IS SHADOW?"

Frustrated, Jesus prayed, "Father, how can I make the people of Earth understand me?"

God sent him an email saying, "This was your idea, not mine. Ask the Holy Spirit. I'm late for a tee time with John the Baptist."

At a loss, Jesus gave up on the Internet and started working for a landscaping service under the name Jose Delsol. However, it wasn't long before Lindsay Lohan tweeted, "Due to Jesus's return to Earth I can no longer hide. I am the Whore of Babylon!" Everyone agreed that explained a lot.

That night, TMZ aired a special called, "Lindsay Lohan: What We Know Now."

Jesus accepted his failure and returned to Heaven. When he arrived at the Pearly Gates he said to God, "Father, they aren't ready."

"Shh," God said. "Things are just getting good down there. One of the Kardashian girls is claiming she's the real Whore of Babylon, and now she and Lindsay Lohan are having it out."

"Which Kardashian?"

"Not sure, I can never tell those girls apart. Popcorn?"

CONTRIBUTORS

Patti Abbott
Patti Abbott is the author of more than 100 stories in print and online. Snubnose Press has published her ebooks, MONKEY JUSTICE (a story collection) and HOME INVASION (a novel in stories). She is the co-editor of the anthology DISCOUNT NOIR (Untreed Reads). She won a Derringer for her story "My Hero" in 2009. She lives outside of Detroit.

Zachary Amendt
Zachary Amendt worked as a bureau chief for City News Service, Inc., the nation's largest regional news wire service. He is a two-time "Notable Story" recipient of storySouth's Million Writers Award.

James Babbs
I have published hundreds of poems over the last several years in print journals and online. I live in the same small town where I grew up. I work for the government but don't like to talk about it. I am the author of Dictionary of Chaos(2002), Another Beautiful Night(2010), Disturbing The Light(2013) & The Weight of Invisible Things(2013).

Cody Badaracca
Cody Badaracca grew up in North Routt County, Colorado, near the town of Clark. He has a B.A. in journalism and is the publisher and owner for Voices Of [the] Goat Publishing, which exists largely in his mind and on his laptop. He's been published in My Favorite Bullet. He sometimes dreams about living in the desert of New Mexico or the bayou of Louisiana. If for no other reason, the variety of reptiles and the mild winters.

Ronan Barbour
Ronan Barbour was born in Canada to an Irish Mother and Canadan father and moved to the U.S. when he was nearly five. He currently lives in Los Angeles, California.

Timothy Bearly

Timothy Bearly currently resides in Sandpoint, Idaho where he likes to eat worms and sing songs. According to his teachers he has an insubordinate attitude (because he raises questions). According to his family he is a communist (because he doesn't believe in laissez-fairy tales). According to his fundamentalists peers he is the antichrist (because he named his dog Darwin). Notwithstanding his frustration with the relentless and groundless ad hominem bombardment, he kind of enjoys his status as persona non grata; he contends that ostracism helps one to write unfettered. Ironically, personal attacks also inflate his ego; it helps him to realize that he is on the right track. He can be lambasted via email: thebearlys@hotmail.com

James Brown

James Brown is an American novelist who has also written short fiction and nonfiction. His acclaimed memoir, The Los Angeles Diaries, was named a Best Book of the Year by Publishers Weekly, The San Francisco Chronicle and The Independent of London.

Kristen Falso-Capaldi

Kristen Falso-Capaldi is a writer, musician and public high school teacher. The latter position has led her to believe she could run a small country if given the opportunity. She has written professionally for local TV, is the singer and lyricist for the folk/bluegrass duo Kristen & J and her essays have been published in The Providence Journal. Currently, she is working on a novel and collaborating on a screenplay. Kristen lives in a small town in northern Rhode Island with her husband and cat. Follow Kristen on twitter @kristenafc.

Jamez Chang

Jamez Chang's work has appeared or is forthcoming in FRiGG, Prime Number, Lines + Stars,Boston Literary Magazine, Poydras Review, and the anthology Yellow Light. After graduating from Bard College, Jamez went on to become the first Korean-American to release a hip-hop album, Z-Bonics (1998), in the United States. He lives in Englewood Cliffs, NJ with his wife and 3 daughters. Visit: www.jamezchang.com

Mark Daponte

DaPonte is a copy/blog writer for an advertising company in New York City and lives in Brooklyn, NY with two boys and one wife. When he isn't sinking down to a 9-year-old's maturity level to make his 9-year-old son laugh and his 14-year-old son wince, he can be found writing short stories and screenplays. One of his screenplays, "The Break In," has (finally) been optioned and is currently being filmed.

José Hernández Díaz

José Hernández Díaz was born in Anaheim, CA (1984). He is currently working on his MFA in poetry at Antioch University, Los Angeles. He earned his BA in English Literature from UC Berkeley. His work has appeared in *The Best American Nonrequired Reading Anthology 2011, Bombay Gin, The Progressive, Kuikatl, Poetry Flash, 3:AM Magazine (UK), Tan lejos de dios (MEX), Merida Literary Magazine (UK), The Delinquent (UK), El norte que viene (ESP), ditch poetry (CAN), Kerouac's Dog (UK), Decanto (UK), Blood Lotus, Haight-Ashbury Literary Journal, Huizache, Counterexample Poetics, Generations, The Legendary, Revista Contratiempo, La Gente Newsmagazine, BlazeVOX12, Emerge Literary Journal,* among others. He has edited five novels for Floricanto Press.

R.C. Edrington

RC Edrington has been a scourge on the small press for years. He's published numerous chapbooks, the first being Whiskey Coma Blues. His scribbles have also appeared in countless journals, anthologies, e-zines and magazines. He offers no graduate degree in any imaginary art form. Nor can he produce a certificate of authentication from any hip writing guild to prove he is an actual writer. He despises hip coffee boutiques and the meaningless flesh that haunts them.

Zdravka Evtimova

Zdravka's latest short story collection "Carts and Other Stories" was published by Fomite Publishing, Vermont, USA, 2012. Her short stories have been published in a number of countries in the world including USA (*Massachusetts Review, New Sudden Fiction, Antioch review, Underground Voices* etc), Canada, UK, Australia, France, Germany, Japan, Russia etc.

JeanPaul Ferro

Jéanpaul Ferro is a novelist, short fiction author, and poet from Providence, Rhode Island. An 8-time Pushcart Prize nominee, Jéanpaul's work has appeared on NPR, Contemporary American Voices, Columbia Review, Emerson Review, Connecticut Review, Portland Monthly, and others. He is the author of Essendo Morti – Being Dead (Goldfish Press, 2009), nominated for the 2010 Griffin Prize in Poetry; and Jazz (Honest Publishing, 2011) nominated for both the 2012 Griffin Prize in Poetry and the 2012 Kingsley Tufts Prize in Poetry. He is represented by the Jennifer Lyons Literary Agency. He currently lives along the south coast of southern Rhode Island. His website: www.jeanpaulferro.com and e-mail address: jeanpaulferro@netzero.net

Simon Friel

Simon Friel lives in Barcelona, Spain. *The Retreat* is an adapted chapter from his first novel, *Murmur*, which will be available in 2014.

Mitchell Grabois

Mitchell Grabois was born in the Bronx and now lives in Denver. His short fiction and poetry appears in close to two hundred literary magazines, most recently The T.J. Eckleberg Review, Memoir Journal, Out of Our and The Blue Hour. He has been nominated for the Pushcart Prize, most recently for his story "Purple Heart" published in The Examined Life in 2012. His novel, Two-Headed Dog, published by Xavier Vargas E-ditions, is available for all e-readers for 99 cents through Amazon, Barnes and Noble and Smashwords (which also provides downloads to PC's). A print edition is also available through Amazon.

Khanh Ha

Khanh Ha's debut novel is FLESH (June 2012, Black Heron Press). He graduated from Ohio University with a bachelor's degree in Journalism. He is at work on a new novel. His short stories have appeared in 2013 February Outside in Literary & Travel Magazine, and Red Savina Review (RSR) in its 2013 Spring inaugural edition (This short story was also nominated for the Winter Literary Award in the Tethered by Letters Journal but was withdrawn because of conflict of interest with RSR.), Cigale Literary Magazine(2013 March issue), Glint Literary Journal (2013 Summer issue), and Lunch Ticket (2013 Summer issue). Visit the author's website at: www.authorkhanhha.com

Rodger Jacobs

Rodger Jacobs is an award-winning documentary writer (SXSW 2000) and co-author of the acclaimed 2004 play *Go Irish: The Purgatory Diaries of Jason Miller.* In 2007, he produced the literary event *The Ragged Promised Land: Celebrating the 50th Anniversary of Jack Kerouac's On the Road,* performed live at Vesuvio Café and the Beat Museum in San Francisco. In 2008 Rodger's short story collection *Mr. Bukowski's Wild Ride* was commissioned by City Lights Books. In 2010, Rodger provided the preface and editorial assistance for *Jack London: San Francisco Stories* (Sydney Samizdat Press) and in the following two years received multiple writing grants. He was a literary essayist and book critic for Pop Matters in 2008-2012. Rodger's first novel, *The Furthest Palm,* was published by Silver Birch Press in 2012. His most recent publication, *"Nazi Noir: The Ghost of the Prophet of Fascism,"* is at L.A. Review of Books.
Author website: http://silverlakeadjacent.wordpress.com/

Ted Jean

A carpenter, Ted writes, paints, plays tennis with lovely Lai Mei. His work appears in *Beloit Poetry Journal, DIAGRAM, Juked, Pear Noir!, Magma (UK), Other Poetry (UK),* and dozens of other publications.

Meg Johnson

Meg Johnson's poems have appeared in *Slipstream Magazine Word Riot, Midwestern Gothic, SOFTBLOW, Counterexample Poetics, The Waterhouse Review,* and others. Her poem "Free Samples" was nominated for Best of the Net. She is currently a poetry student in the NEOMFA Program, a teaching assistant at the University of Akron, and the poetry editor for *Rubbertop Review.* Prior to this, Meg worked for many years as a dancer, choreographer, dance teacher, and actress. She blogs at: megjohnsonmegjohnson.blogspot.com

Thomas Kearnes

Thomas Kearnes is a 37-year-old author originally from East Texas and now living in Houston. His fiction has appeared in *Digital Americana Magazine, PANK, Storyglossia, Spork, The Ampersand Review, Word Riot, Eclectica, JMWW Journal, Night Train, SmokeLong Quarterly, wigleaf, The Adroit Journal, 3 AM Magazine, A cappella Zoo, Johnny America, Prime Number Magazine, Underground Voices, Night Train* and numerous LGBT venues, including *Educe Journal, Diverse Arts Project, Diverse Voices Quarterly, Wilde Magazine* and the *Best Gay Stories* series. He is a two-time Pushcart Prize nominee. His debut short-story collection, "Pretend I'm Not Here," is now available from Musa Publishing and a second collection, "Promiscuous," is available from JMS Books. He is an atheist and an Eagle Scout.

Michael C. Keith

Michael is the author of over 20 books on electronic media, as well as a memoir and three books of fiction. In 2009, he coedited a found manuscript by legendary writer/director Norman Corwin. What he refers to as his "fringe" group series consists of a monograph that examines the use of broadcast media by Native Americans—Signals in the Air (Praeger, 1995), a book that explores the nature and role of counterculture radio in the sixties—Voices in the Purple Haze (Praeger, 1997), a book that probes the extreme right-wing's exploitation of the airwaves—Waves of Rancor (M.E. Sharpe, 1999, with Robert Hilliard), a book that examines the role of gays and lesbians in broadcasting—Queer Airwaves (M.E. Sharpe, 2001, with Phylis Johnson), a book about broadcasting and the First Amendment—Dirty Discourse (Blackwell, 2003, with Robert Hilliard), and a volume that evaluates the loss of localism in

American radio—The Quieted Voice (Southern Illinois University Press, 2005, with Robert Hilliard). Keith is also the author of the most widely adopted text on American radio—The Radio Station, 8th edition (Focal Press, 2010), an oral history—Talking Radio (M.E. Sharpe, 2000), a study of nocturnal broadcasting –Sounds in the Dark (Iowa State University Press, 2001), and The Broadcast Century, 4th edition (Focal Press, 2005, with Robert Hilliard. His most recent books include Radio Cultures (Peter Lang, 2010) and Sounds of Change (University North Carolina Press, 2010, with Christopher Sterling). He is also the author of the critically acclaimed memoir, The Next Better Place (Algonquin Books, 2003), as well as numerous journal articles. He is also the author of five story collections: And Through the Trembling Air, Hoag's Object, Of Night and Light, Sad Boy, and Everything is Epic. He has been invited to lecture internationally.

Dennis Kennedy
Dennis Kennedy is a theatre historian, playwright, and director who has published many books on live performance. His short stories have appeared in a number of literary magazines. He also writes song lyrics for Junk Ensemble, a Dublin-based dance-theatre company. Born in Cincinnati and raised in California, he now lives in Dublin and France.

Mary Krienke
A story of Mary's entitled "Accomplishment," appeared in the journal, Midwestern Gothic, and a short piece entitled, "Maybe it's time for a story" in Two Hawks Quarterly. She received her MFA from Columbia University and lives and work in New York.

Steven Loton
Steven Loton writes stories that are being published here and there. You can catch his writing around various lit mags across London, the UK, worldwide and in certain parts of the Galaxy; or find his blog at http://flamethrowingtheshortstory.blogspot.com.

David Luntz

David Luntz's poems, flash fiction and short fiction have appeared in Andromeda Spaceways, Word Riot, Matter Press: Journal of Compressed Creative Arts, Euphony, The Centrifugal Eye and other online and print publications.

Jenean McBrearty

Jenean McBrearty is a graduate of San Diego State University, and a former community college instructor who taught Political Science and Sociology. She received the EKU English Department's Award for Graduate Non-fiction (2011), and her short stories have appeared in Main Street Rag, Danse Macabre, bioStories, Cobalt Review, and Nazar Look among others. Her novel, Raphael Redcloak, has been serialized by Jukepop. Her website is: Jenean-McBrearty.com

Jim Meirose

Jim Meirose's work has appeared in numerous journals, including the Fiddlehead, Witness, Alaska Quarterly review, and Xavier Review, and has been nominated for several awards. Two collections of his short work have been published and his novels, *Claire, Monkey*, and *Freddie Mason's Wake* are available from Amazon.

B.Z. Niditch

NIDITCH is a poet, playwright, fiction writer and teacher. His work is widely published in journals and magazines throughout the world, including: *Columbia: A Magazine of Poetry and Art; The Literary Review; Denver Quarterly; Hawaii Review; Le Guepard* (France); *Kadmos* (France); *Prism International; Jejune* (Czech Republic); *Leopold Bloom* (Budapest); *Antioch Review;* and *Prairie Schooner,* among others. He lives in Brookline, Massachusetts.

Olyn Ozbick

Olyn's fiction is published and forthcoming in *Fourthirtythree, Crack the Spine* and *Splinterswerve.* He was a finalist in the CBC Literary Prize. His essays, reviews and creative non-fiction have been published in *Chatelaine, Harrowsmith, Equinox, Avenue, Bloom, Journal* and other fine places. He is a recent addition to the *Splinterswerve* editorial team.

Marc Pietrzykowski

Marc lives and works and writes in Niagara County, NY, USA. He has published 5 books of poetry and 1 novel. You can visit Marc virtually at marcpski.com.

Frederick Pollack

Author of two book-length narrative poems, THE ADVENTURE and HAPPINESS, both published by Story Line Press. Other poems in print and online journals. Adjunct professor of creative writing at the George Washington University.

Ken Poyner

Ken Poyner has been appearing in the alternative and small presses for 40 years or so, and is now out and about on the web. His real avocation, however, is being awful eye-candy at his wife's powerlifting meets, from which she holds multiple world records. *Menacing Hedge, Corium, Eclectica, Asimov's, Frostwriting, Gutter Eloquence* and a host of others have been tongue tied with his work of late.

D.H. Schleicher

D. H. Schleicher is an independent author, blogger and film enthusiast from the South Jersey suburbs of Philadelphia. He is the author of the independent novel, *The Thief Maker*, and his writing has appeared in *Scratch, LitNoir* and on *Wonders in the Dark*. He is the founder and editor of the blog, theschleicherspin.com; (http://theschleicherspin.com) and the digital literary magazine, *The Stone*.

Carter Schwonke

Carter Schwonke is a graduate of Syracuse University and University College London. Her short stories have appeared in *Blueline, Snake Nation, Stirring* and *Calliope*. She is a reading volunteer at a California State Prison.

Noel Sloboda

Noel Sloboda's work has recently appeared or is soon forthcoming in *Rattle, Sentence, Harpur Palate, Redactions*, and *Modern Language Studies*. He is the author of the poetry collection Shell Games (2008) as well as several chapbooks. Sloboda has also written a book about

Edith Wharton and Gertrude Stein. He lives in Pennsylvania, where he serves as dramaturg for the Harrisburg Shakespeare Company.

Conor Powers-Smith
Conor Powers-Smith grew up in New Jersey and Ireland. He currently lives on Cape Cod, where he works as a reporter. His stories have appeared in *AE, Daily Science Fiction, Nature*, and other magazines.

Stephanie Smith
Stephanie Smith is a poet and writer from Scranton, Pennsylvania. Her work has appeared in such publications as *Morpheus Tales, The Horror Zine, Pif Magazine, Strong Verse*, and *Poetry Quarterly*. Her first poetry chapbook, Dreams of Dali, is available from Flutter Press

George Sparling
I've been a welfare caseworker in East Harlem, a counselor and reading instructor in the Baltimore City Jail, a lumber yard laborer, a mail carrier, a dishwasher, a crab butcher, and a bookstore manager. I worked a placer gold claim in the northern wilderness of California for a year. One can go crazy living too long in isolation. Madness is like water: we all need it to survive. I've been published in many literary magazines. I live on the north coast of northern California. Sometimes I'm an exclamation point, other times a comma. The better times are when I'm italics in a Jim Thompson crime novel. Or, deadly feet walking through New Orleans in a James Sallis novel.

Evan W. Stoner
Evan Stoner received a B.A. in English from the University of Illinois at Chicago. He studied creative writing and literature as an undergraduate, and has been writing for several years. He currently work as a part-time freelance writer in Chicago. Some of his work has appeared in small literary and arts magazines, including *SAGA*, published at Augustana College, and *The Red Shoes Review*, published at UIC.

David Synder

David Snyder is a writer living in Somerville, MA. He received his B.A. at NYU and M.F.A. at Emerson College, where he was editor-in-chief of Redivider. His work has appeared in *Battered Suitcase, Boston Literary Magazine, Farspace 2* and elsewhere.

Luke Tennis

Luke Tennis has a MA in Creative Writing and his novella, Bernard the Daredevil, won the St. Andrews Press Novella Award. He has also won other awards, most recently a Maryland Fiction Writing Grant. His short stories have appeared in such literary magazines as *ConnecticutReview, Puerto Del Sol, Word Riot* and *JMWW*.

www.ingramcontent.com/pod-product-compliance
Lightning Source LLC
Chambersburg PA
CBHW021956170626
46808CB00001B/182